Into the Forest

A Retelling of Little Red Riding Hood

Jennifer Willcock

En Pointe Press

Contents

To Robin and Brenda

Wolf Names and Meanings

1. Alarick - Noble leader or a Wolf ruler, fierce, supreme ruler over all

2. Bleddyn - Wolf hero

3. Raff - a red Wolf

4. Seath/Seth – Wolfish (Since Seath was hard to pronounce I changed it to Seth)

5. Teowulf - A mighty Wolf

6. Duko - is derived from Doede, meaning a famous Wolf

From https://thoughtcatalog.com/january-nelson/2018/06/Wolf-names/

Prologue

THE FOREST VIBRATED WITH a pulse—*thrum, thrum, thrum*—giving it a life breath of its own. The tall pine trees with their sharp scent waved their branches in the strong wind, which whooshed through the forest, rustling the dead leaves and needles in mini tornadoes a few centimetres off the ground. Chattering squirrels and chirping birds competed for supremacy. The sky, blue only moments before, was now an unfriendly grey.

Battle cries, along with the *thwack* of sticks, added to the cacophony of the afternoon. Rider wrapped her blood-red sweater tighter around her body as she peered from behind the large tree trunk, spying on the game in the clearing in front of her.

Three boys lunged at each other with wooden swords, engrossed in their epic pretend battle. Whooping and hollering, they danced around each other, their weapons swinging and clashing. Rider had never seen the boys before, and she knew most of the people who lived in the forest.

Wood smacked flesh and she winced, then shivered as a breeze swept through the clearing. The boys halted their play, their swords dangling at their sides. The tallest of the three tilted his head toward the sky and sniffed.

That's odd. Could he smell the rain that the dark clouds warned was coming?

"It's going to rain." He beckoned the other two. "We need to get back to the gates."

That explained it. They weren't from the forest.

The second tallest boy frowned as he shoved his white-blond hair out of his eyes. "A little rain isn't going to hurt anyone, Teo. I'm staying here and finishing the Great Battle of Wolf Kingdom." He thrust his sword into the air, waving it around with a flourish. The smallest boy giggled.

The tall one frowned. "No, I'm the eldest, Bleddyn. You have to listen to me. Momma said to come back if the weather turned." He grabbed at his brother's sweater, but came up with a fistful of air. Bleddyn hooted gleefully as he ran away. The oldest boy—what had his brother called him? Ah yes, Teo— growled, "C'mon, Bleddyn." But his brother only widened the distance between them.

The smallest boy ducked to avoid the swipe of his brother's hands, but his long jacket let him down. "No! I don't want to go. I want to play." The boy howled his protests, struggling out of his brother's grasp.

"Do you want a scolding from Momma?"

The young boy thrust out his chin and crossed his arms. "I'm not afraid of Momma. I want to stay, Teo."

A loud sigh echoed through the meadow. "Do what you want, I'm going home."

The boys gawked as Teo headed in the direction of the city. Suddenly a cry rang out, and the littlest one dropped to the ground. Teo spun around, and both older brothers rushed to the youngest.

"What's wrong?" Teo knelt and grabbed the little one's shoulders.

"I think I got stung." A whimper replaced the earlier bravado.

A look passed between the two older brothers. Teo knelt down beside the smaller boy. "Let's see it, Seth. Where'd you get stung?" The swords lay forgotten on the ground.

Seth removed his hand from the base of his neck to reveal a red, swollen lump. Tears streamed down his chubby cheeks. Teo's lips moved. She couldn't hear what he said, although the movement of his mouth suggested it wasn't a very nice word.

"We've got to get him home. He swelled up like a balloon the last time he got stung." Teo carefully lifted his younger brother into his arms.

"We can't let Father find out we were here," the middle boy hissed.

Gathering her courage, Rider stepped out from behind the tree. "I can help."

Three heads whipped towards her and she slowed her steps. Forcing a calm look onto her face, Rider slowly walked over to within a couple of feet of them. The oldest boy's eyes glittered like cold water as they followed her every move. From their conversation and the sniffing, she guessed they were city dwellers, part of the Wolf clan. Though human, the urban dwellers had a keen sense of smell, slightly elongated canines, and a pack mentality. The kingdom was divided up into different clans but ruled by the people in the city or *the Wolves* as everyone dubbed them. She belonged to the Forest clan or, as everyone called them, the *Foresters*. The Forest clan and the Wolf clan lived side by side, but that didn't mean they got along. The complexities of the conflict between the city and forest were beyond her, but the girl knew enough to understand that these boys probably shouldn't be here.

This was her first time being this close to any Wolf. *Never trust a Wolf* had been drilled into her since she could remember. Now, at nine years old, it seemed woven into her very being. The arrogant Wolf Clan thought they were superior to every other clan, especially Foresters, who were less refined and sophisticated. Her insides quivered. *Maybe this isn't a good idea.* Could they smell her fear with their keen noses? When the littlest one cried out, she focused on him. He needed help and she could do that. Rider lifted her basket high, her smile wobbly, and said, louder this time, "I think I can help him."

Ice blue eyes narrowed, following her every step, but the oldest boy didn't try to block her. After slowly approaching the little one, she pressed her fingers to the swelling red lump, warm beneath her touch.

"My father is a medicine man. He knows how to make ointments and salves. He taught me how to make a salve for stings." She set her basket on the ground, so she could reach inside and lift out a handful of leafy greens and break them into bits. When no one stopped her, she knelt, clearing away the dead leaves in front of her. Appearing mesmerized, the boys watched her work, the youngest no longer crying. With water from her bottle, she made a paste using mud and adding the crushed leaves. Working quickly, she made a small ball of mud and leaves. "I'm going to smooth this over your sting, okay?"

The little boy inclined his head.

"It might be cold." She gingerly smeared the mixture on the red welt and then wiped her fingers on dead leaves. "My dad says to leave it on until it dries and crusts. It won't take too long." Her glance landed on one of the discarded swords. "What were you playing?"

"Games. Make-believe stuff." Teo scooped up the handmade weapon and shoved it into his belt.

Her lips turned up as she gave her hands a final swipe on the ground. "It looked like fun," she said. It would've been nice to have joined them, but she kept quiet, unsure. She slid the basket over her elbow and straightened. "My dad's expecting me. He's making medicine and I need to bring these herbs to him. I can't get caught in the rain..." Balling her fists, she slid them under her sleeves.

The oldest boy stepped towards her. "Thank you for your help."

Rider nodded. "Just rinse it off when it dries, and he should be fine." With a curt nod, she turned and ran off into the trees. When she shot a final look over her shoulder, three boys stood still, staring after her.

Chapter One

Rider

❧ ·•✦•· ❧

TEN YEARS LATER

S PEED WAS A DRUG and one from which Rider Hood had no intention of abstaining. Wind tangled its fingers in her ebony locks as she pedalled harder, faster, until her thighs burned, and adrenaline coursed through her limbs. Her full lips widened in a grin, and she tilted her head back, letting the air rush over her face. *Freedom*. Not a soul was around to tell her to slow down, and she jutted out her legs, letting the wheels freely turn as she rushed down the path. Syncing her feet and the pedals again, she checked her watch, pumping her legs harder. Thirty seconds off her personal best for her route as a bike courier for Hood Medicine was unacceptable. Not that the doctors she was delivering her cargo to cared how fast she got to their offices, but she did. Competition—even with herself—was motivating.

Her courier route ran through the thick forest, then along the path into the urban sprawl of Wolf City where she would be forced to come to a halt. Anyone wanting to enter the domain of the Wolf Clan had to first stop and show their entrance papers. Rider clenched her jaw. *Waste of my time*. Usually she wasn't detained, the precious cargo she carried her ticket past the guards.

Rider crested the last hill, the urban centre sprawling before her. A new construction sight appeared near the west end. A deep furrow buried itself between her brows. Why did they need another building? Sections of the huge stone wall that surrounded the city had been torn down and built back up to accommodate the expanding space not once, but twice. Rider and her dad had to dig up a number of plants that had been threatened by the expansion and then transplant them to their garden in their forest home. Since her dad's livelihood depended on the herbs and plants, Rider didn't appreciate the finer points of how progressive Wolf City was seen by its neighbouring clans. One more thing that made the divide between the Forest and Wolf clans gape wide open. The chatter of the squirrels grew louder as she neared the edges of the forest—almost as though they were protesting. Her lips curved up at the thought. They weren't impressed either.

The dirt path narrowed, changing to cement, and the fresh air faded as the city's smells took over—a combination of many people living together in tight spaces, food cooking in spices, and fumes from vehicles. It always took Rider a few breaths to get used to the air here.

Wolf Pack guards, part of the military arm of Wolf kingdom, stalked among the people in line at the pedestrian gate, snatching papers out of hands. Most of the line was made up of couriers and neighbours Rider recognized from the forest. Other guards patrolled the wall, their keen gazes riveted on the people and the horizon. *Do they really believe we're a threat?* Rider resisted the urge to roll her eyes. The Forest clan, or Foresters as they were nicknamed, were peaceful people who lived in harmony with the land and the surrounding clans of the kingdom. They might not trust the Wolves, but that didn't mean they were going to suddenly revolt. *Maybe we should.*

As she drew near the line, her shoulders hiked up to her ears and her rapid breathing wasn't from the city smells anymore. The tall guards in their dark green uniforms and black coats, which accentuated their muscles, wore thin-lipped sneers, glaring as they growled questions. The hair on Rider's neck prickled. *Calm down. You do this every day.* It didn't make it less intimidating, which annoyed her. Heat climbed up her neck, only to pool in her cheeks. She white-knuckled her handlebars. How dare they treat the Foresters like common criminals. But they did. Every. Single. Day.

Maybe they should look in the mirror. *They* were the criminals letting the city sprawl into the forest, not caring that they displaced people, plants, and animals for their own comfort. *They killed Mom.*

The words echoed in her head, but she shoved them down deep. *Don't go there.* Rider needed to focus on getting through the gates.

The line snaked along the wall, and Rider joined the end of it, nodding at a few friends. Mr. Eagleton was a pastry chef for the palace and lived in a modest little cabin just inside the perimeter of the forest. Like many Foresters, he worked in the city. Mrs. Templeton taught a sewing class at one of the kingdom schools. She had taught Rider how to mend holes and sew a straight line. That was about as far as the lessons went because Rider couldn't sit still for very long. Mrs. Templeton had laughed and let her go play. She lived in a bright yellow bungalow near Rider's home. Most of Rider's neighbours were farmers, or entrepreneurs who sold their goods throughout Wolf kingdom. Despite the restrictions the Wolf Clan inflicted on the Foresters, her people still thrived. Rider didn't stop to chat—the gate was not the place to have a friendly conversation.

A guard strutted along the line, barking out commands. Rider hopped off her bike and then snatched her papers from her satchel's front pocket. She ran a hand through her tangled curls. Her fingers slid along her hood before dropping to her side. The Wolves were suspicious—pulling the hood on would make it worse. The desire to hide beneath it wasn't worth the humiliation if the guards decided to make an example of her. *Keep your head down and don't draw attention to yourself.* Her dad's voice echoed in her mind. Repeating those instructions back to him was one of her earliest memories.

"Papers." The growl brought Rider back to the present—the guard's dark eyes glowered as he wiggled his fingers. As she handed the papers to him, Rider schooled her face into a blank canvas. *Keep your head down and don't draw attention to yourself.* She focused on his left elbow, the mantra running through her mind like a ticker tape as he riffled through the documents. Her toes curled in her running shoes. "These have expired," he said, barely sparing them a glance before pressing them back into her hands.

Her eyes snapped to his face and narrowed. "No, they're good for another six months." The words were out of her mouth before she could snatch them back.

He closed the distance between their noses. His hot breath hit her between the eyes, making them water. "Not as of today. New rules. Go to the Forest Business Centre and get them in order. You've got twenty-four hours." He roughly slapped a sticker on her hoodie, which noted her expired papers and the time frame she had to obtain new ones. "Show some respect, or next time I won't be nearly as pleasant," he hissed as he strutted away.

Rider sagged against her bike, her heart pummelling her rib cage. The busy entrance was her saving grace because any other day she'd be hauled to the offices for her bad attitude.

"I see you got an expiry date too."

The boy unfolded himself from his bike, his long legs untangling themselves. A weight lifted as she recognized familiar hazel eyes framed by thick, dark glasses. Messy blond hair hung over his forehead. He pushed his glasses up his nose with his index finger. Rider smiled. "Ethan, am I glad to see you."

Ethan was a courier for a farm that specialized in wild mushrooms and truffles, and he was also one of her oldest friends. Wolves had expensive tastes when it came to their food—truffles were a prized commodity. He bowed slightly, "I aim to please."

"The lines are gonna be long at the FBC, and I've got to have this medicine delivered yesterday." She jammed her papers into her backpack, sighing loudly. They hustled through the gates, the city enfolding them into its busyness and noise.

"Me too. I'm glad my boss was late today getting his delivery together because now I can wait with you."

She scowled. "That's the only good thing about this. Waste of our time."

"Is there a choice? If we go anywhere without our proper papers, we'll be in trouble. Remember when Rosie Prescott got thrown in jail for making her delivery first before getting her papers renewed?"

Rider nodded. Rosie had quit her job as a courier after that. Sitting in a lock-up cell for two days was not worth even the nice salary the fresh produce farm paid her.

The two friends picked their way through pedestrians and bikers, all trying to get away from the congestion at the gates. Since the

Forest Business Centre was only two blocks away, they decided to walk their bikes. The crisp breeze blew a ratty paper across their path, catching Rider's attention. An advertisement for the upcoming ball that the king put on for everyone in the kingdom. Even Foresters were welcome—for that one day. Other pieces of paper, food wrappers, and dead branches lay scattered in the gutters and stuck in shrubs. "Where arc thc garbage pickers? Usually the streets are pristine."

Ethan shrugged. "Maybe they have to renew their papers too. Aren't most of them Foresters?"

She nodded. "Wonder what made the Howell Family paranoid this time?"

He snorted. "Who knows with the royals?"

Rider kicked a stone out of her path. She jabbed Ethan with her elbow. "You know the forest is a dangerous place with dangerous people who have dangerous ideas. The only things we're good for are our meds and our food."

"Right? We are the epitome of all that is bad in the Wolf world."

Rider scanned the throng of pedestrians. A food cart selling kabobs was parked nearby, and the owner was setting meat on the grill. The sizzle of the fat sent fragrant steam into the air. "We should probably be careful of what we say. I don't need more trouble today." Rider sighed. "I've already been warned about being disrespectful." *Never trust a Wolf.*

"I heard your sass at the gate." Ethan wrapped an arm around her shoulders. "You were awesome." He picked up his pace, grabbing her elbow to pull her along. "C'mon we better hurry up or we'll be in a mile-long line."

Rider lengthened her strides to keep up. People on bikes, pedestrians, and other vehicles mobbed the streets around the FBC—no one was going anywhere fast. Honking horns competed with people shouting. Rider's temples pounded as the exhaust fumes choked. They locked their bikes to a post that already had two other bikes chained to it. The plain FBC building was small, and the line-up was around the corner.

"Oh no." Rider halted, her chin dipping. "We'll be here all day."

Ethan studied the line. "It's not that bad. I'd say we got here just in time. Another ten minutes and we would've been here until closing." They trudged to the end of the line and settled in to wait their turns. Rider wasn't as optimistic as her friend as they walked past a lot of people already in line.

"Hi, Rider, Ethan. How are you today?" An elderly gentleman sagged against his cane, but his smile was bright as sunshine.

"Morning, Mr. Birch. I'm good. You?" Rider grinned at the man, but her gaze wandered over his frail body. He shouldn't have to wait in a line for hours.

"I'm very well, thank you, dear." He motioned with his free hand at the line. "I guess we better settle in for a bit. It's gonna be a while. I'm glad I brought my book."

Ethan snorted. "It's ridiculous."

"Never trust a Wolf," muttered Rider.

Mr. Birch's blue eyes studied them. "Hm. Not much we can do. I've always wondered what life would be like if we all got along."

Rider snorted. "That's not possible, Mr. Birch. The Wolves are too arrogant and selfish."

The old man shuffled a few steps forward. "Maybe so, but I still hope I live to see the day we're all unified."

"I don't think that's ever gonna happen." Rider faced Ethan. "Not in any of our lifetimes." She whispered so the old man wouldn't hear. The line snaked along and Rider gritted her teeth, imagining her day vanishing into thin air.

Chapter Two

Teo

P RINCE TEOWULF GLARED AT the middle-aged man who stood before him. After flipping through the man's documents, he slammed the Approved stamp on them. He shoved the papers forward with two fingers, then called, "Next." A middle-aged woman stepped forward, her blue eyes wide, and his scowl deepened as he motioned her closer with an impatient wave of his hand. Her timidity irritated him more than he already was. Which was saying something. A low growl emitted from his throat as he snatched the papers out of her hands. *I hate my father.* He quietly repeated the refrain to the beat of the stamp hitting the paperwork. He pushed the newly approved papers back to the woman.

As she vanished into the crowded room, he stared at the line threading all the way outside. A puff of air escaped his lips. The day stretched endless. A cool draft of air wafted in from the open door. The constant arrival of people let in the chilly air, which kept the office cold. Teo didn't mind. The fact that the coolness had the waiting Foresters wrapping their jackets closer around themselves didn't bother him either. He turned his attention back to the line, one side of his lip curling up. *Let them freeze.*

"Private joke, Prince?" His co-worker's bright yellow eyes locked on his as she swiveled in her chair.

His curved lips straightened into a thin line, and he growled, "Shut it, Maya." His ice-blue eyes narrowed. "I'm undercover, spying on the common people of the forest. And maybe you too. Better be careful."

The lie spun out of his mouth. He was incognito, that much was true. Even his father understood what would happen if people recognized the crown prince, working in a grunt job—utter chaos. Girls falling over themselves to get a glimpse of the very gorgeous, very single prince, hoping he'd notice them. People slipping messages for the king into Teo's hands and pockets. His presence would have turned the FBC into a circus, which wasn't the point of Teo working today. To avoid said circus, as well make a point to his son, his father had instructed his press secretary to disguise Teo. Eyeglasses and a red wig that covered Teo's very short, military-style cut changed his appearance drastically. Even Teo hardly recognized himself. Discovery wasn't a worry—as long as Maya or one of the other soldiers he worked with didn't let it slip.

"Yeah, right. That's really why you're doing menial work here at the Center." She pressed her own *Approved* stamp into the ink pad. "It has nothing to do with you getting kicked out of school for brawling."

There it was. The reason Teo was working here today. His father's version of punishment for "unprincely" behavior. It may have been "unprincely" to punch the moron's lights out, but the dude deserved it. The image of the guy getting handsy with a girl, who obviously wasn't his girlfriend and who was clearly uncomfortable with the advances, made Teo's blood boil. He shook his head. His father hadn't bothered to ask questions when security summoned him to the school. He never did, always assuming Teo was to blame. Most times Teo *was* guilty, but occasionally it was the other's guy's fault.

Right. Like good old Dad cares about the details. Or me. Teo closed his eyes. When he opened them, Maya was still gazing at him. She blinked. "Maybe you should just accept it and start acting like the prince you are."

"Like I said, Maya. Shut it." He turned to the next person in line, waving them forward. The day was as endless as the line. All due to his father—conveniently declaring all forest papers expired and doubling the work of the FBC on the day his errant son was working out his punishment. Teo ran his tongue along his incisor, his eyes focused on the people in front of him. He straightened, eyes alert. *Who's this?* Instead of yet another elderly person standing in front of him, a girl around his age, curly black locks nearly covered in a red hood, filled the space. She studied him with eyes so green they made his mother's emeralds seem dull. Teo's dry mouth forgot how to work. *Stop staring.* He picked up his stamp. "Papers," he barked, holding out his hand.

The girl pushed them across the counter with a little more force than necessary, her fingers whiter than the papers they clutched. *Did she just give me attitude?* Teo narrowed his eyes and found his words. "Name and occupation."

"Jenna Rydell Hood. Courier for Hood Medicine."

"Place of residence?"

Her gaze slowly flicked to the sign above them that stated this was the Forest Business Centre, then her eyes locked on his. "The forest."

Was that sarcasm? She better show me respect. His nostrils flared as blood pounded through his veins. How dare a Forester talk to him or any Wolf like that. "Want to repeat that in a different tone?" he snarled. Her eyes widened slightly. He sniffed. *Fear. Good.*

"The forest." She tugged at the string of her hoodie, as she lowered her gaze to the stamp in his hand.

Better. Teo slowly perused the half of her he could see above the counter. She shifted her weight under his stare. She was taller than average with a slim build. "Remove the hood."

The girl shoved it down off her curls, freeing them from their confines. They bounced to life. Her hand shook slightly and she stuffed it in her pocket as though afraid he'd notice. He did.

The inky curls framed her porcelain face while the blood-red hood accentuated the contrast. And those eyes. When he reached them, she was staring into his once more, even though she risked getting reprimanded for being disrespectful. Again. *Feisty.* It should annoy him; instead, he was drawn to her, intrigued. Would she back down? Her eyes never left his as he straightened to his full height of six feet, three inches. He spread his fingers on the counter, resting his weight on them as he invaded her space. "Wolves are due respect. I could make your life difficult for that little show of insolence." His lip curled up at the corner. "However, I'm feeling generous, so I'll let it go this time. I won't the next." He stamped her papers with a loud thump and nudged them in her direction with one finger. "Jenna Rydell Hood." He enunciated each word. *I've got your number, sweetheart.*

The girl picked up the documents and turned away from the counter. She glanced back once before vanishing into the packed room. *Now that was interesting.* His lips quirked up. The day had been somewhat redeemed. At least for the five minutes he'd spent with her. Even if she was forest. His father would have a fit if he ever found out Teo had put up with that kind of disrespect from one of her kind. "Next."

As an elderly gentleman filled the space vacated by the young girl, Teo closed his eyes so he wouldn't roll them. His small moment of victory vanished, like the girl. *I hate my father.* "Papers." He opened his eyes, held out his hand, and sighed.

—◦—

The work day had lasted an eternity, extended by the long line of people needing papers renewed. At the end of his shift, Teo tossed the wig onto the floor of the staff room, then rubbed his fingers through his hair. After flinging open his locker, he scooped up the wig and shoved it onto the top shelf. He reached for his glasses but hesitated. Returning to the palace with his usual escort was not on his agenda tonight, so maybe he'd better keep the glasses. Hopefully that would at least lower the chances of him being recognized.

After grabbing his military-issued coat and hat, Teo slammed the locker shut, the metal clanging. He angled his hat low on his brow. Darkness had blanketed the city, which might help too. Slipping his arms into the sleeves, he stalked to the rear exit, not bothering to say goodbye, as he didn't want to alert his guards to the fact he was leaving. *What a waste of a day.* He picked up his pace as he put more distance between the building, his day, and himself. *I need fun.* A distraction from the lecture that was sure to come from his father when he got home. *Gonna delay that for as long as I can.*

Teo stepped off the curb into the street. The object hit him full force, knocking him to the pavement. His glasses were knocked askew, cracking against his face. He ripped them off and tossed them away. Out of his peripheral vision he saw whatever it was that had collided with him divide into two and then hit the pavement, hard. Moaning, he rolled into a sitting position and tentatively touched his throbbing leg. *Great.* He eyed the twisted bike that lay a short distance away, its back wheel still spinning. A groan came from that direction. The cyclist. At least he or she wasn't dead. That was all he needed as an ending to this stellar day.

He crawled over, his leg protesting the movement. As he neared the body, dark hair and pale skin came into view. The hoodie the biker wore was blood red. *Wait a minute...*

Slowly, she raised herself, shaking out one limb at a time. Definitely the feisty girl from the FBC.

"Take it easy. You had a quite a fall." He reached out to steady her.

She slapped his hand away. "Watch where you're going! You don't just step out into a busy street." Her words snapped at him like an elastic.

Teo frowned as he scanned the empty street. When he turned back to her, he raised an eyebrow.

Her eyes wandered down his body, widening as they took in his military coat. She scooched away from him. Of course. Since she was a Forester, this incident weighed heavily in his favour. Obviously she hadn't recognized him as either the worker from the FBC or the crown prince. Another bonus.

Her face was ghostly in the dying daylight, but those green eyes were huge. Against his better judgment, Teo moved closer. The obvious thing to do was to haul her in for disrespect or bodily harm to a royal, or...really, the list was endless. Blood trickled down her temple, and he sighed. Since when had he ever done the obvious thing? Still, even if he wasn't going to arrest her, that didn't mean he'd put up with the mouth. "I can see that the street is *super* busy," he drawled, gesturing to their barren surroundings. "And is that really how you want to speak to me?"

She thumbed dirt off her shoe.

Blood rushed to his head. All he had to do was snap his fingers, and she would be at his mercy. But she only recognized him as Wolf Pack.

Did he want to bring attention to his status? His father wouldn't be pleased if something like this happened to him. But Teo wasn't his father. *Do I want to be like him?* Teo didn't know; regardless, he was too tired to march this girl, whoever she was, to the guard offices at the gate. And she *had* been interesting at the FBC, made his day more enjoyable. In a twisted way. He'd let it go. "Are you hurt?" His tone was gruff, and he cleared his throat. "Let me help you." He offered his hand.

"Fine. I'm fine." She gritted out as she gingerly straightened, ignoring his hand.

"You're bleeding. I don't think you're fine," he huffed. Heat crept up his neck and he rubbed it. That was what he got for trying to be nice. Maybe he *should* try to be more like his dad...

The girl felt her forehead, smearing the dark blood that trailed down her white skin. "I told you I'm fine. My father is a doctor. No need for you to worry." She swayed slightly.

"Easy." He reached for her elbow, but she stepped out of his grasp. Teo frowned; he wasn't used to being given the cold shoulder by a girl. Or anyone.

She surveyed the area around her. "My bike."

The cycle lay a few feet from her, the front tire no longer circular. *It's not my concern. She's forest. I'm a Wolf. I don't owe her anything. Go.* Teo planted his weight on the ball of his foot, ready to pivot away. The girl slumped onto her knees beside the bike, looking so pathetic that Teo limped over. Against her protests, he hauled the bike upright. The tire was warped where it had hit him. Wow, she'd been booking it. No wonder his leg ached. No doubt there were tire marks on his skin. He wrapped his fingers around the tire and gripped the bar between the handles with his other hand.

"Don't touch it!"

He let go of the bar and held up his hand, palm facing out. "I'm just going to straighten the wheel." Setting the bike carefully onto its side, he grasped the steel rim and tugged. *Better.* "I think you can ride it now. If you take it to Fang's Garage tomorrow, I'll see to it that they install a new tire for you."

Her eyes widened. "Why would you do that?" She cocked her head. "You're a Wolf and I'm a Forester. I don't need any handouts from *you*."

He straightened abruptly. He was doing her a favour, wasn't he? "You should be grateful I'm not calling the Wolf Pack on you."

"Right. Because I'm the one who stepped into the street without looking," she scoffed.

"Fine, suit yourself." He shoved the bike at her and she grabbed it before it fell to the ground. His eyes locked on her green ones. "Watch where you're going from now on." The sharp intake of her breath at his words made him smirk as he hobbled away, trying hard to cover up the fact that he was limping.

The memory of the feisty girl combined with his smarting leg nagged at Teo as he made his way to the palace. Why hadn't he called the Wolf Pack? He shook his head. The defeated look on her face as she stared at the bike had done him in. Not the greenest eyes he'd ever seen. Definitely not.

I'm going soft. He was nothing like his father. Which was the answer to his question. Nor could he let his father find out that he'd been a wimp and let the girl go. If the king found out, Teo would suffer more unwanted consequences—the last thing he needed after the day he'd just had.

A group of young people ahead of him stopped to talk to another couple passing by. Teo ducked behind a metal pole that held decorative flags, not wanting to be recognized. His coat was dirty from his fall into the street, and he probably looked a mess. No need to invite more bad press. Thankfully, no one had witnessed the bike crash. *That would have been a nightmare.* It *had* been his fault. He hadn't looked as he stepped out into the street. Not that he would have ever admitted that to the spitfire.

The group in front of him didn't appear to be moving on, so Teo backtracked and slipped down a side street. The walk had worked most of the ache out of his leg, but he'd still be sporting a bruise tomorrow. At least the limp had eased. One less thing for his father to question him about. Now, if only he could enter the palace unseen. A slide show of last night flicked through his mind. His father's thin lips and narrowed eyes. Teo's own bloodied knuckles. The girl crying as Teo shoved the cocky moron up against the wall after his fist had delivered the *Hands Off* message. She'd run off before Teo had a chance to ask if she was okay—leaving Teo looking like the instigator. He blew out a breath.

Wishful thinking hadn't stopped the incident from making the headlines, probably how Maya knew about it. The school had not called the cops, opting instead for the palace head of security. *I would've preferred the police.*

The wrought-iron gates surrounding the palace rose up before him like a sentry, keeping out Foresters and general riffraff. Golden light shone through every window, illuminating the building. His stomach dropped as he halted. *No, no, no. The state dinner.* The clock tower chimed. He had minutes to get dressed and get down to the ballroom. *Stupid. How could I forget?* He scrubbed his hands over his face before jogging to the family entrance and his unwanted obligations for the night.

Chapter Three

Rider

W*HAT JUST HAPPENED?*

The bike forgotten in her hand, she stood staring stupidly as the guy she'd hit limped away. He'd stepped off the curb right into her lane. True, she'd been in a hurry to get out of the city and home, as the time she'd been forced to spend at the FBC had made her day twice as long. Then suddenly he was right in front of her. He hadn't checked for traffic, only walked into the street as though he owned the place. *Typical of a Wolf.*

What confused her was the concern in his eyes for her well-being, belying his snarl. *And* he had tried to fix her tire, then offered to buy her a new one. *Not typical of a Wolf.*

Rider sagged against the frame of the bike, the ache overtaking her body. Her stomach growled, reminding her she hadn't eaten since breakfast and she still had a long ride home. Breathing deeply, Rider examined the front wheel—the guy had done a good job of straightening it. She flung a leg over the bar and lowered herself gingerly to the seat, and the bicycle stayed upright. *That's a good sign.*

Something sticky slid down the side of her face, reminding her that she was bleeding. She touched her fingers to her forehead. *Just a scrape, but heads bleed. A lot.* The hanky her dad made her carry was stuffed in her pocket and she withdrew it, her lips lifting. A handkerchief was better for the environment than tissues, and he was fond of reminding her that a person never knew when they might need one. *Right again, Dad.* After tying it around her head to stop the flow of blood, she scanned the area, searching for her backpack. A pair of broken glasses, along with crumpled papers and food wrappers, were scattered across the cobblestones. She searched the other side of the street. When she spotted her pack, lying in the gutter next to the curb, she steered the bike over and then leaned down to scoop it up. As she threaded her arms through the straps, she grimaced at the pain shooting through her shoulder. *All I want is to soak in an herbal bath.* Groaning to herself, she pushed her bike forward. It wobbled only slightly.

The steady, albeit bumpy, rhythm of the wheels relaxed Rider as her mind sorted through the day's events. The inconvenience of "expired" papers had more to do with the king wielding his authority than anything else. Either someone had ticked him off, probably a Forester, or he was paranoid about a power grab. King Duko was extremely vigilant about keeping his throne safe. Precise records were kept of troublemakers, new immigrants, and forest people. One of the ways he kept tabs on everyone was through the issuing of documents. Or making everyone renew them whenever he felt powerless. She couldn't remember her papers ever coming close to an expiry date.

So glad Ethan was with me. The mass of people in the line-up had provided great entertainment. Young and old, a few families, several other teens, all had waited to get a stamp before they could move on with their day. She and Ethan had filled the time people watching, making up stories about everyone's lives. They'd also mocked the Wolves running the desk. Of course, that was done in whispers because if they ever got caught disrespecting a Wolf, they'd be hauled down to the guard's offices. Rider shuddered.

The guy at the desk had been on a power trip. She needed to be more careful. *Keep your head down and don't draw attention to yourself.* Her father's deep baritone echoed in her ears. She hadn't done a good job of that today—first the dude at FBC and then hitting the military guy in the street. Not her finest moments, but those arrogant Wolves deserved it. *Wait.* A thought niggled her. Her mind jumped back and forth between the two guys. Back and forth, back and forth, to the rhythm of her feet pedaling.

The bike slowed as she drew up to the guards patrolling the city gates, but they waved her through with barely a glance at her papers. She shook her head at the inconsistency of it all, which kept the Foresters on edge. Like the guy tonight—he hadn't acted the way she'd expected. She pumped her legs hard as she left the city behind, the urge to get home giving her a shot of adrenaline. The farther Rider got from the city, the deeper the night sky darkened, until it was a velvet canopy over her. The moon shone like a large diamond with smaller stars twinkling throughout. The desk clerk's eyes flashed through her mind. They had glittered like diamonds behind his glasses when she had ticked him off. Hmmm. Come to think of it, so did the bike wrecker's eyes, although he didn't have glasses.

Rider hit the brakes. *Glasses.* That was it. How could she be so dense? The desk clerk and the bike wrecker were the same guy. His hair hadn't looked red, but it was too dark to tell for sure. The broken glasses in the street, though? She'd bet they were his. He wasn't as much of a jerk as the FBC dude. When he'd offered to have her bike fixed, he'd gone way beyond what was required of a Wolf to a forest person, according to Wolf law. Confidence faded as she rode on. Maybe he wasn't the same guy. But those eyes... *If he was one and the same, why the schizophrenia? And why the disguise?* She frowned. *Why do you care?* None of it made any sense, but then the Wolves rarely made sense.

Rider pumped her legs harder, eager to be home where the world sat correctly on its axis. Her dad wasn't prone to fearful fancies, but it was late enough he'd be checking the front window. And she was too tired to try and figure out the mystery of that guy tonight. Whoever he was. A prickling ran over her scalp. *He was the same guy.*

The lamplight from her front window greeted her, easing her anxiety as she cycled up the path to her childhood home. The house wasn't big but it was cozy, and the cheerful red door welcomed everyone. Rider shivered, glad to see smoke rising from the chimney. The curtain rippled as she approached. She waved, letting her father know she was okay, then steered around to the back of the house, dismounted, and locked up her bike. She strode into the warm kitchen, where her dad met her with a big hug. She threw her arms around him.

"What happened? Are you okay?" He kissed the top of her head.

When she spoke, Rider's voice was muffled against his chest. "I'm fine. I had a minor accident, and our papers expired today, so I spent two hours waiting in line at FBC."

"I heard about the papers. Mrs. Templeton dropped by to pick up medicine for her father and she filled me in. Everyone's been speculating as to why. But what's this about an accident? Are you hurt?" He held her at arm's length, searching for injuries, his gaze landing on the handkerchief. He let go of her and lifted it away from her wound, prodding it gently with his fingers. "Just a scrape, but head wounds—"

"Bleed a lot," she interrupted. "I know, Dad."

"I'll clean it up and put salve on it. How did it happen?" He opened a cupboard and pulled down a brown glass bottle and then selected another container of ointment and a clean cloth. "Sit down and tell me what happened. It's not like you to fall off your bike."

Sighing, Rider sank onto one of the wooden kitchen chairs. "A jerk stepped out into the street without even looking. I barrelled right into him and we both went flying. At least I was on my way home." Her dad dabbed at the cut and she inhaled sharply. The pungent odor of the ointment filled her nostrils, waking her senses. "I got the raw deal, though. My front tire is bent, and I feel like I got hit by a truck."

Her dad gently smoothed lotion onto her cut and covered it with a small bandage. "You'll live. I'll take a gander at your bike tomorrow. If you rode it home, it's probably within my abilities to fix it." He capped the bottles. "Since you're sitting here and I'm not bailing you out of a cell, I take it that you didn't hit a Wolf?"

"That's the weird part, Dad. The guy was from the city—Wolf Pack from the cut of his coat—but he *offered* to replace the tire. He said to take it to Fang's... I refused, but it surprised me. Then he straightened out the tire for me. Even stranger, I'm pretty sure he was the same arrogant guy who stamped my papers earlier in the day at the FBC, except something was different about him. He had red hair there and glasses. When I rammed into him with my bike, he had short, dark hair, military style. But I'd recognize his voice and eyes anywhere." Those glittery diamond orbs that pierced right through her. It was definitely the same guy. The more she thought about it, the surer she was. "It doesn't make any sense."

Her dad rubbed the stubble on his chin. "Maybe you were more dazed than you realized from the accident. Why would a Wolf go out of his way for you? Especially Wolf Pack? Maybe you misunderstood, and he was simply suggesting a garage to take it to."

"Hmm, maybe." Rider tapped her fingers on the table, thinking.

"You need to eat. You'll feel better after a good night's sleep, and your brain and body will be rested and ready to go." He opened a cupboard and grabbed a bowl.

Only then did Rider notice the enticing aroma of beef and vegetables coming from the pot simmering away on the stovetop. Her dad filled a bowl and brought it over to the table, along with a piece of crusty bread. Her stomach grumbled loudly.

Her dad laughed. "I think your body is telling you it needs food." He ran his fingers over her head and smiled at her.

She picked up the spoon and dug into the steaming bowl, savouring the bite of rich gravy and tangy veggies. It burned her tongue slightly, but she didn't care. As she chewed, she thought about the Wolf she'd met that day. She couldn't put her finger on it, but things didn't add up. *Why would a Wolf behave that way? Strange.*

Rider shovelled the stew into her mouth, scraping up the remaining bits with a crust of bread before washing the bowl at the sink. After grabbing a tea towel and drying her hands, she braced herself against the countertop, fatigue washing over her.

"G'night, Dad. I'm beat."

"Sweet dreams, honey."

Groaning, Rider dragged her body up the stairs to her room, flopping face first onto the soft bed. She sighed, snuggling into the soft blankets, her eyelids drooping. Her mind drifted as though meandering along a lazy river. Three boys playing in the forest, their shouts grabbing her attention. The image faded as the shouts died, replaced by mud mixing with green, leafy bits as her small hands made a salve. Then she stood staring into ice blue eyes at the FBC. Those eyes, familiar, faded to a dark glow as a hand reached out to help her on a dark city street.

Rider jolted upright out of her sleepy daze. Her eyes skittered around her room, then she scrubbed her face. A dream. Wasn't it? She swung her legs over the side of the bed and stood, grabbing her pyjamas off the floor. After changing, she sat on the edge of the bed, willing her mind to bring the dream back, but it was lost to the fog of sleep. She fell against her pillow, her mind roving over her very weird day and strange dream.

Chapter Four

Teo

TEO RAN DOWN THE hallway, his footfalls silent on the thick carpet. A guard tapped his watch and then shook his head as Teo passed. Teo frowned—he didn't need any reminders that he was in hot water.

At the large wooden doors, Teo skidded to a halt and straightened his tie and jacket before pulling them open. His fingers trembled as he fiddled with the tie's knot. His tux had been nowhere to be found—he hoped his father wouldn't notice. *Who am I kidding?* The king never missed a detail, and he would assume Teo's lack of proper attire was an act of rebellion. The day before, Teo had argued in favor of wearing his military dress uniform, but his parents vetoed that idea, telling him it would give too aggressive an image. Tonight, the Howell family wanted to play nice, which confused Teo. Usually, his father showed off his strength and power so no one would doubt who was in control. A subtle warning not to cross the king.

A quick glance at his own watch told him he was ten minutes late. If he was lucky, cocktails had gone long and his lateness would be unnoticed. He gracefully slid into the crowded room, the sweet smell of wine and champagne tickling his nose. The light reflecting from the chandeliers on the gold-painted walls and gleaming hardwood floors made the room glow. People from the four most powerful clans—Wolf, Bear, Deer, and Fox—filled the room. Color from every shade of the rainbow flooded his vision. Women dressed in gowns of ruby red, royal blue, purple, and green dotted the room. The men wore black, mostly tuxes. Teo yanked at his collar as he scanned the room. His gaze locked on his youngest brother, Seth.

A frown creasing his handsome features, Seth zig-zagged his way through people, tables, and chairs, his amber eyes never leaving Teo. His brother, tall and muscular, had raven hair like Teo, but that was where the similarities ended. Seth's confidence and purpose drew people to him. He embraced his role as prince. Teo, on the flip side, wanted to run the other way. From the crowds and from his responsibilities.

You should inherit the throne. Teo fingered a button of his suit jacket as he contemplated Seth's pristine tux and clean-shaven jaw. *I can't even find my tux.*

His parents, along with his Uncle Alarick, his father's brother, stood chatting with guests on the other side of the room. A fortunate break for Teo. As a waiter ambled past, Teo snagged a glass from his tray. After emptying it in one gulp, he set it on a table before his brother invaded his space.

"What do you want, Seth?" Teo wasn't in the mood for games.

"Where have you been? Dad's seething. And guess who's been on the receiving end of that wrath, Teo? Me, that's who. You're the crown prince, pull it together." Seth hissed the words through clenched teeth. "And where's your tux?"

No excuse was going to make this better. His brother grabbed his arm and dragged Teo to a secluded corner.

"Is that make-up on your face?"

Unfortunately, his cheek had been bruised when he'd hit the ground after being side-swiped by the bike. He'd swiped some kind of powder from his mom's suite and thought he'd done a good job with the stuff.

"Funny thing happened on the way to the ball tonight." Teo chuckled humourlessly. "I got hit by a bike courier on the way home from FBC. That's why I'm late."

"You escorted him to jail yourself? Why didn't you call the Pack?"

"No, it wasn't like that. It was an accident. I wasn't paying attention when I stepped into the road, and she was right there." Teo clamped his mouth shut. Why had he admitted that to Seth, of all people?

The sound of tinkling glasses and laughter filled the awkward silence that descended between the two brothers. "Were you still in disguise? How do you know it was an accident? Maybe she recognized you. You could have been targeted."

Teo shook his head. "It wasn't like that," he repeated.

"You should have called the Pack. Arrested her. You're Prince Teowulf. You know, the *crown* prince."

"Call the Pack? I might as well put out a press statement that the crown prince had messed up again. I don't need any more bad press. Besides, it's a scratch. She was in worse shape than me. Dazed and confused. She didn't recognize me."

"You're sure?"

"Yeah, so don't tell Dad."

"Teo." Seth drew out his name, ending it with a sigh.

"Seth," Teo grabbed his brother's elbow. "He'll sentence me to a year of palace arrest."

His younger brother popped a knuckle. Teo grimaced. He hated that sound. Seth glared at him. "This is the last time I'm covering for you. I mean it."

Teo locked eyes with his brother, waiting until Seth blinked. There was no way his youngest brother was going to win a staring contest. Teo was oldest, and the alpha next in line to his father. Seth had to cave or challenge him—rules of the Pack.

Seth's jaw clenched, but he flicked his eyes away first.

At least his brother knew his place in the family. Teo opened his mouth to speak, but Seth huffed away. With a glance around the emptying floor, Teo decided to follow his little brother. As people seated themselves at tables, leaving less of a crowd, Teo was exposed, and he didn't want to get cornered by his father. A groan escaped as Teo slid onto his seat. His other brother, Bleddyn, lifted a glass in a *cheers* gesture but asked, from the corner of his mouth, "What's the matter?"

"Later," he murmured. Bleddyn would drop it for now. It was not the time or place. Seth seated himself on the other side of Bleddyn. Their father preferred to line them up from oldest to youngest at these dinners. *What are we, five?* Teo contemplated his siblings. Bleddyn had a wildness about him. The grey hair didn't help—an inherited gene from their mother. He used to be white blond, but, as he grew older, his white turned a silver grey, striking with his hazel eyes.

Bleddyn quipped about a trivial event, and Seth laughed. A warmth stirred within Teo. Despite the occasional friction, they were his best friends, and he knew they had his back—unlike outsiders who didn't understand the pressures of the palace. His father ran a very tight and strict kingdom, his family being no exception.

A shadow fell across the table, and the warmth he'd enjoyed suddenly turned to a cold chill. His father, intimidating in his black tux, his long black hair slicked off his forehead, towered over Teo. A thin silver crown nestled on top of the king's head. Teo and his brothers stood. The king gestured with his hand for them to sit, but he didn't move away. Instead, he spread his fingers on the table and leaned in to Teo, who met his father's intense stare steadily.

The smile curving the king's lips didn't reach his golden eyes. "You're late, Teowulf."

Teo gripped the edges of his chair, hidden under the tablecloth. "My deepest regrets, Sir. The lines were long at the FBC…"

His father's eyes narrowed. Teo was pushing it—his father knew why there had been long lines, meaning that Teo's words could be interpreted as an accusation. The king frowned at his eldest son before making his way to the middle of the table where the queen was already seated. Teo untangled his fingers one by one from the death clutch he had going with the chair.

Bleddyn elbowed him in the ribs. "Seriously, Teo? Putting the blame on Father for your lateness? Are you nuts? Get your act together, or Dad will have more than your hide."

"Don't remind me." Teo wiped his sweaty palms on his pants. "But the lines *were* long because of him." He picked up his goblet of water and gulped down the contents. A waitress set a steaming plate of roasted meat in front of each of them, cutting off anything else his brother might say. Teo's mouth watered at the smell of garlic and meat juices. He picked up his fork and knife and dove into the delicious red meat.

After the five-course meal, each plate more decadent than the one preceding it, their father rose to his feet, lifting a glass towards the guests of honour, who sat to his left. Until now, Teo hadn't paid attention to the people sitting there. He didn't recognize anyone. *What clan are they?* Their uniforms and dress were not ones he'd seen before. Instead of the usual glitz and glamour that guests typically wore to the palace, these people were plainly dressed in black suits or dresses except for the hair colour of the men. Purple, blue, and white hair adorned the men. Wigs or dye? It definitely wasn't natural, which was odd.

A chorus rose around him, and Teo hastily grabbed his wine glass and lifted it. He'd missed his father's toast, but he didn't care. It probably wasn't important—more boring politics.

Wait staff descended upon the room, cleaning up the debris from dinner and magically transforming the room from dining hall to ballroom. The strains of a violin competed with those of a bass, as a string quartet warmed up in the corner. Teo wasn't in the mood for festivities tonight. His body ached from being hit, and it had been a long day. Stifling a yawn behind a hand, Teo searched for the nearest exit that wasn't in his father's field of vision. Sleep was at the forefront of his mind. He took one step, only to be grabbed by Bleddyn and steered in the opposite direction.

"Are you crazy?" Bleddyn whispered loudly. "You can't escape yet."

Teo scowled at his brother. "I've put in my appearance. Let me go."

"Nope. That's not happening."

Bleddyn steered him over to a group of young people—the guests of honour. The suits and dresses may have looked plain, but close up the fabrics were fine wool and rich satin. Obviously expensive and well cut. He fingered his own tie. *Didn't need the tux anyway.* He studied the strangers with their unique appearance. These were not the sort of people his father usually had dealings with—a bit too fantastical for the uptight king. What was dear old dad up to?

"Teo, I'd like you to meet Tania, Frederick, and Hansel. They are from the Falls District. Part of the small Peacock clan. My brother, the crown prince, Teowulf."

Peacock clan explained their hair, but a bell rang somewhere in Teo's brain. As the crown prince, he was privy to a small number of reports about surrounding districts. The Peacock clan had made some significant strides in scientific research, most notably in chemistry and pharmaceuticals. Was that why his father had invited them?

The young woman curtsied as the guys bowed. Heat flushed up Teo's neck, and he tugged his collar again. This was the part he hated. What was wrong with a simple handshake? He acknowledged them with a slight dip of his head before taking Tania's hand, drawing it to his mouth, and kissing the back of it lightly. Flowers mixed with a chemical smell wafted up his nose. An odd mix and not at all pleasant. He cleared his throat, hoping to displace the aroma. "Pleasure to meet you. I've never met anyone from the Peacock clan before." The boys' hair colour was eye popping and definitely dyed. *Obviously trying to mimic their namesake.*

Tania smiled, dimples showing in her cheeks. With hazel eyes and blonde hair that hung to her shoulders, she was pretty, but not Teo's type. A flash of red and dark curls hijacked his mind. *Whoa.* He forced his attention to Tania, who was staring at him, her head cocked. "I'm sorry, can you repeat that?"

"I think this is a great thing our fathers are doing."

Her brothers nodded eagerly beside her, so Teo did as well, although he had no clue what she was talking about. Would she say more? Bleddyn stood across from him, his keen interest apparent in the way he leaned forward slightly. The king didn't divulge information to his sons like Tania's father did.

"Our product is superior to the forest's in every way. It mirrors their medicines and salves, but ours are much more effective and reliable. Nor are we dependent on Mother Nature to supply them. We depend on ourselves."

Teo blinked. "What exactly is it you do for your father?"

"I'm a scientist. We all are. My brothers are chemists and I'm a botanist. I pick the plants that need to be imitated, and then the boys create a synthetic copy of them." She fingered the string of pearls around her neck. "Brilliant, isn't it?"

This was what the king was up to? Images of all the Foresters who'd come into the FBC that day flipped through his mind. The red hood who delivered medicine. What would it mean for her? He sipped his drink. *Why do you care?* He didn't. He didn't care one iota about a girl from the forest. He was the crown prince of Wolf kingdom. One day he'd rule it all.

The king and queen glided onto the dance floor, halting all conversation. A melodious waltz invited dancing, and the royal couple gracefully made their way across the space cleared for dancing. Oohs and ahs echoed around the room as they glided over the shining hardwood floor. Teo politely watched, but, when the music ended, he made his excuses and left the party.

His body desired rest, but his mind had other ideas. The clock chimed two before he fell asleep.

Chapter Five

Rider

A COOL BREEZE BLEW through the forest, ruffling the red and yellow leaves. Autumn in the forest was Rider's favorite season, although no season was bad in her beloved home. Her bike glided swiftly over the hard ground as she passed by a small brown cottage with a bright orange door and red shutters. The Wilders, the older couple who lived there, grew squash, pumpkins, and gourds in fields on the other side of the forest. They were a kind couple, and Rider had spent many hours helping them harvest vegetables. Today they sat on their porch swing, steam wafting from the mugs they held in their hands. She waved as she biked past them.

A slight breeze loosened a strand of hair from her ponytail. Shivering, Rider pulled her hood up over her hair to ward off the chill. The warmth of the wood stove in her kitchen beckoned her home.

"Rider." Ethan rode up beside her.

She braked, skidding to a stop. "Hey, Ethan, what's up?" It'd been a week since they'd waited in line at the FBC, and she hadn't seen much of her friend since then. Fall was harvest time for the truffles, so Ethan worked a lot, helping with the harvesting when he wasn't making deliveries.

"Hey, I knew that was you. I can always tell because of the colour of the hood. It's different than other red coats or jackets."

"You too can own a Rider original. I've told you over and over I'll dye one of your shirts using the special dye I make from chokecherries and red autumn leaves." She eyed his empty bike bag. "Are you returning from a delivery as well?"

"I am. The fall is always crazy." He tugged on her empty bag. "For both of us. The Wolves need their truffles and their medicine."

"Yeah, especially as we enter the cold weather and flu season. But, unlike truffles, the herbs don't grow in the winter. Dad and I are harvesting soon before they all die off."

He fiddled with his handle bars, avoiding her eyes.

"What?"

"Did you hear anything in the city today?"

"About what?"

Ethan slouched on his seat, balancing on his one leg and the bike. "Rumours... I think." A bird chirped, then swooped out of a tree. Ethan's eyes followed the movement. "There's talk another company is providing Wolf kingdom with meds."

Rider jerked at the words. "What?"

Ethan reached out a steadying hand, gripping her handlebars to hold her bike in place so they both didn't end up in a heap on the ground.

"What did you hear, exactly?"

"King Duko made a deal with the Falls District and ChemTech to provide synthetic medicine."

"Synthetic medicine? They think they can replicate a plant's healing powers? How would that work?"

Ethan pointed to himself. "You're asking me? I failed chemistry. Your dad might know more. Maybe they've consulted him?"

"No, he would have told me. And no one said anything at any of the doctor's offices I delivered packages to today. I need to get home. C'mon."

Heart pounding, Rider raced through the woods, her dark ponytail flying like a flag in the wind. Ethan puffed behind her. Stupid Wolves. They may be the landowners, but that didn't mean they could dictate her life or the lives of her neighbours. *That's exactly what it means.* They controlled everything—trade, livelihoods, travel— keeping the Foresters under their thumb. When she careened into the driveway of her house, her dad stopped raking the colourful leaves that swallowed up the front yard.

"Dad!" Rider jumped off her bike before it had completely stopped.

Her father dropped the rake and jogged over to her, concern etched on his face. "What is it? Are you okay?"

"Did you know King Duko's made a deal for synthetic drugs with someone else?"

Her dad's jaw slackened. "Are you sure?."

"Ethan heard it in the city. The king has agreed to trade for synthetic drugs."

Her father patted her shoulder. "Breathe, Jenna-girl," he said. "Hey, Ethan."

"Hey, Dr. Hood." Ethan eased off his bike and then kicked down the stand.

"How's the truffle business?"

"If Caps'n Stems gets any busier, they'll have to hire more people."

Dr. Hood chuckled. "I bet the Capwells aren't complaining."

Rider set her bike against the house. *Who cares about truffles?* "Ethan, tell my dad what you found out in the city today."

"I was at the small corner store where the couriers hang out if we have a second between jobs." He rubbed his gloved hands together. "One of the guys, who lives near the border of Wolf kingdom and the Falls District, said he heard the news from a friend who works at ChemTech."

Dr. Hood frowned. "That's disturbing information, if it's true."

"You didn't know, Dad?"

"This is the first I'm hearing about it. No one said anything to you as you made the deliveries?"

Rider threw her hands up. "Not a word. Why wouldn't they?"

"They might not have the green light from the palace to say anything. Too bad you didn't have to deliver any meds to Dr. Lupine's today. His office always seems to deal with us fairly and honestly."

"Yeah, it's been a week since I was there." Rider chewed the inside of her cheek. "Would Dr. Lupine go along with this?"

"I doubt any of the doctors have a choice, if the order is coming from the king." Her father rubbed his chin. "I wonder what Duko's endgame is? He's playing with fire, trying to mimic the healing power of nature. Plants can't be impersonated. People have tried before, with destructive results. You two are too young to remember, but we had a sickness go through here thirty years ago. The Wolves came up with a drug that, in the end, only made the sickness worse. Shortly after that, they left making medicine in our hands because we'd been doing it for years. Duko fought it, but his council forced his hand. Too many Wolves had died."

"Did the sickness affect us too?" Rider shoved her cold hands into her jacket pockets, but she wasn't about to go inside.

"Yes, but we used our own remedies, and we fared much better than the Wolves. That's why Duko had to give up the fight. We'd already proved our medicine worked."

"What are we going to do, Dad?"

Dr. Hood kicked loose leaves into the pile he'd raked earlier. "I'll go see Dr. Graham at the Forest Apothecary this afternoon. He may have some news. Not much goes unnoticed by him in the pharmaceutical society. Don't worry, Jenna-girl. It'll be okay." He wrapped his arms around Rider, and she squeezed his waist. In her dad's arms, she always felt safe. After a moment, he pulled away, then nodded to Ethan before heading around back.

Ethan fiddled with the band of his watch. "I better go. The Capwells will be wondering where I am. Your Dad's right; don't worry. It'll work out." He picked up his bike and slid his long leg over the bar until he straddled it. Pushing off, he waved goodbye.

She bit her bottom lip, trying to let go of the worrisome thoughts flooding her brain. *Never trust a Wolf.*

⸺◇⸺

Teo

Teo trudged along the wooded trail, his gut clenched into a tight ball. Two other Wolf Pack guards followed behind. In his hand, he held a letter for Dr. Hood, sealed by the king. Wolf kingdom no longer required the pharmacist's services. His father thought it would be more effective if the message was delivered in person, and since Teo had been tardy last night for the dinner, he'd been elected the messenger boy. The red wig and new glasses were in place because this wasn't a duty for the crown prince but an errant son. According to his father, anyway.

Dr. Hood. Teo's mind flicked to the courier who had graced the FBC the other day. Jenna Hood. Teo assumed she must be related to Dr. Hood. Would she be at the house today? Maybe he could deliver her a message too—Wolves deserved respect. Would she even recognize him? Probably from the FBC. Sometimes Wolf Pack filled in when the FBC were short-staffed, so him showing up in a uniform as the FBC guy shouldn't raise her suspicions.

The Hood cottage came into view, and Teo breathed in deeply through his nose and out through his mouth. *Pull it together*. There was no need to be nervous; Foresters served the king. It was their privilege, and if the king decided to take away their livelihoods, so be it. Although, in Teo's opinion, the king should be the one delivering the news in person. His fingers tightened around the scroll, crumpling it slightly.

The two guards placed themselves at the edges of the lawn as Teo rapped on the door. A middle-aged man with piercing green eyes answered. Those eyes were familiar. Definitely related.

"Dr. Hood?"

The man nodded, eyeing him. "Yes, that's me."

Teo handed over the papers. "On behalf of the king, I'm letting you know that your services as pharmacist to Wolf kingdom and Wolf City are no longer required, as of the first of next month."

The man took the papers Teo handed him. As he backed away, Teo spotted a flash of red behind a sheer curtain, but it disappeared as quickly as it had appeared. It was probably his imagination. As Teo hurried down the path, he heard the click of the front door closing. He ignored the desire to glance behind him to see if he could see her. The red hood. Teo shook his head. He hated being his dad's lackey.

———◆———

Rider

"It's true." Dr. Hood's words fell flat as he stared at the papers in his hands. "Duko really did make a deal with the Falls District and ChemTech to produce their synthetic versions of natural healing herbs and plants. The palace is holding a press conference tomorrow." He waved the letter. "At least the palace had the courtesy to let me know before they announced it."

Rider studied her father as he slumped into a wooden chair at the harvest table. His strawberry-blond hair was greying at the temples, and he needed a haircut. His green eyes, the only thing, physically, that Rider had inherited from him, had shadows under them, and his crow's feet had deepened.

"Why would King Duko do this? It makes no sense." Rider sat beside her dad, setting her elbows on the table and resting her head in her hands. Her temples throbbed from the blood pounding through her veins. But it wasn't the letter that had caused that. At the sight of the messenger, her heart had gone to the races. It was the guy from the FBC, who may or may not be the same one she'd hit later that night. Rider bit her lip. What kind of coincidence was that? She blew out a breath into her hands. Had he had some ulterior motive in coming here? She lifted her head. He wasn't going to intimidate her, even though that was exactly how she felt. "Scratch that. It makes absolute sense. It's another way the Wolves can lord themselves over us." Her jaw tightened. She wouldn't give in to her fear. How dare they?

Her father folded his arms across his stomach. "It's not your worry, Jenna-girl. I'm going to call Dr. Graham and we'll figure something out. Maybe we can meet with Duko, convince him he's making a mistake."

"Do you really think Duko will listen? He hasn't ever before. The Wolf clan doesn't care about us—that it's our livelihood. They haven't even offered any kind of compensation. We need to stand up to them. Make them see us. Show them we are equals."

"We'll try talking to them first. It probably won't make Duko change his mind but... I'm not giving up yet." His smile didn't reach his eyes. "I'm gonna start supper. How does soup sound?"

"I'll make it, Dad. Why don't you finish raking the yard. By the time you're done, the soup will be ready." Rider rooted around in the fridge and found celery, onions, and carrots. Chopping vegetables would keep her hands busy. *I'd like to chop up King Duko.*

"Okay, sweetie. Thanks." He grabbed his coat off the hook and headed outside.

Rider diced the vegetables with gusto, sending a piece of carrot scurrying to the floor. She pretended it was Duko's head. If she worried about the king, then she couldn't focus on the FBC guy. Arrogant Wolves. *They think they're smarter and stronger than everyone else, as if that gives them permission to do what they please. It's got to stop. Someone has to stand up to Duko. To the Wolves.* She shuddered, thinking about the consequences of losing their livelihood.

If we can't provide medicine, why would they let us stay here? Rider froze, the knife in the air. Would Duko make them leave? Did the king hate the Foresters that much? Rider white-knuckled the knife. There was no way she'd let the Wolves, or Duko, get away with stealing their jobs and homes. Forest people were not less than Wolves, and it was time the Wolf clan got that message.

Chapter Six

Teo

T EO STOOD BESIDE HIS mother on the platform, his uncle Alarick, an advisor to the king, on her other side. A thousand tiny ants crawled over his skin, although Teo knew it was all in his imagination. He resisted the urge to jump off the stage and run, instead straightening his shoulders, his hand grazing the ceremonial sword at his right side. His brothers stood to the left side of the stage while his father, front and centre, waited at the podium. The sound person adjusted the mic on the stand.

Teo shuffled his feet, then stilled as his mother's blue eyes lasered through him, an effect she'd mastered over the years. She could communicate an entire speech through one pointed stare, a cock of the head, or a raised eyebrow.

People crowded the front lawn of the palace, filling every available space. Curiosity about the king's announcement had brought them out in droves. Rumours had been flying since the ball—mostly wild speculation about ChemTech's products. From what Teo had heard, you'd think they had cured all the world's ills. Lacing these tall tales was a smugness that finally they would be independent of the forest and their medicines. Hood's medicines mainly. As a result, before him stood not only the palace courtiers but most of the inhabitants of Wolf City, eagerly waiting for his father to speak.

Teo kept his features blank, willing the time to pass. So what if they got meds from another county? The important thing was to do what was best for Wolf kingdom. They didn't need the forest—not now. A memory of Dr. Hood's disappointed face as Teo delivered the news flitted through his mind. He shoved it away. Wolves were superior to everyone, especially to those nature-loving, berry-picking Foresters. He'd heard it so often growing up it was now a voice-over in his head, in his father's voice, of course.

What exactly makes us superior? He'd always been told his people were stronger, smarter. Yes, Wolves were taller than most Foresters, who were leaner and shorter, but did that measure superiority? Perhaps physically, but Teo doubted it. He'd seen many Foresters haul heavy loads into the city as he patrolled the gates.

As for intelligence, Teo wouldn't bet on Wolves being smarter. Dr. Hood was an example of a very smart Forester. Teo side-eyed his father, who was engrossed in conversation with his press secretary. One didn't question King Duko, especially not his sons. But the absence of a good answer to that question nagged Teo.

The mic screeched. His dad glowered at the sound guy. *Yikes.* Sympathy for the techie washed over Teo because the sound team would hear about it later. Probably the man would be demoted for that little gaffe. The king hated to be embarrassed. He didn't put up with any show of weakness at all. Even a screeching mic.

The tech guy closed his eyes and humbly gave his dad the go-ahead sign. The king stepped up to the podium. A hush fell over the crowd, all eyes turned to the man who led Wolf kingdom. His family had been in control for a hundred years, making it the prosperous empire it was today. Duko never missed an opportunity to take credit, either.

"My great people, I have exciting news for you today..."

Teo tuned out his dad's voice, scanning the crowd as he'd been taught to do in the military, looking for threats or anything unusual, suspicious. He wasn't on duty, but he'd take surveillance over listening to his father drone on. Teo's bored look belied the fact that his body was alert and wired, ready to move if need be. His eyes swept over the crowd, snagging on ... The sunshine glared and he lost sight of whatever had caught his eye. Retracing his visual path, he searched the crowd again. *Where was it?* An old woman leaned against a man next to a kid on his dad's shoulders. No, before that. *There.* A red hood.

Squinting against the sun, Teo strained to get a better look without giving himself away. *I wish I'd worn my sunglasses.*

Were those dark curls under the hood? He was too far away to be certain. She wouldn't come out here, would she? The person's face was in shadow, but he'd recognize that unique colour anywhere. He'd never seen anyone else wear that exact shade of red. Jenna Hood. The girl with the attitude from the FBC. The girl who'd smashed into him on her bike. A courier for Hood medicines. Of course, she'd want to hear the king's address to the Wolves. The spin he'd put on it for his people. At the FBC, Teo had actually read the words on her papers, taking his time in order to annoy her. And he had seen a flash of red the other day while delivering the news to her family home. *Yes, she would come to Wolf City. And she was right in front of him.*

Teo slowly shifted his weight from one foot to the other. This announcement would radically affect the way the Forest clan and the Wolf clan interacted. The forest depended on trade with the Wolves, and the Wolves depended on the forest's primary exports—medicine and food. His father hated that dependency on the forest, especially for something so important. There wasn't much to be done about food, because the Foresters farmed a lot of the land, something Wolves weren't too interested in doing. But the medicine seemed to irritate Duko, and he ranted every chance he got about Wolves needing to be self-sufficient. Nature was too unreliable, which somehow made it the Foresters' fault. The kingdom needed to find another medicine source, hence the deal the king had made. Technically, the meds coming from ChemTech didn't make the Wolves self-sufficient, since they still depended on outsiders to supply them, but Duko seemed to have no problem overlooking that fact. Teo wasn't fooled; he knew his father. This new trade deal with the Falls District and ChemTech was about more than reliability. His father wanted revenge. Teo's forehead wrinkled. *Revenge for what?*

Duko smiled from the podium. He cracked a joke and the crowd roared. Teo blinked to avoid rolling his eyes. The people of Wolf kingdom thought their king was accessible, but, in reality, if they got too close, they nursed bite marks. Only the queen was allowed that kind of access, no one else, not even his sons. Reflecting on it now, Teo wasn't sure if his father let his mother in all the way either.

The area where Teo had glimpsed the hood was now void of that particular shade of red. Somehow, Jenna Hood had magically disappeared, like a poof of smoke. His shoulders sagged slightly, but he straightened when his mother cleared her throat. Teo didn't need another lecture about his posture and what people would read into it.

Clapping and whistles filled the air as his father wrapped up his speech. The fanfare faded, and Teo fell in line behind his parents, following them through the palace entrance.

Other government officials slapped his dad on the shoulder, smiling and laughing. Teo's head throbbed. He turned to his mother. "I'm going to my room. I've got a headache." He didn't wait for her permission. After striding around a corner, Teo bolted up the servants' staircase and jogged to his room. As soon as he was inside his suite, he stripped off his uniform and shrugged on a T-shirt and dark jeans. Then he grabbed his coat and beanie off the hook and sped along the corridors, back to the servants' staircase. He needed freedom from the confines of the castle.

"Where you going, big brother?"

Teo startled, whirling around to see a blur of muscle move around him and block the staircase. Bleddyn.

"Jumpy? Not good for a Wolf to be on edge. Where are you going?"

"I need fresh air—I've got a booming head. If you'll excuse me." Teo started to move down the stairs, but his brother was quicker, grabbing his shirttail.

"Not so fast." Only his brother's grip on his shirt kept Teo from falling. "Tell me what's going on. You seemed distracted at the press conference." His hazel eyes pierced Teo, like lasers cutting him in two, exposing him.

Teo jerked away from his brother's grip. "I told you, I've got a headache. That's it."

Bleddyn pursed his lips and then held up a small envelope. "Mother sent me to give you this."

"What is it?"

"Medicine for your headache... from ChemTech. She thought you looked a bit pale. We all recognize the signs of your migraines by now, and she thought this might help." Bleddyn jiggled the envelope and then held it behind him. "But first, tell me what had your attention at the press conference."

"Nothing. I was bored so I was scanning the crowd as if I was on duty." Teo lunged at Bleddyn, but his brother side-stepped him.

"Hmmm. I'll figure it out eventually." He held the envelope out to Teo, who snatched it.

"Mind your own business," he muttered as he shoved past his brother.

Teo jammed his beanie over his head as he headed out of the palace, walking behind bushes to avoid the guards. The Wolf Pack were thorough in their duties, but Teo was smarter. As a member of the Pack, he knew their habits and where they were lax. Growing up in the palace, Teo had learned all the good hiding places, places the Wolf Pack didn't know about or didn't bother to check. That combination helped Teo slip in and out of the palace without any problems. He arrived at the service gate as a white delivery van approached it. While the guard checked the driver's papers, Teo snuck around the far side of the vehicle and jogged away from his home and into the city's centre core. People still mingled around after the press conference, eating at restaurants or having coffee at cafés. Snatches of conversation wafted through the air.

"Glad we aren't going to depend on the forest for our medicine anymore."

"Duko always looks out for us."

"Like Hood has the only say in medicine. He can't be trusted."

Teo hurried on, his head throbbing to the beat of his footsteps. Remembering the envelope from his mother, he turned into a nearby café and bought a soda. After swigging down half of it, he popped the two tablets in his mouth, downing them with the rest of his drink. He needed to lie down, but the fresh air had cleared his foggy brain, so he headed home. Teo would look into Hood medicine and whatever he could find out about Jenna Hood. The fact that she'd been skulking around at the press conference nagged him. Why had she been there?

She knew what it was about—he'd delivered the message himself. What was she up to?

He wasn't going to rest until he figured it out.

Chapter Seven

Rider

❧ ·◆· ·◆· ·❧

THE PEOPLE ASSEMBLED ON the front steps of the palace were mostly government officials, members of the king's court, and city dwellers. Wolves. Rider slouched, letting her hood fall forward as she skulked towards the middle of the crowd. *I should have worn a different hood.* The red stood out. In a hurry to leave this morning, she'd forgotten to grab a different one. She furtively cast a glance around her. No one paid her any attention.

Around her, people murmured, snippets of their conversation drifting by her. "The king always looks out for us first."

"We rely too much on the forest."

"Hood Medicine has gotten cocky."

Why bother making a public announcement when everyone knew about the trade already? Rider shook her head. At least it kept people's attention off her. As a Forester, she wasn't really supposed to be there. Wolves frowned upon the Foresters sticking their noses into Wolf affairs. Occasionally Rider had witnessed press conferences, when she'd been in the city, but she'd always been on the fringe. Today she was right in the middle of the crowd. The last thing she needed was someone questioning why she was here. She'd end up in an interrogation office with a member of the Wolf Pack, where they would inevitably discover her identity. She slouched a little lower.

The royal family strode out onto the steps of the palace to a podium with the royal crest on it, followed by more government and palace officials. Rider studied the Howell family. King Duko was an imposing

45

figure in his military uniform. Although handsome, his demeanor challenged anyone who might consider messing with him. Up to this point, Rider had only seen Duko in pictures, never in person. Those pictures didn't do justice to the regal aura that surrounded him. Despite herself, Rider was drawn to him, to the whole family. A chill ran over her scalp, and she hugged her jacket closer. *Never trust a Wolf.* She'd better not forget that.

The queen was elegant with her grey hair knotted in a bun. Even as a child, she'd been grey with a prominent black stripe along the left side of her styled head, which added to her unique appearance. Although the queen was too far away today, Rider remembered those mesmerizing, ice-blue eyes from magazines and school texts. A thought snagged but she couldn't quite grasp it before it flitted away. Rider had read that the animal wolves, canine lupus, communicated with their eyes, a trait the Howell family appeared to share.

An older man stood on one side of the queen—an advisor, perhaps. But the person who captured her attention was the crown prince, who stood on the other side of the queen, dwarfing her with his height and broad shoulders. With the exception of that height, he was unlike his lean and wiry father in physical appearance. Confidence oozed off the heir, combined with a dash of arrogance. His gaze roamed the crowd, as though he remained alert to any threat.

Rounding out the family were the two younger brothers. All three of the princes wore military uniforms and ceremonial swords. All three belonged to the Wolf Pack. *Duly noted.* Rider usually didn't concern herself with the royals, but she hadn't been impervious to the gossip that flew when she was in the city. According to rumour, the crown prince managed to get himself in a fair bit of trouble. *I wish I'd paid more attention. I need to know who we're up against.* Today they stood right in front of her. She scanned the platform again, but the crown prince drew her to him like a magnet.

Rider took a step forward and squinted. *No... it couldn't be.* She shaded her eyes from the blaring rays of the sun. *He's the guy I hit.* Why would the crown prince be out in the street alone? Where was his security detail? *Maybe I'm mistaken.* She bit her lip.

Another thought slammed Rider. If it had been him, that meant he was probably the guard from the FBC because she was positive they were the same person. Why would he be working at the FBC? Rider clapped her hand to her mouth. *I was so rude.* She gawked at the royals. *I wish I could see his eyes. Then I'd know. No one else had eyes like that.* A thought clicked. *Except his mother.*

The prince seemed to look right at her, and Rider hunched her shoulders, bending her knees so she was less visible. *Please don't see me.* Her eyes widened. *I hit the crown prince with my bike. I hit the crown prince with my bike!* She gulped in air and then forced it out.

Wait ... He'd been totally to blame. The invisible hand squeezing her windpipe relaxed. Rider snuck another glance at him. His attention was directed towards his father, so she slunk away, hiding behind the mass of people, not willing to take the risk of staying.

She had the information she wanted about the trade deal, but the royal family was a puzzle. She'd physically assaulted and been rude to the heir to the throne, but she wasn't in jail. It didn't make any sense. Duko was untrustworthy, but maybe his son wasn't like him. Could it be?

Rider cast one last glance at the steps of the palace and the family standing there. They could be any family in any setting. A sense of déjà vu smacked her but quickly vanished. She headed home to the forest, the plan to save her dad already running through her mind.

———◦———

Ethan slouched against a tree, his bike on the ground nearby as Rider entered the forest. She slowed to a stop, straddling her bike. "What are you doing here?"

"Funny, I was about to ask you that same question." He crossed his arms. "What are you up to?"

She schooled her face into a blank canvas. "Nothing."

"Yeah, right," he scoffed. "You didn't run into a press conference, did you?"

"I don't know what you're talking about." Rider kicked her pedal and started to move away, but Ethan's arm on her handlebars stopped her momentum.

"You're a lousy liar, Rider. I *know* you went to that press conference."

"Okay, I did." She gripped her handlebars tightly. "You didn't tell my dad, did you?"

He rolled his eyes. "We're not in grade school."

"Thanks. I appreciate it. Dad worries too much. He'd kill me if he knew I went." She tugged her bike along the path, Ethan following.

"With good reason." Ethan huffed. "Why didn't you ask me? I'd have gone with you... I checked our old hiding spot to see if you'd left a coded message asking me to come."

Heat washed over her face. Why hadn't she asked him? "I was less conspicuous on my own. I wanted to get all the facts, make sure we were told the truth." She ignored the hurt in his eyes. "Did you really check the old hiding spot?"

"Yeah." Ethan picked up his pace, catching up with her. "I get wanting to go on your own, but it's not a smart or safe move."

"I know." She did know, but somehow she hadn't been able to help herself.

"Did you find out anything? No one saw you, right? You stayed on the fringe of the crowd?"

Rider kicked a rock out of her way. It tumbled a few feet and then stopped.

"Rider." Ethan groaned and halted his bike.

After braking, Rider turned and said, "I couldn't see anything. I had to move into the crowd."

Ethan drove his fingers through his hair. "Are you insane? If anyone spotted you, you'd be arrested for spying. Then they'd arrest your dad and half the forest."

Rider scratched her neck. "No one recognized me." *I hope.*

Brown leaves crunched beneath their feet as she relayed what the king had said at the conference. She left out the part about the crown prince being the victim of her bike accident, or that he'd been the officer at the FBC.

"What do you think your dad will do?"

"He and Dr. Graham are planning to try and talk to the palace. But we both know that Duko won't listen. I doubt they'll even get an appointment."

The crossroads where they went in separate directions neared. Ethan hopped on his bike. "I need to get home. I'll talk to you later?"

Rider nodded.

"Don't do anything stupid." Ethan glared at her before riding away.

Ethan didn't need to worry. Rider didn't plan on doing anything stupid, but she was going to do *something*.

Chapter Eight

Teo

T EO GROANED AS HE rolled over onto his side, opening one eye and then jamming it shut. His bedroom was dark, but it spun, regardless. Or maybe Teo was spinning. His stomach flipped over, churning, and he breathed deeply in through his nose, afraid he'd lose its contents if he opened his mouth. He clutched his pounding head, pressing his palms in where it hurt. ChemTech's medicine hadn't eased the pain; if anything, Teo felt worse than before.

He felt around the bedside table, toppling a book and a stack of papers before finally finding the drawer. After pulling it open, he fingered paper and pens and then clutched a smooth, small glass bottle. *Please don't be empty.* He jiggled the bottle, breathing a sigh of relief as liquid sloshed around. Leaving the drawer open, Teo rolled onto his back. His hands trembled, but he managed to get the top off and take two slugs of the gross tasting medicine. After capping the bottle, he leaned against the headboard and closed his eyes, willing his rebellious stomach to settle and the vice squeezing his skull to cease.

"Teo?" Bleddyn's voice roused Teo from a deep sleep.

"Hmmm?" he mumbled.

"Mom sent me to check on you. You missed dinner."

Teo rubbed his eyes before blinking. He squinted at the clock. "What time is it?"

"It's after seven o'clock."

Teo gingerly sat up, testing for pain and dizziness. Nothing. Only the hangover from the migraine remained. "I passed out."

"That ChemTech medicine was potent, eh?"

Teo flicked on the small table lamp on his bedside table, the dim glow not bothering his eyes. "No, it didn't work at all. My headache got worse. A couple of hours ago, I found leftover medicine of Dr. Hood's and took it." The bottle lay beside him. He held it up.

Bleddyn stepped farther into the room. "And now you're feeling better." Not a question.

Teo ran a hand over his head and rubbed his neck. "Yeah." He locked eyes with Bleddyn. "ChemTech's medicine was useless."

"Are you sure? Maybe it took a while and coincided with taking Hood's medicine."

"No. There was at least four hours between doses. And, as always, Hood's medicine worked."

Bleddyn sank onto a nearby chair. "Maybe it was a one off."

"Maybe."

"Are you going to tell father?"

Teo winced. That wasn't a conversation he wanted to have. "I probably should."

Bleddyn grimaced. "Good luck...Want me to go with you?"

"Nah. I'm going to be the future king; I should probably learn to stand up to my own father. He'll respect me more if I do, right?" *Maybe? I can hope.*

"Your funeral."

Or not. "Funny." Teo set the bottle in the nightstand's drawer. "I'll talk to him first thing in the morning." His stomach rumbled. "I need to eat." He swung his legs over the side of the bed and stood on shaky legs.

"Lots of leftovers." Bleddyn studied him. "I'll walk you to the kitchen—that way I can disperse any rumours you're drunk. You don't seem too steady."

"Ha ha." Although his wobbly legs certainly would make people doubt his sobriety. "Let's go. I'll feel better with food in my stomach." Teo followed his brother out of the room. Eating would help his head, but it wasn't going to erase the knot in his stomach. The last thing he wanted was to tell his father that ChemTech's drugs didn't work.

◆○◆

The king sat at the breakfast table reading the daily newspaper. The *Wolf Times* headline was about ChemTech taking over the production of medicine for the kingdom. Teo cringed. His cutlery rattled on his plate as he set it on the table.

"Good morning, Teo. You're up early." His father kept reading the paper.

"Morning, Sir."

Duko folded his paper in half in precise lines. "Missed you at supper. Your mother said you had a headache."

Teo cut into a piece of sausage. *I guess we're having this conversation now.* "I had another migraine."

"I'm sorry to hear that. Your mother said she gave you the new pain meds from ChemTech. Must have worked brilliantly since you're sitting here looking the picture of health this morning."

Teo stabbed a piece of meat. "It didn't work. After taking the drugs, I felt worse. Only after I found Dr. Hood's medicine and took it did I start to feel better." He chewed, but his eyes never left his father's face.

The king's eyes narrowed, and his jaw tightened. "What are you implying?"

"ChemTech's medicine didn't work—at all. Hood's did."

"And you know that because you took his medicine *after* taking ChemTech's? Obviously ChemTech's drugs were kicking in when you took Hood's fairy concoction." His father waved his hand in the air as if brushing away an annoying gnat.

"What? No. I'm telling you the new meds didn't work. My headache got worse, and I was nauseated."

"ChemTech is one of the most up-and-coming pharmaceutical companies in the kingdom. They would not make a bogus product. As I said earlier, it probably kicked in when you took Hood's."

"Four hours later? What's the point of a pain killer if it takes four hours to work?"

"You were out of it with pain. You've probably mixed up the times. Could be you need a stronger dose for a migraine. I'll talk to ChemTech about providing a more potent dose next time." His father stood. "As the crown prince, it won't do to have you whining about a bit of pain and disappearing for a whole evening because your head hurts. Be a man. Your mother has turned you into a wimp." He departed, his words echoing around the empty room.

Teo glared at the empty space where his father had sat, then slowly unclenched his fingers, one by one, from around his fork and knife. The king wasn't going to listen to him, not in the past, not now, probably never. Teo shoved his half empty plate away and then stood, his chair scraping the wooden floor with a loud screech. He'd done his part; someone else would have to get through to Duko. But Teo was going to make sure he was stocked up on Hood's pain medicine for future headaches.

Chapter Nine

Teo

T EO SLID HIS SUNGLASSES over his eyes, hoping it would be enough that he wouldn't be recognized. The city gates were swarming with people and guards. It had been a couple of days since the announcement about the medicine contract. Anxious Foresters flooded the city, stockpiling supplies as well as selling off their goods in case further cancellations of contracts and restrictions were put in place. Teo tried to ignore their worried faces, but one woman, clutching a small child, had tears streaming down her face. Why was she crying?

There's nothing you can do to help them. Forcing his gaze away, Teo flipped his hood up and then slipped by the guards. Unlike the Foresters, Wolves could come and go as they pleased, but today Teo didn't want anyone asking questions about where he was headed. He slipped through the gates to the other side, his step lighter now that he was outside the chaotic city gates.

Tall, elegant pine trees spiralled to the sky, their spiky needles colouring the forest green and tickling Teo's nostrils with their strong, bold scent. Most of the deciduous trees had lost their leaves, and their limbs pointed bony fingers to the sky. The hairs on Teo's neck stood at attention. He quickly moved along the dirt path, the only way into the forest, keeping a watchful eye on his surroundings. All vehicles except for small, solar-powered carts were prohibited in the wooded area. Only the farmers used the solar carts at harvest time. Most of the farms were on the other side of the forest where the soil was fertile.

What am I doing here? Dad will kill me if he finds out. Information—that was Teo's mission today. If he found out anything useful, then maybe his father wouldn't have his head. Would he be pleased? Spying was right up the king's alley. Teo's stomach turned, and his steps faltered at the thought. *It's smart to know what your enemies are doing.* Curiosity about the Hood girl was not what was driving him today. No, he was on a mission to find facts.

Teo inhaled deeply, the forest breathing with him. *It feels alive.* It'd been a long time since he'd been in these woods. His lips curved at the memories of playing here amongst the trees with his brothers. Oftentimes they picked berries when they were in season, stuffing themselves until their tummies ached. Their mom had secretly allowed them to come into the forest as young kids—until their father found out and put a stop to it. Teo frowned. His father had been so angry, yelling at both his mother and him. He padded along the dense carpet of dead leaves and pine needles. Small cottages—red, yellow, green—dotted the landscape. The contrast with the cold steel and cement of the city struck him. The Foresters lived a very different lifestyle than the Wolves.

Teo's racing mind slowed, the sun sifting through the tree branches warming his face. Beauty surrounded him. A calmness overwhelmed him. Why had he stopped coming? *Oh right. The bee sting.* Seth's bee sting had put an end to their forest adventures. His mother hadn't been able to hide the sting from their father. Teo halted. *The girl in the blood-red shawl!* How had he forgotten about her until this minute? He'd only seen one other person wear that colour. *No, it couldn't be. Could it?* The pieces all fit—she'd made a salve that day, told them that her dad had taught her how. Teo smacked his forehead with his palm. The red hood should have given it away. But he'd tried not to ever think about that incident. So, of course, he hadn't put the puzzle pieces together.

He checked his surroundings. If he remembered correctly from the other day, he was close to where she lived. Hood Medicine was located in the Hoods' home. *There.* The side of the house rose in the distance. Scanning the area, he spotted a hidden place to keep an eye on the small dwelling. Teo jogged to a clump of underbrush and then eased closer to the Hood home. When he'd been there before to deliver his father's edict, Teo hadn't paid much attention to the building or the area. Now he studied it. The structure was simple in design but had a welcoming feel. The front yard was neat, with several gardens in it. What grew there? Herbs, flowers? Whatever had been there was gone. A cool breeze flew through the area, as if reminding Teo that winter was coming. Blowing on his hands, he searched the property, but no one appeared to be around.

The memory of that day when he was a kid flitted through his mind. Why had she helped them that day? Why had he let her? He knew even then that he shouldn't have allowed her to aid Seth. Teo shook his head, shaking the memory away. It didn't matter because, in the end, his father had blamed Teo for Seth's injury. As if Teo had command over the bees. But they weren't supposed to be in the forest. His mother had defended him, saying she'd given the boys permission. In his father's eyes, Teo should have known better. He was trained to be the ruler—disobeying orders, allowing his brother to get hurt, all proved Teo was a failure in his father's book.

The girl's motives were a mystery, but things had definitely changed. The attitude she'd given him the two times they'd interacted proved she was a hardcore Forester. *I'm a hardcore Wolf. Wolves don't mix with the Foresters.*

Finding a clump of dead logs and brush where he could easily see the front entrance to the house, Teo squatted down, out of sight. This part of the forest was thick with trees and underbrush, which provided an excellent hiding place. Teo settled in to wait. He'd catch the Hoods at whatever they were up to.

⊸◆⊷

He didn't have to wait long. Ten minutes later, Jenna Hood stepped onto the porch. She grabbed a rake propped against the house and ran down the steps. Her long curls were tied up away from her face, and, for once, she wasn't wearing the red hood. She dragged the rake across the ground, gathering up the dead loose leaves. After raking them in a neat pile, she dropped to her knees as though searching in the grass. Had she dropped something? For several minutes she combed through the lawn, occasionally picking what appeared to Teo to be weeds and laying them aside.

Teo scooted closer, squinting to get a better view. What was she picking?

After gathering up the greens, Jenna entered the house, only to come outside again a minute later, wearing the red hood. Grabbing the rake, she headed around the side of the house. Teo straightened, scoping out other hiding options that would take him closer to the backyard. But his search was cut short when she re-appeared around the front with her bike. Teo dropped to the ground, his leg protesting the quick movement. *Stupid bike.* He rubbed the spot where he'd been hit while he studied the bike's front tire. It was straight with no bend. She must have repaired it or bought herself a new one. There'd been no bill from Fang's Garage, so she hadn't taken him up on his offer. Curious. He'd assumed she'd jump at the chance to let a Wolf pay.

"Dad, I'm going now. See you in a couple of hours," she called out. "Dandelions are in the sink for the salad. But I think that's the last of them."

Dr. Hood, pushing a wheelbarrow, walked around the side of the house, waving her off.

Teo's body stiffened. Should he stay and keep an eye on Dr. Hood or follow the girl? As Dr. Hood parked the wheelbarrow and then stepped into the house, Teo decided to follow Jenna. Crossing his fingers that he didn't trip on a root, he crept quickly through the brush. Once Jenna arrived at the edge of the forest, and Teo was certain she was headed into the city, he switched to the path, pulling his hood lower. His long legs kept him close but not enough to raise suspicion. He knew how to track prey.

A long row of people stood waiting at the gates. She slowed her bike, lining up behind an elderly couple and chatting with them for a minute. Always so neighbourly, those Foresters. Unlike anyone in the city. Most people in the city didn't pay attention to those around them, let alone stand around talking to them. Teo searched the guards' faces around the entrance and on the wall. There was Bleddyn. Groaning,

Teo inched over into the bushes before they ended at the edge of the forest. If he kept going, he'd be in the open and Bleddyn would spot him. Had his brother already seen the Hood girl? Would he know who she was? Teo wasn't sure if his brother had ever seen a picture of her or met her at the gates.

Teo ran a thumb over his lips. He needed to get through the gates without Jenna or Bleddyn seeing him. He didn't want to answer the questions Bleddyn would fire at him if he was found out. If he went through the secret entrance down the wall a way, he'd lose the girl. *I'm going to lose her anyway.* Only two people waited in front of her now. She'd be inside and he'd be stuck out here. What was the best path?

He strode to the line, keeping the girl in his sights. He'd cut through the offices, but he needed Bleddyn to do that. Hazel eyes locked on Teo's blue ones. *Let me in* Teo mouthed. Bleddyn nodded and met him at the officers' entrance. Teo moved to enter, but Bleddyn blocked his way. Teo ducked around his brother's bulk with a quick, "I gotta run!" He raced through the officers' quarters and out the other side of the wall.

The red hood was still visible, which made her an easy target. His chest tightened at the thought. She turned down a narrow, cobble-stoned street. A frown creased his brow as he slowed his pace. They were in an older part of the city, with brick or stone buildings rising only two or three stories. A far cry from the more modern steel and glass structures in the newer sections. Ironically, this part of the city reminded Teo of the forest. A wind whistled past him, carrying with it the smell of spices, roasted meat, and freshly baked bread. Teo's watering mouth reminded him he'd missed lunch. A favourite bakery was farther up and around a corner. Often, when Teo was on duty, he'd eat lunch there. Best smoked meat sandwiches in Wolf kingdom, they boasted. They weren't lying. He breathed deeply, hoping the smell alone would hold off the hunger as he pushed on after the red hood.

Afraid he'd lose her, Teo sped up. She turned onto the street where the bakery was located, and he careened around the side of the building. The round wheel of a bike shoved into his leg. A sense of déjà vu came over him. *This is getting old.* He landed on his butt, peering up into a face hidden by a red hood. All he could see was the glint of her eyes. He thrust his chin up and glared at her.

Chapter Ten

Rider

*D*OES HE THINK *I'M an idiot?* Since Rider had entered the city, she'd sensed him behind her. *What kind of Wolf lets himself be noticed?* Had this guy, whoever he was, been spying on her in the forest? *Time to find out.* After rounding the corner, she jumped off the moving bike and used her momentum to turn and face the way she'd come, ready to intercept the stupid Wolf. His footsteps echoed on the cobblestones and then his long legs came into her crosshairs and she rammed her bike into him.

"Ugh." He cursed as he landed on his butt. The hood of his sweatshirt fell to his shoulders, revealing a strong jaw, straight nose, and eyes the color of ice-cold river water. A black beanie covered his hair.

Oh no. The crown prince. Although Rider's stomach plummeted to her knees, she refused to let him see her sweat. Gathering up all the bravado she had, Rider hissed, "Why are you following me?"

He eased back on his elbows, casual, as though he sat on the ground chatting with girls every day. Maybe he did; what did Rider know about princes? Nothing.

He smirked. "What's with you hitting me with your bike? Again."

"So, it *was* you that night. And at the FCB building. Am I right?"

He picked something off his jeans, ignoring her question. Which was all the answer Rider needed. She thrust the bike forward again, threatening. "Answer me. Why is the cr—" She stopped and cleared her throat. "Why are you following me?" Would he have her arrested? Where was the Wolf Pack?

Slowly he lifted his gaze, his lips curling in a wolfish smile. He pressed a palm to the asphalt and pushed to his feet, leaning in so close that Rider noticed for the first time that indigo ringed his blue-grey eyes. They drew her into their depths and she couldn't look away.

"Who says I'm following *you?*" His low voice was calm, smooth.

The sound sent delicious shivers up her neck, the electricity heating her cheeks. She blinked, stumbling back. Fury at herself for letting his good looks enrapture her coursed through her veins. Liar. He was totally following her.

He sniffed the air and motioned to shops down the street. "I was on my way to Grey's Bakery and Sandwich shop for a snack. It's up the street."

"I don't believe you," she croaked.

He ran his tongue over his canine and her mouth dried up like a river in a drought, but she wouldn't give him the pleasure of showing her fear. Or anything else she was feeling, for that matter. Even if his lips looked soft and full.

His teasing expression faded as he backed away. "Believe what you want. Not my problem." Pointing to the bike, he warned, "Better be careful with that—it might be construed as a deadly weapon. Wouldn't want the Wolf Pack confiscating it now, would you?"

His mocking tone raised her hackles. She clenched the handlebars. "Scared of a little old bike?" she taunted, then snapped her mouth shut.

He cocked his head. "Nope, but you should be scared of big old Wolves."

"Why? We may have different heritages, but we're all human. What makes you so superior?" Rider blinked. Where had those words come from? They spewed out as if someone else was in control of her mouth.

His ice blue eyes probed hers. "Watch it—that's not a popular opinion here in the city. I could have you arrested for a lot more than the reckless handling of a bike."

Sweat trickled between her shoulder blades, leaving a cold trail on her back. He could indeed have her arrested, yet he hadn't. Why? He'd had ample opportunity. She tamped down the fear threatening to crawl up her throat. He wasn't going to do anything. Right?

He bowed slightly and then turned toward the bakery.

"I know what you're trying to do, but it's not going to work," she hissed.

Still facing away from her, he said, "You don't know anything about me... Hood." Then he strutted up the street until he reached the bakery, the wooden sign swinging in the breeze. After opening the charcoal-colored door, he threw her a smug smile before disappearing inside.

Rider propped her bike against the wall and sank onto the sidewalk next to it, all the adrenaline seeping out of her like blood oozing from a wound. Was she insane? *He's a Wolf prince, and I threaten him with a bike?* She chewed a nail, wincing when she bit too close to the quick. She stuffed her hands into her hoodie pocket. Time to get out of here. She didn't understand why the prince hadn't arrested her, but waiting around for him to change his mind was not high on her priority list.

Where are his bodyguards? Obviously, he was sneaking around with his own hoodie obscuring his face, like she was. Why? *Had* he been spying on her? She'd been so sure, but when he looked at her the way he had, her thoughts got all confused. Yes, it was definitely time to leave.

Her bike flew through the streets as though it had sprouted wings. Her errand forgotten, Rider focused on getting home as quickly as possible. *What are you playing at, Wolf prince?* He'd recognized her, all right. Questions riddled her brain but she had no answers, which left her stomach tied up in knots.

Why hadn't he called the Wolf Pack on her?

Chapter Eleven

Teo

I'T'D BEEN A WEEK since Teo had followed the Hood girl, and she still haunted his thoughts like a spirit in one of his childhood tales. A cool wind riffled through his hair, but Teo was glad for the refreshing air. He'd come out to the courtyard to reinvigorate his mind and body. However, the breeze hadn't blown away his wayward thoughts. Why hadn't he called the Wolf Pack, especially since she'd threatened him? *With a bike.* Not that he'd felt intimidated, although—he rubbed his leg where a big, tire-size bruise marked his leg—she had impressed him with her bike-wielding skills. He grinned at the memory of her feisty expression, her white knuckles gripping the handlebars. Had she guessed who he was? Although she hadn't admitted it, he suspected she had, that she'd actually started to call him the crown prince, but she still hadn't backed down, which intrigued him. And she'd called him a liar. Were all Foresters that bold, or only her?

He shook his head. *I'm going soft.* His father would not approve; he'd think Teo was weak for having such traitorous thoughts. He flicked his fingers as though the movement might shove the thoughts away. Why did he care so much about his dad's opinion? It didn't matter what Teo said or did, it was never enough for his father. Teo didn't measure up.

He prowled around the palace court yard, the pristine fall day lost on him, thoughts swirling through his mind like the dead leaves on the ground. Had she recognized him as one of the boys she'd helped in the woods so long ago? He wouldn't have made the connection if it hadn't been for that unique colour of red. As a girl, she'd worn a shawl in that shade; today it was a hoodie. He kicked a stone out of the way, staring at the spot where it had disappeared into a puddle. Why couldn't he vanquish her from his thoughts as easily? His life was complicated enough, given his relationship with his father. Besides, she was forest... *She's not worth your time.*

He scrubbed his hands over his face. Had she bewitched him? Did Foresters have magical abilities? He snorted. He was definitely losing his mind. Jenna Hood didn't have magical abilities, she was simply the most maddening person he'd met in a long time.

Standing there in the middle of the street, she'd been ready to ram her ridiculous bike into him again. Even so, he'd been drawn in by her wild beauty. All his defenses had fled like cowards. He *should have* escorted her to the jail; instead, he'd engaged her in *conversation*. And that scared him, so he'd run to the bakery like a sissy. No, the threat of another tire mark didn't bother him—what terrified him was the fact that he couldn't keep himself away from her, despite the lies she spewed. Foresters and Wolves were not the same. *Remember that.* But his mind had other ideas. It was consumed with images of her wind-blown curls framing her face, her flushed cheeks and pink lips begging—*for nothing*. Teo violently shook his head to clear it. Foresters were beneath Wolves and definitely beneath a crown prince. That message had been drilled into him since he was little, so why was he finding it so hard to remember now?

The sounds of footsteps on the flagstones drew Teo's attention. He sank onto a small stone bench as Bleddyn sauntered towards him. Maybe his brother could steer him back to the world of the sane. But the specter of emerald eyes with long, dark lashes refused to budge from his memory.

Bleddyn dropped onto a nearby rock. As children, they'd played here—games of checkers, cards, and then, later, reading adventure and ghost stories. Lately, it'd become a sanctuary to Teo, since his father seemed to have forgotten about it and never came here.

The mild day was welcome, this late in the year. The large courtyard boasted a variety of trees—evergreens, maples, birch—all surrounding a pond where large koi swam in the summer months.

Bleddyn sifted through stones at his feet. After picking one, he threw it into the pond. It skipped at least four times. "Bet you can't beat that."

Teo scoffed. "I'll bet I get five." He found a nice round, slim stone. It skipped five times. He smiled smugly at his younger brother.

Bleddyn picked around for another stone. "Who's the girl in the red hood?" he asked.

So, his brother *wasn't* going to help distract him. Teo stared at the pond, schooling his features into a bored expression. "Who?"

Bleddyn tossed the stone from one hand to the other. "I'm not an idiot. I followed you last week, after you ran from me at the gate. I've been waiting seven days for you to come and talk to me. Nothing. We're brothers, Teo." He hurled the stone into the pond. It jumped six times, like a bug dipping its toes into the cool liquid. "And don't get me started on the fact that I was able to tail you. You're Wolf Pack, for crying out loud. You let your defenses down because you were engrossed with the girl, who then tried to take you down *with a bike.*" He glared at Teo. "Help me understand why you didn't call the Wolf Pack."

"Please," Teo huffed. "As if she could hurt me. I'm twice her size; the bike barely makes a dent." He unconsciously touched his leg. "I wasn't about to bring the Wolf Pack into such a minor incident. She didn't know who I was." Not that she would admit, anyway. Besides, Bleddyn couldn't have been close enough to hear them speak or Teo would have smelled him. Still, his brother wasn't wrong. Teo'd had no clue Bleddyn had followed him. He silently cursed himself. That was a mistake he couldn't afford to make again.

"Is she the same person who hit you the night of the dinner with the Falls District?" Bleddyn's tone was mild, as if he were only now fitting the pieces together.

Teo shrugged. "Why would you think that?"

"Because it's too much of a coincidence that you're threatened with a bike by two total strangers." He smirked. "By the horrified expression on your face when I followed you, it looked like that bike made you uncomfortable—as if you already knew it intimately." His brother's eyes danced merrily.

Teo punched his brother lightly in the shoulder. "You're imagining things. If I looked horrified, it was because I ended up on my rear end in front of a Forester. Never a good position."

"Am I imagining things, Teo? Because that didn't look like a stranger-to-stranger conversation."

Teo locked eyes with his brother. "Yes, you are imagining everything."

"I hope so. I'm all for a little fun and flirting, but in case you've been blinded by her looks or whatever, just remember that she's a Forester and you're a Wolf. The crown prince, in case you've forgotten. None of those things go together. If Father ever catches wind..." Bleddyn blew out a breath, leaving the warning dangling, "... let's just say that her world and ours don't mix. They never will. We're too different."

But what if they weren't?

We're all the same, she'd said.

Teo chewed the inside of his cheek. That kind of thinking only led to one thing: trouble. He definitely didn't need any more of that. "You don't have to worry. Nothing's going on. I know what's expected of me." The sun's reflection glittered on the surface of the pond. A bird chirped happily in the trees. The churning in Teo's stomach didn't reflect the serenity around him. "Father has made sure of that."

Bleddyn's eyes softened. "Father wants the best for you."

"Right." Teo's voice was low. Did Bleddyn really believe that?

"He's tougher on you than the rest of us because you're going to rule one day. He wants you prepared."

"Maybe." The doubt in his voice echoed through the air.

Bleddyn stood. "I'm heading inside. You coming?"

"No."

"See you later then." His brother wandered up the path, apparently in no hurry to get anywhere. Teo wished he was more like Bleddyn, who seemed to let the world roll off his shoulders. Instead, Teo felt the weight of the world weighing down his whole body.

Their conversation played back like a recording. The king wanted his heir prepared, but it didn't matter what Teo did, his father was unhappy. Why bother?

As for Jenna Hood, so what if she was forest? Maybe he'd seek her out to spite the king. Teo's lips curled at the thought of him bringing home a forest girl. His father would blow a gasket.

Tempting.

But Bleddyn was right. Teo had no business associating with her. *But why not, really?*

Teo jumped up, wandering over to the edge of the pond. What if Wolves and Foresters did engage? What was the worst that could happen? He shook his head. *Leave it alone.* Except Bleddyn's observation about Teo's interest in Jenna Hood was no joke. His brother was too observant; he'd seen what Teo had barely admitted to himself—he was attracted to the girl. Spiting his father aside, if the king found out about either bike incident, there would be consequences. The crown prince did not let people harass him. His father would feel the need to make him an example to his brothers, as well as his leaders. Who knew what the king would do to the Hood girl? A shudder ran through his body.

What to do with Bleddyn? His brother would nose around until he came up with answers, and Teo couldn't let that happen. He'd have to find a way to distract him somehow. Teo ran a hand over his head, his thoughts centering on the Hood girl. What was she up to? Her actions did not bode well.

His earlier question needled its way into his thoughts. Why didn't Wolves and Foresters mix? Only one place could give him the answers, and Teo intended to find them.

⎯⎯◆⎯⎯

"Find anything interesting?"

Teo jumped in his seat, his heart in his mouth. His uncle's words boomed in the quiet royal library. Shelves filled with books lined the large room, but Teo wasn't interested in leisurely reading. Also housed in the room were histories and accounts of Wolf kingdom; these were the volumes that had drawn Teo to the room today. A small pile of books lay off to the side, while Teo perused the most recent history book. A pen and paper were ready if he needed to take notes, but, so far, Teo had more questions than answers.

Alarick chuckled quietly. "Teowulf, military are not supposed to let anyone sneak up on them." The rebuff was gentle.

Teo stood and saluted the man. "Uncle Alarick, it's good to see you. I'm... I was bored, so I thought I'd read." The lie fell flat, even to Teo's ears. The younger brother to Duko, Alarick was an advisor to the king, and no fool. The same blood flowing through their veins was where the similarities between the two brothers ended, though. Alarick was short and rounder than was healthy. His hair was more grey than red these days, but his yellow eyes glowed. He'd always been a favourite with Duko's sons because of his gentle ways and ready laugh. Teo knew not to underestimate him—beneath the soft exterior existed a fierce warrior. Alarick would fight for his family to the death. He was also the wisest man Teo knew, and today, that made him uneasy.

His uncle held a mug of steaming coffee with one hand while he lifted the book Teo had been reading with his other hand, turning it to read the cover. "*The History of the Wolf and Forest Clans*," he read aloud. A grey, bushy eyebrow lifted. "A little light reading?" The question behind the words echoed around the large room.

Teo resumed his seat, unsure where his uncle's loyalties lay. *Will you tell me the truth or will you protect my father, toe the line of lies?*

Clear yellow eyes met Teo's.

"Why does my father hate the forest?" The words rushed out like water pouring forth from a crack in a dam. The heaviness in his chest lifted. The question that had reverberated throughout much of Teo's life was finally out in the open. His shoulders sagged.

Pointing to the chair next to Teo, Alarick asked, "May I?"

Teo nodded.

Alarick sat quietly for so long, Teo wondered if he would refuse to answer his question. Finally, his uncle spoke. "A long time ago, the forest took something precious from our family."

How could a forest steal something? "I don't understand. What did it steal? Why haven't I heard about this?"

"It was another time—long before you were born." Alarick drew in a deep breath. "We had a younger brother, Raff."

Teo's head jerked. "What?"

His uncle shrugged, as though that was explanation enough. "Raffy was curious, always pestering us with 'why this' and 'why that'. It drove your father nuts." The lines between his brows and along his lips softened. "But we loved him. He was so full of life and love, and he worshiped your father. Duko could do no wrong." Alarick swiped dust off the cover of the book Teo had been reading, then he wiped his fingers on his sweater. No one had looked at these tomes in years. "When Raffy was four, your father was eight and I was six. We often played out in the woods—but not with the kids who lived there. Our father didn't like Foresters, either. I think he was jealous of them."

Teo's jaw dropped. "Jealous of a Forester?"

"Seems outlandish, right? I believe our father envied them their freedom, for one thing. Your grandfather loved to hunt, but he rarely had time for it. His mother, your great-grandmother, said he spent hours in the woods studying the wildlife, plants, and trees as a young boy. The other issue was that our dad didn't trust the Foresters—he was afraid they could take control of the kingdom. Several prominent forest men led the way in the research of medicine, pharmaceuticals, and environmental concerns. Dad didn't like that because it meant he wasn't in control. Despite that, we did have better relations with the Foresters than we do now. When Raffy died, everything changed." Alarick's face darkened. "Before that, when we were kids, we played all kinds of imaginary games in the forest—mighty warriors, brave knights, and anything else we could think of. Much like you and your bothers did."

Teo bit his lip. "How did you know Mom let us go into the woods?"

"I make it my business to know. I was worried that if your father ever found out, well, what did happen would happen. I wanted to be around to protect you and your brothers and your mother, but I didn't do such a great job. I'm sorry you got so much blame when Seth was stung."

"It's okay. It wasn't your fault." Teo clicked the end of the pen with his thumb.

"Anyway, one day it rained hard while we were playing there. We'd gone much farther in than we usually did, and we'd discovered a ravine, which provided all kinds of adventures, since it was steep with rocks and broken branches. That day it was also slippery, from rain and mud, and Duko was trying to get us up out of it.

Raffy was too little and kept falling behind. Duko lay on his stomach at the top and reached down for him. Raffy grasped his hand and made it almost to the top, but their hands were both wet and slippery. Duko couldn't hold on, and Raffy slipped and tumbled down to the bottom. He didn't get up. Duko and I frantically slid down to him. His head was covered in blood from striking it on a rock. I stayed with him while Duko went for help, but Raffy never moved. Alarick cleared his throat. "Even after all this time, I can still see him lying there. His hand was ice cold." A shudder shook his body.

His stomach churching, Teo studied his uncle. He'd never seen the man lose his cool. "You don't have to tell me any more."

Alarick held his hand up. "No, I'm fine. You need to know this history, Teo. Anyway, Duko ran to the palace, and the king himself came back with him, along with several Wolf Pack members. They got Raff out of the ravine, but they couldn't save him; he was already dead. Our father blamed Duko—he was the oldest and responsible for us. I'm not sure your grandfather ever forgave him. He always seemed to be punishing him in small ways after that, and he never let Duko forget it."

How awful for Teo's father. Teo's heart hurt for him. A little. "But that doesn't explain why father hates the forest so much."

"Duko went to the Hoods for help first, because they lived close by, but old Dr. Hood and the king had had a falling out a few years earlier. According to Duko, Old Hood wouldn't even listen to him, just sent him on his way. Duko always blamed the Hoods for the delay, believing that contributed to Raff's death."

Teo threw the pen on the table, his lips pressed together. Old Dr. Hood? Was that Jenna's grandfather? Who would do such a thing?

"I can't believe the old guy would send dad away. He was a kid." A fire rose in Teo's stomach. "I can't blame Dad for hating the Hoods."

"It's certainly a puzzle, and not like the old doctor, who had a reputation as a good man. I think there's more to the story than we know. But Duko needed to blame someone, and he took aim at the Foresters. Especially the Hoods. Personally, I don't think it would have made a difference if the old guy had come. I believe Raff was already dead." The man's fingers trembled as he traced the circles on the surface of the wooden table. "But, to your initial question, Duko was inconsolable. He turned that anger on the Foresters and the Hoods. With the foundation of distrust already in place, his anger and bitterness built on it. But, Teo, that kind of hate—whether it comes from us or the Foresters—is never going to do anyone any good. It's tit for tat, and look where we are today. Your father is bitter and angry still. I can't help but think what kind of man he'd be if he'd only let it go and forgiven Hood."

Alarick picked up his coffee mug, took a sip, then cradled it in his hands. "Besides blaming Duko, your grandfather became paranoid about safety. He forbade us to go to the forest after Raff died and then started putting safety acts in place for Wolves, starting with a curfew. Wolves couldn't be in the forest after dark or after heavy rains. He built the wall and gate to monitor that."

Teo's brow furrowed. "Wait. You mean the wall and gate were built to keep Wolves away from the forest, not the Foresters out of the city?"

"Ironic, isn't it? Only after Duko took over the throne did the wall become a way to keep the Foresters out of the city."

A thought poked at Teo's mind. "It's like Seth's sting on a much bigger scale. Dad's never forgiven me for letting that happen to him. That's why he believes I'm irresponsible, isn't it? I let him get stung just like he let his brother get hurt." With much more dire consequences. Teo grimaced.

"Yes, I believe that has something to do with his impatience."

Teo laughed, but it came out sharp and bitter. "Impatience is a mild word for how he feels about me."

"He believed his father's assertion that he killed Raff. There were too many similarities between the circumstances of Seth getting stung and Raff's accident. Thankfully, the outcome was much different. Still, I think you remind Duko of himself, and he hates himself so much that he projects that onto you." He clapped a hand on Teo's shoulder. "Neither Seth's sting nor Raff's death were anyone's fault—not yours, or your father's."

"He's believed I'm a screwup ever since that day."

Alarick sat back in his chair, drawing his palms together as if in prayer. "You aren't a screw-up. And you aren't your father. But consider this, haven't you gone out of your way to prove him right? Getting in fights, suspended from school?"

Teo slammed the book shut. "He believes it already, so why bother trying to prove him wrong?"

"You're satisfied with showing him he's right about you? That, as you say, you're a screw-up?"

Teo shrugged.

"Your father is complicated, but you don't have to be. Be the person you want to be, not a wannabe rebel who's always chasing his father's approval in a twisted way. Be a man, Teo. A good one. Whether or not your father gives you his approval, that's on him. Your behaviour? That's on you. Who do you want to be?"

The answer should have been a no-brainer, but Teo wanted his father's approval. Still, at what cost? Would hate get him that proud pat on his back? His bad behaviour had only brought about his father's scorn. But somehow Teo believed that being like his uncle Alarick, who was a good man, wouldn't score many brownie points with his father either. He might try all his life and never please him. Sighing, Teo shook his head. He didn't have an answer for his uncle.

Alarick squeezed his shoulder before pulling back his hand. "You've got time to figure it out."

"Why is this the first time I'm hearing about Raff?"

"Your father silenced everyone. No one spoke of Raffy and his accident."

"Why?"

"I think he thought that, by not talking about Raff, he'd forget him, but he never has. I don't think a day goes by that he doesn't remember him. I know I think about him every day, wondering what he'd be like, what he'd be doing. He'd love you boys. But, instead of focusing on the good, the tragedy only fuels Duko's hatred." Alarick tapped the cover of the book. "This conversation is our secret. Your brothers don't know. It would not be wise to say anything to your father, at least for now, considering your status with him at the moment."

Teo ground his teeth, resisting the urge to bolt for his father's office and confront him. Uncle Alarick was right. Rushing in like a fool to face off with his father was not going to help the situation. He nodded once.

His uncle clasped his hands over his stomach. "I have a question. Why the interest in the forest?"

Silence filled the book-lined room. Dust motes danced on the beams of sunlight streaming through the floor-to-ceiling windows. Teo knew he owed his uncle the truth, since Alarick had trusted him with one of the biggest secrets of the Howell family.

"After father passed the trade deal, I got curious because it didn't make business sense. No one's ever complained, that I know of, about Hood Medicine. But my whole life I've been told, 'Stay away from the forest'. It's been drilled into us that Wolves are superior to the Foresters. Then, all of sudden, father is doing this trade deal. He's trying to screw the Foresters. It made me wonder why." Teo folded the corner of one of the pieces of paper he'd been using. Would that response satisfy his uncle's curiosity?

"I'm getting old, Teo. I've seen many things, but one thing I've learned is that people, no matter where they're from, are still people. That includes the Foresters." He paused. "You're a noble and honourable young man. You're intelligent. Those attributes will take you far if you don't let your father's hate seep into you. If you ask your own questions, like you're doing." Alarick glanced at the clock on the wall, then pushed away from the table. "I need to go. Meetings, they're never-ending."

Teo stared at the book in front of him. His mind whirled with all that Alarick had shared with him. He'd come to this room pursuing answers; instead, he had nothing but more questions.

Chapter Twelve

Rider

◆◆◆ · · ◆ · · ◆◆◆

IN THE WEEKS FOLLOWING the trade deal, Rider spoke to as many nurses and doctors as she could, hoping to learn more about the new drugs. The deadline was fast approaching when it would become illegal for her to bring medicines into the city, and any chance to glean information would be gone.

So far, what she'd found out chilled her to the bone. A number of doctors weren't happy with the trials of the synthetic drugs. Duko was rushing them through, not allowing time to study the data; many feared the repercussions could be disastrous. Several in the Wolf medical community claimed the drugs didn't work at all. Rider made a mental list of those who had expressed their worries, but with the Wolf Pack now guarding every medical office in the city, as well as the hospital, Rider could only nod in sympathy. The Wolf Pack's presence was to make sure that the turnover to the synthetic drugs went smoothly. That was the official line. Unofficially, it was a not-so-subtle warning to the Foresters, especially her father, to avoid causing any disturbance. The Wolf Pack didn't take kindly to troublemakers.

Rider got off her bike in front of a small, plain office building. She couldn't deliver this last package for the day fast enough. The only signage on the building was a red cross in the window. Despite its poor advertising, it was one of the busiest medical offices in the city. She entered, frowning at the sight of the guard standing off to the side near the front desk. *Is the crown prince pulling guard duty at one of the doctor's offices? Is that beyond a prince?* She closed her eyes. *Stop.*

Prince Teowulf was taking up way too much real estate in her brain. Even now his handsome face and ice-blue eyes floated across her mind like a mirage. He was confusing—why had he let her go unpunished for insolence on multiple occasions? She couldn't solve the puzzle of him, and that was a problem.

Rider blew out a breath, hoping to chase the memory of those eyes away as she approached the desk, smiling at the woman manning it.

"What's with the guard inside? I thought they were mostly outside or at the front doors, not practically sitting on your lap." Rider kept her voice low as she handed over the package of meds.

The administrative assistant's smile didn't reach her eyes. "Making sure the transition of meds goes smoothly." She angled her body closer to Rider and whispered. "It's a message for you. Don't cause trouble or else. Be careful." The woman widened her brown eyes before turning her attention to the package. She signed for it, then handed the paperwork to Rider.

"It's really busy here today." Rider nodded towards all the sick people.

The woman grimaced. "Yeah, I guess flu season came early."

Shoving the papers into her bag, Rider glanced around the office. Time to leave. She'd have liked to get more info about the drugs, but it wasn't safe. The guard was too close. Even she wasn't that crazy. After wiggling her fingers goodbye, Rider hastened to the exit. Several people waiting to see the doctor sweated profusely, their faces as pale as a winter sky. Holding her breath, Rider hurried outside, crossing her fingers she wouldn't get sick too. At the click behind her, she let out her breath and immediately sucked in more air. Between the obvious sickness and the stress of trying to find out more about ChemTech's medicine, the knot in Rider's stomach had coiled tight. Deep breathing helped a little. Quickly she unlocked her bike, stopping when a shout broke through the everyday noise.

"Rider!"

"Hey, Ethan, how's it going?"

He cruised to a stop beside her. "S'ok. Done for the day?"

Rider nodded, straddling her bike. "You?"

"Yeah. I'll ride with you. I heard there was a commotion at the gates today. The Wolf Pack gave a couple of the couriers a hard time. Mostly from your father's place. Did you have trouble?"

Rider shook her head. She had breezed through the gates this morning. "I wonder what happened to make them snarly?"

Ethan chuckled. "Maybe there's a pea in their mattress, messing with their beauty sleep."

She grinned at the reference to the fairy tale, but the smile faded as the gates came into view. Wolf Pack guards prowled around, questioning several people. The tendons in Rider's neck tightened like a marionette. She slowed, dragging her foot.

"Uh oh." Ethan braked too.

She tucked her cold fingers into her hoodie pocket as she studied the scene in front of her. "Ethan, go on ahead. They won't stop you for delivering truffles. They love truffles. If you're with me, you're sure to get detained." She tugged her hands out of the warmth, hopped off her bike, and moved a step away from him.

"Nope. I'm not leaving you alone with the Wolves." He stuck close as they trudged toward the line of people. A Wolf guard approached them. Ethan froze beside her. Several people still waited in front of them, so why was a guard advancing toward them before they reached the front of the line?

"Papers." He snapped his fingers. His pristine black uniform outlined his stocky frame. Other than a grey strand hanging over his eyes, his hair was covered by his military cap. *This guy is way too young to be grey.*

Yellow eyes, the color of butter, lasered in on her. Her fingers trembling slightly, Rider fumbled with the bag's zipper. Ethan handed his papers over. She managed, finally, to open the compartment where she kept her documents. Pulling them out, she breathed deeply.

The guard scanned Ethan's papers and then handed them over. "You can go."

Ethan side-eyed Rider, and she tilted her head to the gates. *Go.* Ethan took his time, tightening the straps on his courier bag before straddling his bike. Finally, he pedaled away, disappearing through the gates. He didn't dare ignore the order to be on his way.

Rider held her papers out to the guard, who had waited for Ethan to leave. He grabbed them, his yellow eyes never leaving her face. A shiver snaked down her spine as she lowered her eyes. Heat crawled up her neck and she cursed her fair skin. Clenching her fists at her sides, she resisted the urge to smack the guard's face and then run as fast as she could. Who did he think he was? *Keep your head down.* Her father's voice echoed in her mind, and she flexed her fingers. Not worth it. She'd only bring down more trouble on her father and his work.

"Name." The word was more of a bark.

"Jenna Rydell Hood." Her voice was even, strong. She wasn't about to be cowed by the bully. The guard paused, causing her pulse to spike. *Don't show fear. He'll smell it.*

He ran his finger down the paper. "Why were you in the city?"

"I'm a courier. I was delivering packages for Hood Medicine." Her voice wavered on the last word. *Darn.*

"Follow me." He took hold of her bike with one hand while grasping her elbow with the other. They walked to a long, low building where the guards' offices were located.

Rider's heart hammered against her rib cage, but she willed her features to stay blank. The blood was pumping so fast through her veins that she felt light-headed. What was going on? Legally, she had until the end of the week to deliver medicine. The guard's face was stony, but the malice on other guards' faces was absent from his. She stumbled when he hurried her along, righting herself as another guard stalked toward them. She couldn't see his face, but he was definitely giving off an angry vibe. *Uh oh. This isn't good.* Rider's throat clogged and she coughed. Where had all the oxygen gone?

The new guard ignored her, angling so that he stood between her and her escort, who had released his hold on her. Both knew she wouldn't run. Not in a place crawling with Wolf Pack.

She still couldn't see this new guard's face, but his hiss was audible. "What are you doing?"

His voice was familiar. Where had she heard it before?

"Keeping away trouble." The grey-haired guard reached for her arm again, but the new guy blocked him. Grey-haired guy peered around the taller guard at her. "I want answers. She's a Forester, and I intend to find out what's going on."

Yeah, you and me both. Rider's head throbbed. Maybe she could try and make a run for it. She contemplated the distance between her and the gate. At least a hundred metres away, and there was a maze of people between her and the exit. It wasn't going to happen.

The second guard stepped sideways, turning to her. Everything clicked into place. It was him—the crown prince. Her stomach knotted. Why was he making an issue *now*? Had he changed his mind and wanted her arrested for the bike accident, her disrespect? And who was this other guard? Did he know about her "crimes" against the prince? Would he arrest her? She sucked in air.

Ice-blue eyes locked with hers, but his blank face didn't give away his intentions. She thought she might vomit, so she swallowed, hard. *Was he coming to her rescue or did he plan to turn her in?*

Chapter Thirteen

Teo

N*o, no, no.* T**EO** ground his teeth, scowling at his brother. *I will kill you, Bleddyn.*

Teo had seen Jenna Hood approach the gates with the other courier from the FBC and had watched in horror as Bleddyn locked in on her, as though she was dinner. Yelling to his fellow patrolman that he was taking a break, Teo had flown down the tower stairs where he'd been patrolling the top of the city wall.

Now he stood in a staring contest with his brother in front of the courier. He'd tried to keep her from seeing his face, but his brother was too stubborn. Her eyes widened as recognition dawned. Then, just as quickly, her two delicate eyebrows furrowed. He couldn't blame her; he'd have questions too if he were her. He glared at Bleddyn until his brother blinked. *I'm in charge here.*

"Why are you questioning her papers?" Teo hissed under his breath.

Bleddyn thrust out his chin, his bravado making an appearance once again. "Random check. Out of my way." He pulled Jenna and the bike past Teo.

The other guards near the building stared at them, not bothering to hide their curiosity. Teo clenched his jaw. Wolves didn't undermine each other in front of Foresters. He knew better.

"Fine then. I'll come along." He cut off Bleddyn's rebuttal by leading the way to the offices. Bleddyn had no choice but to follow or let the girl go. His brother sighed loudly as he ushered Jenna along, leaning her bike against the side of the building before following Teo inside.

"Have a seat, Ms. Hood." Bleddyn pointed to a wooden chair on one side of a table. Teo stood next to him, silent, allowing his brother to lead the questioning, so he could observe the girl. She sat down and jerked her hood off, her curls bouncing out of control. Bleddyn blinked, appearing to have forgotten what he'd planned to say. Teo smirked. *Smart girl.* He hoped she would give his brother grief, like she'd done to him at the FBC.

There was no reason to hold her that Teo knew of, but Bleddyn, once he'd found his voice, asked question after question. *Why are you being so nosy?* Teo only half listened, leaning against the wall and studying her while she responded to the interrogation.

She sat with perfect posture. Her voice had a nice timbre to it, low and soothing. She wasn't oozing attitude, but she wasn't cowering in a corner either. Green eyes locked with his. The colour startled him every time he got a glimpse, like living emeralds that sparkled and glowed, hypnotizing him.

Finally, Bleddyn waved a hand toward the door. "Okay, Ms. Hood, you can go." He didn't offer any explanations or apologies for detaining her. He didn't have to. Guards could randomly check and question anyone leaving the city who was not a Wolf.

"I'll escort Ms. Hood out, while you do the paperwork." Teo's tone challenged his brother to disagree. Bleddyn opened his mouth and then closed it, nodding once instead.

The girl stood, following him out. He grabbed her bike before she could take it and run. "A word of advice," he growled. "Get rid of the red hood. It makes you stand out."

"I like it. It keeps me warm. Besides, I don't have a closet full of items to choose from."

Like you do. Teo filled in the obvious insinuation. "My brother," he paused, giving the words time to sink in, "might not be so generous the next time. And I might not be around to rescue you."

Her mouth dropped open. "Did I ask you to rescue me? In any way, did it appear I needed a knight in shining armour? I'm quite capable of taking care of myself. The last thing I need is *you* to be my protector." She poked his chest with her finger. It kinda hurt. She packed a lot of energy in that tiny body.

His nostrils flared as he grabbed her hand. He glared at her, but she stood her ground. Sparks ignited that Teo could almost feel zapping back and forth between them. Then she ripped her hand away and yanked the bike from his grasp. Anger and frustration roared through his veins. He wanted to throttle her, he wanted to ... His eyes dropped to her lips. He swallowed, his stomach doing a weird roll. To cover his confusion, he leaned into her personal space. "I'm not protecting you. I'm warning you. The next time you might not get off so easy."

Her jawline hardened, and the smell of fear was strong, but her expression didn't change. Teo had to give her kudos for her courage, even if that kind of stupidity could get her in trouble. The air around them thickened again. This close to her, the freckles on the bridge of her nose stood out, and she smelled like soap and herbs. Heat fanned through him. He channeled the unwanted emotion into a snarl. "The king doesn't like Foresters. Anytime. And right now, Ms. Hood, you're in his crosshairs. I would not advise you or your father to make a false move."

After shooting him a dark look, she rode off. The other courier waited for her farther down the path, near the entrance of the forest. They vanished into the woods together. Who was he? A friend? A co-worker? Or something else? Teo clenched his fingers into fists at his sides. Why did he care what a Forester did or who she was friends with?

"Gorgeous... in that natural, granola, kind of way." Bleddyn stopped next to his brother, his arms folded across his chest. Teo resisted the urge to smack him.

"Stay out of my business," he warned. "She doesn't concern you."

"*Au contraire, mon frere*; that's where you're wrong. If you want to keep her out of trouble, because she *is* trouble, then you need my help keeping her off dear Dad's radar."

"The little stunt you pulled today is not keeping her off the radar."

"I needed to find out who she was. Someone has to vet her, since you are a babbling idiot when it comes to her."

"Why do you want to help her? She's a Forester."

"An important fact that I hope you keep in mind." Bleddyn held up a finger. "The trade deal. The Hood family is, or was, our primary supplier of those goods. You're no fool, Teo. Dad claims to be keeping an eye on them to make sure they stay in line, but he's hoping they won't. They make one mistake, and he'll teach them a lesson—a lesson that will resonate with all Foresters. It'll be humiliating and very public. How much more so if it involves you? He'll milk it for all its worth. Is that what you want for your little crush?"

Teo shoved him. "She's not my crush." *She isn't.* He was only keeping an eye on her to make sure she didn't do anything stupid to threaten the trade deal.

Bleddyn guffawed. "You better get over her real quick because that would not end well for the Hoods or yourself. And, for the record, I'm trying to help *you* stay out of trouble. I don't give a whit about her."

Teo removed his cap and ran his fingers through his short hair. "You've got a great imagination, Bleddyn. Why aren't you working for Dad's PR office?"

His brother rested his shoulder against the stone wall of the office building. "Is it my imagination? You moved pretty quickly once you saw her from your patrol post. On. Top. Of. The. Wall."

Teo tugged his hat low over his eyes. He didn't want to answer Bleddyn's questions and insinuations right now. But the only way to get him to back off was to give him a bit of truth. "You're right; she's the one who hit me that night. Oddly enough, she was at the FBC earlier that same day. For a Forester, she seems okay. A little on the feisty side, which is why I didn't want her to make a scene here today. I understand what our father is capable of, despite your doubts to the contrary. I'm not a total idiot. However, she's not guilty of anything but being Hood's daughter."

Bleddyn flicked lint off Teo's jacket and then pressed his finger into the thick fabric. "You're going soft. For a girl. A Forester. Like I said, she's pretty in a natural kind of way, but she has *Beware* written all over her." He straightened his own jacket. "We need to get to work before people start asking questions."

"Bleddyn, you're blowing this situation way out of proportion. It has nothing to do with her. I'm only concerned about the trade deal. We both know ChemTech's pain killers don't work. We can't have the Hoods doing anything stupid, since they are the source of the medicine that works. It's going to take Father time to realize that, though, and we need to make sure we give him that time." That was the truth. Partially. It didn't matter if those green eyes haunted his thoughts.

"Sure, Teo, you keep telling yourself that. Ask yourself one question though: Is she worth the trouble?"

Is she worth the trouble? Teo's mind ran that question on a loop as he patrolled the wall. The city's lights lit up the horizon. Old design mixed with new, sleek buildings. Dusk was turning into darkness, and the lights of the city shone like the stars they blurred out. But Teo was blind to it. A chilly wind whipped his body. Being up high on the wall made it seem ten times colder. Shivering, Teo picked up his pace, pivoting at the end of the wall. The forest was dark. He made out the shadows of houses, but the dense underbrush and large trees blocked any lights in windows. *What's she doing? What does she eat for supper? Is she a vegetarian like most Foresters?* He kind of hoped not. Meat was the main staple in his diet. He couldn't fathom only eating veggies. He marched a few steps farther along the wall. What did it matter? He wasn't going to do anything with his crush. He couldn't.

Too many differences separated the Wolves and Foresters. Most days, those differences seemed insurmountable. Other days, like today, standing there listening to her answer his brother's questions, he wondered more about their similarities. He'd always been told that Wolves were superior. Stronger. Smarter. Better. Yet they breathed the same air, needed to eat and sleep. Blood flowed through her veins like it did through his. He understood now where part of the hate came from, thanks to Uncle Alarick. The Hoods hadn't saved his young uncle, but was that a good reason to punish and oppress all Foresters?

Teo sighed. It was easier to go along with what he'd been taught his whole life. Stay away from the forest. Yet, he couldn't erase Jenna Hood from his mind. The dark, curly hair and those jade eyes had sunk their hooks into him. Even Bleddyn noticed. Who else had? *No one.* He'd only ever seen her when he was disguised and mostly alone.

Teo turned in the opposite direction, keeping vigil on the city as he patrolled. Was it worth the risk to get to know her a little? Against all reason, his gut told him *yes*.

And Teo had learned to trust his instincts.

Chapter Fourteen

Rider

T HE WIND WAS BRISK and cold, but Rider didn't care. She welcomed the discomfort as she sat on a lawn chair on the back lawn. Behind her, yellow light streamed out the kitchen window, illuminating the area around her. Decaying leaves gave off an earthy smell that filled her nostrils as she breathed deeply. City people thought it stank; to Rider, it smelled like home.

I'm not protecting you. I'm warning you. The next time you might not get off so easy. Prince Teowulf's words chilled her blood. What did he mean? She'd go to jail? Worse? Even more alarming—why had his brother targeted her? Or was it a coincidence that he'd picked her? *He let Ethan go. No coincidence.* Was that why the crown prince had high-tailed it over? Did they see her as a threat? It didn't make sense. Teo had let her go after she'd hit him and threatened him with her bike. Maybe his brother recognized her name and that was why he'd questioned her. That was plausible. But it still didn't explain why the prince had interfered. Again. Rider scrubbed at her eyes.

The back door opened and closed. Her father strolled over to her, holding out a steaming mug. "Chamomile."

She cupped her hands around the warm ceramic mug, enjoying the warmth it gave off. Her dad juggled his own mug as he tugged a chair over beside hers.

"Everything okay?" His mild tone suggested he was trying to be nonchalant, but she knew he was concerned. Ethan had blabbed the whole incident as soon as they got to her place.

"Yeah, Dad. I'm good." She patted his knee. "I'm not scared of Wolves."

He sipped his tea. "No, you're very brave, loyal, and protective. I love those qualities about you, but now is not the time to act rashly. The Wolves will be vigilant. I need you to stay safe."

Rider balanced her mug on her knee. "It's not fair that Duko is taking away our livelihood. The Falls District and ChemTech can't compete with you. He's not only punishing us because of his hate, he's going to end up hurting his own people."

"I know, but what can we do? It is what it is. I'll find another way. This isn't your responsibility to fix or worry about." He laid his hand on her arm and gave it a squeeze. The palace had refused her father's request for a meeting. "Duko isn't safe. Perhaps the city isn't either. Maybe I should send another courier to do the rest of the deliveries."

"Dad, it's only a few more days until the trade deal ends. I'll be fine. I'll keep my head down and won't draw attention to myself." *Maybe wear a different hoodie.*

"They still picked you out today." His tone was doubtful as he turned the mug around in his large hands.

"Dad, it was a random check. Stop worrying." Her dad wouldn't believe that any more than she did, but she said it anyway. "Do you think they'll force us out of the Forest?"

Her father pursed his lips as he set the mug on the ground beside his chair. "I hope not, Jenna-girl. But I'm not sure. If they do force us out, Duko might find himself in hot water from the other clans. We supply many of them with meds too, and us being forced to leave the forest would not go over well."

"Would we rise up against him?" Rider was hopeful.

Her father laced his fingers together. "How can we fight the Wolf Pack? It'd be a bloodbath."

Rider's stomach tightened into a knot. "It's not fair," she repeated.

Her father kissed the top of her head. "I know. I'm sorry. I wish I had a better answer."

She wove her arm through his. "Let's go inside. It's freezing out here." Rider was as anxious to leave her thoughts in the cold as she was to get herself out of it.

———◇———

Her bedroom was dark and quiet and should have been conducive to sleeping, but Rider's mind had other ideas. *I have to do something. King Duko can't get away with this.* Her dad's medicines were superior to everyone else's in the kingdom. No one disputed that, yet Duko was forging a deal with foreigners. Was that solely to spite and make life miserable for the Foresters, especially the Hoods? *We have to show him we are equals. But how?*

She sat up, her blankets dropping around her. *Compare the drugs.* Somehow, she had to find a way to obtain a sample of the foreign medicine. *Then I can show those Wolves that Hood medicine works better than that synthetic junk, like Dad told us he did with that other epidemic.* Rider smiled into the dark. Finally, she had a plan.

———◇———

With only a few days left until trade with the Wolves ended, Rider kept her eyes open for any chance to take possession of the new medicine. ChemTech's first shipment of the new meds had already arrived in Wolf City so there would be no gaps in the supply chain.

Rider had spotted packages sitting in the doctors' offices with the ChemTech logo on them, detailing what the meds were and how to use them. Her deliveries had decreased to half of what they'd once been. A couple of the doctors submitted full orders to Hood Medicine while they still could because a lifetime partnership with the Hoods had instilled trust. Maybe allies in Wolf City and kingdom weren't as elusive as Rider had thought. At the very least, these doctors had questions about this new medicine too. She hoped Duko didn't confiscate any remaining Hood meds after the new trade deal took effect.

Rider wound her way through patients standing along the outer edges of the waiting room of Dr. Lupine's office. Every chair in the room was filled by men, women, and children. Babies cried, while younger kids squirmed on their parents' laps. Several people held tissues to bleeding noses. The desire to turn and run outside overwhelmed Rider. She hurried to the desk and handed the package to a woman, who took it before grabbing a ringing phone. While waiting for the receptionist to sign for the package, Rider noticed the small ChemTech package on the desk, sticking out from underneath a few folders. ChemTech's logo, along with the flag of Falls District, was stuck to the envelope. The label indicated it was a sample of their over-the-counter pain medicine. Her fingers wiggled as Rider peered at the woman who was still talking on the phone, her back to Rider. Did she dare take it? Or was Dr. Lupine an ally? Would he give it to her if she asked? Rider's heart thumped against her rib cage. *Never trust a Wolf.*

Glancing quickly to her left and then her right, she slid her hand over the counter and down towards the brown package. A door opened down the hall. Rider snatched her hand back over the counter, her hearting pounding against her ribs.

"Rider, how are you? I didn't recognize you without your red hoodie." Dr. Lupine smiled. The man always appeared calm and collected amidst the chaos of his office. Maybe that was why he was one of the best doctors in the city.

Rider forced her lips into a smile. "It's in the wash. Here's your package. I'll only have one more delivery for you before the trade deal ends."

Dr. Lupine's amber eyes darkened. "I know. Thank you for bringing this today." As he spoke, the doctor picked up the brown package Rider had been eying and tucked it inside a larger envelope. He slipped it under the payment for the day's delivery and slid it across the counter to Rider. "Give this to your father. It's the final payment for today and next week. Tell him I've enjoyed our partnership."

Her eyes widened.

The doctor kept his voice low so the Wolf Pack guard standing nearby couldn't hear him. "Be careful going home and put that in a safe place. It's the first samples of painkillers from ChemTech's labs for your father to look at. Take care, Rider. Not all Wolves hate the forest."

Those quiet words still hanging in the air, he vanished into one of the patient rooms. The receptionist was still talking on the phone. Rider stuck the envelopes into her bag, hiding the one with the pills beneath the false bottom of her backpack. The Wolf Pack would have to tear her bag apart to find it.

———◇———

Rider stifled the urge to hop on her bike and ride past the line at the gate. What was the rush to leave the city today? Guards wove in and out of the lines, checking documents, but Teo and his brother weren't among them. Her shoulders sagged. Several minutes later, Rider handed the guard her papers. He skimmed them before shoving them back at her, barely registering her presence. Rider kept her head down as she pushed her bike through the gates and then hopped on and pedalled hard all the way home. Breathless, she dropped her bike on the front lawn and ran into the house. "Dad!"

Dr. Hood ran from his office. "Jenna-girl! What is it?"

Ripping open her bag, she yanked the envelope free and held it out. "Dr. Lupine says he's really enjoyed your partnership."

Her father reached out and took the envelope, then slid a finger under the lip of the envelope and tapped the contents onto his palm.

Rider moved closer for a better look. "Look what he's given you. He said it's the first samples from ChemTech's lab. They're painkillers. We can compare theirs with ours to prove ours is better. Like you did in the last epidemic."

A smile slowly spread across Dr. Hood's face. He clutched the bag to his chest. "It's a priceless gift, and from a Wolf, no less."

Rider chewed her bottom lip. *Don't trust Wolves.* The mantra came unbidden. *What if it was a trap? Was Dr. Lupine setting them up?* No, they would have stopped her at the gates. *Maybe he's alerted the Wolf Pack to come here to the Forest to pick her dad up.* "What if it's a trap? I didn't think," she gulped.

"Easy, Jenna-girl. I believe Dr. Lupine is one of the good ones. He cares about people, whether they're Wolves or not, although I still didn't expect him to side with me. Still, we need to be cautious. Dr. Lupine took a great risk giving you this, so our silence keeps everyone safe."

"What do you plan to do? How are we going to expose the Falls District?"

"I'll put this in a safe place while I set up a few tests." He retreated to his office. Something had shifted. Rider smiled. They had an ally in Wolf kingdom.

Are there more?

Chapter Fifteen

Teo

I T WAS THE LAST day for medical trade deliveries from the forest, specifically from Hood medicine. Teo paced behind the alley
dumpster, breathing through his mouth. The stink of rotting veggies
and meat soured his stomach. The dimness of the alley gave him good
cover, though. Any of the guards looking over would only see a dark
hole, yet he had a full view of the city gates from this hiding spot.

Bleddyn worked the crowd, checking papers and asking questions.
He had never doubted his brothers before, especially not Bleddyn,
who'd always had Teo's back. But the Forest brought out the worst
in the Howell family. He hadn't expected Bleddyn to pull Jenna in for
questioning either. *I should take Bleddyn's advice and stay away.* Yet
here he hid, waiting. For her. He couldn't help himself—she'd clearly
lured him in with some sort of forest magic. At least, that was the
excuse he told himself.

He scanned from one side of the gates to the other. Nothing, nothing... *there.* The red hood had been replaced with a grey one, but he'd
recognize those curls anywhere. The bike had undergone a paint job,
no longer teal but a sleek black. Warmth spread through his chest; she
had listened to him. The warmth was quickly replaced by a sliver of
doubt. *Why* would she listen to him? Was she up to something? Until
now, Jenna Hood had been her own person, making her own decisions.
What had changed?

Bleddyn sifted through the family of five's documents, oblivious to
the courier on the bike with the grey hoodie. One of the kids was

wailing while another ran circles around Bleddyn's legs. Teo smiled as his brother's face reddened. Then he focused on Jenna again as she handed over her papers to a different guard. His shoulders loosened. Flipping up his own black hoodie, Teo hopped onto the bike he'd borrowed from a stable boy. The sunglasses and ball cap would help him to blend in with the other couriers, he hoped. After slipping out from behind the dumpster, he maneuvered the bike into the cover of the shadows of the tall buildings and followed Jenna.

Once they were out of sight of the gates and away from the busy main streets, he rode alongside her.

She scowled, but her eyes remained focused on the road ahead. "There's enough road here that you don't need to crowd me." She sped up.

She doesn't recognize me. He smirked while keeping pace with her. The wind, along with the irritated vibes coming off her as she ignored him, invigorated Teo. The girl was feisty. Deciding he'd played long enough, he cleared his throat loudly and then flipped down his glasses. She glanced at him then quickly looked away, her bike wobbling slightly.

"What do *you* want?" Her voice was low, quiet.

"Just taking a bike ride."

She snorted.

How refreshingly unlady-like.

"I really need to deliver my packages, so, if you'll excuse me." She pedalled harder, zipping too fast through the pedestrian-heavy streets. They wheeled around a corner.

"Slow down!" Teo tried to keep the panic out of his voice. She was a much more accomplished cyclist than he was, and the fear of crashing was becoming real. "Please. I need to talk to you."

Jenna stared straight ahead and sped up, if that was possible. Teo swallowed, afraid he was going to lose her. Suddenly she braked, motioning for him to turn right onto a side street. He stopped when she did, his chest rising and falling rapidly.

"Out of shape, Prince?"

He couldn't get a word out, not even to put her in her place for that comment. She chuckled. The faint smells of cabbage and urine invaded Teo's nostrils, and he switched to struggling to breathe in through his mouth.

"What do you want? You've got one minute." She tapped her foot on her pedal, her curls bouncing with the movement.

"It's the last day for deliveries and..." he huffed.

"And?"

"You know the saying, keep your friends close and your enemies closer." He glowered at her, but his heart was racing. Probably from the vigorous biking. It had nothing to do with that hair or those green eyes. "I see the red hood is gone."

"It's in the laundry." She lifted a shoulder then let it drop.

"Riight, well, good thing. Finish your deliveries and go home. Consider this a friendly warning."

"I don't take orders from *enemies*." She eyed him. "You're just full of warnings and advice, aren't you? Which makes me wonder why you care, Crown Prince. It's your father who's forcing my dad out of a job. Shouldn't you be upholding his laws?"

"You're mistaking care for mistrust. I don't trust you. The sooner you leave the city, the better." *Call it protecting my own interests.*

"*That's* the problem. If you would trust us, none of this would be happening, But you're so arrogant. You think you're better, smarter, than Foresters, but you aren't. You'll be sorry you forced my dad out when your synthetic medicine doesn't work."

Teo stilled. What did she know? Had the doctors complained that ChemTech's medicine was a bust? Not good. If she knew that ChemTech's medicine didn't work, she could make trouble. Big trouble. Keeping his features blank, he met her stare. She didn't flinch. "The medicine works fine," he lied. "Have you heard otherwise?" He rubbed his thumb along the hand grip of his bike, as though he didn't have a care in the world.

"I'm a courier, a lowly Forester. What would I know?" She tried to shove past him, but he blocked her with his bike. The gesture filled him with an inordinate amount of pleasure—for once he was the one wielding the bike as a weapon.

She sighed loudly.

"Be careful, little Red Hood." He pressed his front tire against her leg. "You need to show respect when talking to a prince."

Her quick intake of breath reeked of fear. *Good—fear would keep her safe. She'd be arrested for that kind of talk by any other Wolf.* He needed to keep her on her toes and out of trouble. And if she knew anything about ChemTech's medicine, he had to find out what.

Teo studied her. Behind the fear was a steely resolve that shone through those eyes glaring at him. Daring him. To what?

"The problem with Wolves is you never think about anyone but yourselves. Maybe if you opened your eyes, you'd do the right thing."

"What's that supposed to mean?"

"If you're so smart, figure it out for yourself."

Teo's nostrils flared. "Explain yourself."

She titled her head to the sky, then focused on him. "My father is the best pharmacist around, yet you fire him. He's treated your sick and injured for years with dignity and compassion. Have there been any major complaints or lawsuits? No, but this is how you treat him?"

"I haven't done anything. It's my father," Teo sputtered. Why was he defending himself to her? He was a Wolf.

The girl huffed out a laugh. "Really? Has anyone, including yourself, stood up to your father and asked him to reconsider?"

Teo shifted his weight. He didn't need to answer to her.

She shook her head, the hood falling away from her curls. Dark tendrils framed her face, making her porcelain skin more pronounced. His fingers itched to push those curls behind her ear. Instead, he gripped the handlebars tighter, telling his trouble-maker heart to stop racing.

"That's what I thought."

She had no idea how helpless he was. Teo couldn't continue this conversation. He backed his bike up so she'd be free to leave.

The girl shook her head. "You're a coward. Or a narcissist. Only thinking about yourself." After piercing him with a final stink eye, she rode away, vanishing into the city. Her words echoed off the tall buildings. Alarick and several other leaders had asked Duko to reconsider the trade deal before announcing it publicly. The king had refused. Jenna Hood didn't understand that Teo was powerless, that his title meant nothing. Anyone who could and wanted to help had tried. It was pointless. As was his growing infatuation with this girl.

What am I doing? Forget her. But that was a problem because he couldn't forget her. He ran his hand over his short hair before biking to the end of the street. How could one person be so irritating yet also intriguing?

He spotted her up ahead as he eased into traffic and tailed her. She wasn't derailing him from his mission that easily. If she knew something about ChemTech's drugs, he had to find out what. The only way to do that was to keep her in his sights.

As Teo rode, he checked every corner and alley entrance, making sure they weren't being followed. His father wouldn't hesitate to pull in the courier if she stepped one toe over the line he'd drawn. Teo had to keep that from happening because he was terrified of what would happen if she got caught and accused the king of making medicine that didn't work. He loosened his fingers from the death grip on his handlebars.

Jenna zig-zagged around people and vehicles. He didn't bother to conceal himself because so what if she saw him? She pretended she didn't notice, but Teo caught her rolling her eyes at him at least once. Her irritation sent waves of warmth through him. If she meant to detract him, she was failing miserably; her ire was a pleasant change from girls falling at his feet and catering to his every whim. *She's trouble.* He should let her go; that was the smart thing to do, but when did he ever do the smart thing?

At the third stop, she glared at him as she stalked into the office. He couldn't help chuckling, which only seemed to irritate her more. Jenna Rydell Hood was like no one he had ever met. Was that the attraction?

He waited in the shadows of the buildings for her to come out, his gaze darting around the quiet, empty streets of this neighbourhood. Was he trying to save his own skin or the Hoods'? He wasn't sure.

Jenna strolled out of the building, her backpack in her hand. After settling on her bike, she turned toward the city gates. The bag settled in on itself; clearly she had delivered all her packages. Teo caught up to her.

"You're still here." Her tone was flat.

"Just making sure you leave safely."

She kept her speed at a normal and safe clip this time. Her cheeks and nose were pink from the chilly air, and her dark curls, wind-blown. Bleddyn was right that she was gorgeous in a granola sort of way. No make-up or pretty clothes to hide behind. Her beauty was raw and untamed, beckoning Teo closer. This could be the last time he saw her.

He frowned. "Will you be back in Wolf City?" The words were out before he could think better of them.

"I have no reason to unless it's to make deliveries. Since that's no longer happening, *thanks to your family*, I have no business here. Forest people, as you know, aren't welcome to wander the city."

He ignored the dig and ran through his options. Five minutes before they reached the gates and he had to disappear. He couldn't follow any closer than the alley he'd hid in this morning or he'd be recognized by his brothers and the other members of the Wolf Pack, increasing the possibility that someone might rat on him to his father.

Blood rushed through his veins. Pain though she was, he didn't want this to be the last time he saw her. Plus, he needed to find out what she knew about ChemTech's medicine.

A purple flyer flapped against a lamp pole, catching his attention. *That stupid ball. Ugh.* The flapping continued, like a waving flag attempting to capture Teo's attention. *Wait, that's it!* The lame ball was the answer. King Duko held a ball every year for all the kingdom, including the Forest people. It was a charade, but it worked. Wolves believed the king was a generous benefactor to all people, looking out for everyone's best interest. What a farce. Teo didn't know what the Foresters thought about it. Guess he was about to find out. An image of him and Jenna Hood dancing flickered through his mind. He shoved it aside. *Keep her close so you can get any information she has about ChemTech.*

"Are you coming to the Wolf Ball?"

She laughed. "That's a good one. Why would I? It's a joke." She clamped her mouth shut, toeing the ground with her shoe. So, the Foresters didn't think highly of the ball, but they still came out to it. For the free food and drink, probably. Teo didn't begrudge them that.

They got little else from the Wolves, but he wasn't about to admit that to her.

"I'll ignore that comment if you'll come. If not, I might have to arrest you for insolence."

Rider snorted. Teo bit his lip to keep from smiling.

"Oh, so *now* you're going to arrest me? For refusing to go to the ball with you? That's rich." A pink flush spread up her neck and pooled in her cheeks, adding to her appeal. "Ugh, I know you aren't asking me on a date, so what are you up to?"

"Wouldn't it be interesting if I did ask you on a date?" he muttered quietly. His father would have a cardiac arrest. And it would be a chance to hang out with this girl... *Stop it.* "Technically, I'm under Palace rules and can't pick my own dates, so no, I'm not asking you on a date. But it's not a trick, and you actually might have fun." *Definitely not allowed to date a Forester. Or a Hood.* "It's a masquerade ball. Everyone wears a mask. You won't be recognized."

She stopped her bike abruptly and wheeled it to the side of the street. Teo followed, pulling his hood farther down over his brow.

"If it's masquerade, you won't even be able to tell if I'm there."

"I'll find you. Tell me what you'll be wearing."

"I have no idea what I'd wear because, you know, I have so many ballgowns to choose from." Sarcasm dripped from her every word.

"Come. I'll find you."

"I'm not promising anything." She pushed off and Teo followed.

"I'll take that as a yes."

She glanced over her shoulder, and he flashed her his best charming smile.

She shook her head, but he caught the slightest curve of her lips before she turned around. The gates loomed ahead so he didn't follow her, instead drawing into the shadows of the alley. The guard motioned for her papers and then searched her bag. Teo frowned. The guard released her and Teo unclenched his jaw. *What am I doing?* Did he have a death wish? Mesmerizing eyes and a feisty temperament had rattled his brain. He ran his hand over his face. *If* she came, he had to keep her away from his father and brothers. He'd created more problems for himself than he needed. But the thought of holding her as they danced did weird things to him. What would it be like to dance with a woman he wanted to instead of having a dance card filled with names of the girls who only wanted something from him or whose parents were trying to marry them off?

Suddenly the lame ball didn't seem so lame. Teo's lips curved up. He couldn't wait for Saturday night.

Chapter Sixteen

Rider

I'VE LOST MY MIND.

Rider tore along the forest path on her bike, oblivious to her surroundings.

"Watch it, girlie, or you'll be having an accident!" An older woman jumped off to the side.

The brakes whined, Rider hit them so hard. "I'm so sorry, Granny. I was lost in thought."

The woman shook her head, her short, grey curls bouncing. "What's got you so pent up? Are you worried about your dad?"

"There's a lot going on, what with the new trade deal. I'm concerned for us and the rest of the Foresters who are affected."

Granny's pale blue eyes studied her. "Hmmm. Why don't you come in for tea, and maybe we can relieve some of those anxieties. Tea works wonders."

Rider grinned at the woman as she fell in step beside her, wheeling her bike between them. The woman's cottage wasn't far, and it was one of Rider's favourites in the forest. Perhaps because she had so many good memories of the place. Everyone called Mrs. Willow Granny because of her short, grey hair and small eyeglasses that she liked to wear around her neck more than on her nose. The woman always had time for a chat served with a cup of tea and cookies. Rider had spent a lot of time on the porch of Granny' house over the years, sipping dark, spicy teas with lots of milk and sugar. The older woman had filled a void after her mom died.

Inhaling the smells of vanilla and cinnamon, she followed Granny into the quaint house.

Granny pointed to a chair by the small table. "Sit. It's too cold outside for the porch." After turning the gas on the stove, she filled the kettle and set it on the burner. *Granny* was a misnomer. The woman was spry for her age, moving better than most people half her age. She plucked two china cups from the cupboard and set them on the table. Rider smiled as she fingered her delicate cup. Tea was better in real china was a motto Granny lived by. After the tea was made, the woman brought the teapot over to the table along with a plate of oatmeal cookies.

Rider's stomach rumbled and she rubbed it, laughing. "I skipped lunch."

"Well, then, it's a good thing you almost ran into me." Granny's eyes danced.

"I'm so sorry again."

"No need to apologize. I'm glad to see you; it's been a long time. How are you?"

"I'm okay, considering what's going on. But Wolf kingdom is our main importer of medicine. I don't know what dad's going to do once this trade deal goes into effect."

Granny poured fragrant tea into the cups. "Your dad is very re-sourceful. He'll figure it out. And we'll support you until he does. That's what we Foresters do. We are a community. When one of us is in need, we all are in need."

Rider knew that was true. The Foresters always helped each other. If a farmer's crop failed, they all pitched in with meals and food. If a person was sick, they took care of them, or babysat kids so the parents could rest. Neighbours made presents at holiday time for children whose parents couldn't afford them. Rider remembered the plethora of food that came to their house when her mom died. It wouldn't be any different now.

"What else has got that intelligent mind riled up?"

Rider chewed a piece of cookie, hedging for time. Should she mention the prince? "A guy. A Wolf."

Granny bit into a cookie, her face calm, no judgment on her features that Rider could see. "What did he do?"

"That's the problem. He hasn't acted like a Wolf. I've run into him a couple of times with my bike. That seems to be a bad habit of mine." She met Granny's eyes, which sparkled. At least she had a sense of humour about the narrowly missed run-in. "I was mad at him because he stepped out into the street like he owned it. But he didn't report me, and he offered to pay for the repairs. Then today, I saw him again. He invited me to the ball. Not as a date," she was quick to add, before Granny got the wrong idea. "Why would he do that?"

"Does this Wolf have a name?"

"Teo." Rider jiggled her teacup, swirling the reddish liquid around, hoping the older woman wouldn't make the connection between the name and the prince.

"Maybe he wants to be friends."

"With a Forester?" Rider scoffed. "I doubt it."

"Maybe he's different. It's a pity we can't all get along. In my opinion, I think we'd do so much better if we worked together instead of fighting one another. Maybe this Wolf is providing an opportunity to build bridges between the two clans rather than tearing each other down."

"He's not interested in helping us."

"No?" Granny sipped her tea, her little finger crooked as though she were royalty herself.

"Pretty sure." Rider broke a cookie in two. "He's the enemy."

"But I thought you said he hasn't acted that way. Maybe you need to change your perception of him."

Rider set the cookie pieces on her plate. "They're the ones taking away my dad's livelihood. Why do *I* need to change? We haven't done anything wrong."

"No, but someone has to make the first move. Why not you?" Granny smiled. "But that's an old lady's thoughts... Now tell me, if you go to the ball, what will you wear?"

Rider sighed. Another problem. She had nothing to wear.

⚬

Rider kicked at an old T-shirt lying on the floor of her room, which looked as if a clothing hurricane had blown through it. Jeans, shirts, and hoodies littered the floor and bed. The one dress she owned she held in her hand, studying it. It was too small. She never dressed up. After tossing the garment onto her bed, she ran her hands over her face. She'd decided to go primarily so she could spy on Duko and get more information about the trade deal. People would be gossiping, and she might hear something useful. Some piece of information they could use against the Wolves. The tests her father had run on the medication from Dr. Lupine had been inconclusive.

Maybe this Wolf is providing an opportunity to build bridges between the two clans rather than tearing each other down. Granny's words echoed. No, Prince Teowulf wasn't trying to build anything, let alone a bridge. What he was up to was a big question mark, but Rider was going to find out. And this ball provided a perfect opportunity to spy. The idea of dancing with the prince had no influence on her decision. None whatsoever.

Thump, thump, thump.

"Come in." Rider opened the bedroom door.

Her dad peered into the room. "Whoa, what blew through here?"

Rider scrambled, kicking clothes off to the side and picking up other piles to allow her dad to enter. She swallowed over the small mountain that suddenly crowded her throat. *It's a dumb dance.*

Her dad moved a T-shirt so he could sit on the edge of her bed. "What's going on?"

"That stupid Wolf Ball. A friend asked me, and I was thinking of going." Not quite the whole truth. "I don't have anything to wear."

Her dad held up a finger. "I might have just the thing." He hurried out of the room. Rider folded a pair of jeans, sliding them into a drawer. What was her dad up to?

"Will this do?"

Red filled her vision. The long, crimson dress he held out to her was straight out of a fairy tale. She grasped the gown by the hanger and held it out in front of her. The dress was the colour of poppies, with a halter neckline and a long chiffon skirt. It was delicate and the most beautiful article of clothing Rider had ever seen. "How... where did you get this?"

"It was your mother's. She was wearing it at the ball the night we met. Friends surrounded her, but she was all I saw. I thought she was a shining star. All the young guys, including a few from the Wolf clan, were drooling over her, but I don't think she noticed. I didn't think I stood a chance, especially since Duko was circling."

Wait. What? "The king?"

"He was the crown prince then, and he had that entitled gleam in his eye, but she ignored him." He chuckled.

"Duko was interested in a Forester?" That made no sense.

"Your mother was so breathtaking, I think even Duko forgot for a moment where she came from. Anyway, I gathered up my courage and asked her to dance. We danced the rest of the night together. She could have had anyone she wanted, but she chose me." He fingered the dress. "I kept it after she passed, thinking maybe there'd come a day you might have a use for it. I think the ball is a good place to wear it, don't you?"

Rider blinked. He was giving it to her? After carefully draping the dress over her bed, she threw herself into her dad's arms, hugging him tight.

He squeezed her. "You remind me so much of her. You have her spunk. She'd be proud of you, as I am."

She pressed her forehead into her dad's chest, inhaling his earthy smell of sage and soap. They rarely spoke of her mother. She had died in the city when Rider was thirteen. She had been delivering medicine to one of the offices when she was hit by a vehicle. The driver didn't stick around to help, and her mother had died there on the street alone. Not one Wolf stopped to help. It had taken a long time for both Rider and her dad to move forward.

"Thanks, Dad," she whispered.

"I think it will fit, but if it needs alterations, I'm sure Granny can help. Try it on." He left her room.

She carefully removed the dress from the hanger and lifted it to her nose, breathing in deeply the scent of rose oil, a fragrance her mom had worn every day. Stroking the soft material, Rider closed her eyes, remembering her mother laughing, her hazel eyes glowing. She was pushing Rider on the tire swing that used to hang outside on the big tree in the backyard. Rider loved that swing. She'd been fearless yelling, "Higher, Mommy! Higher!" Her mother's dark hair hung in waves around her shoulders, but a few loose strands blew in the breeze. Rider recalled the soft wool sweater she'd worn and how, as a little girl, Rider would cuddle next to her mom as she sorted herbs from the basket on her lap. *I miss you, Mom.*

Rider opened her eyes and sighed. Quickly, she shed her jeans and T-shirt, carefully lifting the dress over her head. It slid down her body like a glove, showing off curves that Rider hid behind her bulky sweatshirts and jeans. She twirled around, enjoying the feel of the skirt swirling around her legs before smoothing her hands over it. Rider had never worn a ball gown before. Her uniform of hoodie and jeans was comfortable, but she didn't mind feeling pretty either.

Her dad knocked, peering in after Rider answered. His eyes glassed over as she stood before him. "You're beautiful, my girl."

"Daad, you're only saying that because you have to."

"No, sweetie. You are prettier than any wildflower out there."

Rider tilted her head, studying her reflection. Her dad set a box on the floor. "Shoes."

Rider knelt and opened the box. Pulling out a pair of red heels, she raised an eyebrow. "I'm not sure I can walk in these." She held one in her hand and turned it around like a scientist examining a new specimen.

"I can understand why. They look like torture devices to me, but your mother managed, and I have no doubt you will too. You've got a couple of days to practice." He smiled encouragement.

She set the shoe back in the box. "Thank you. For everything."

"Have fun." He hesitated. "But be careful. Duko is not to be trusted."

She knew that, but what about his son? Fantasies of waltzing with the crown prince tripped through her mind, leaving her breathless. *Wolves aren't to be trusted.* Her chest tightened. Was Teo different, like Granny suggested? She twirled, staring at her reflection in the mirror. *Forget him.* Her mission was to gather information and try to find out what exactly Duko planned for the Foresters. It was best to keep her mind on those things because there was no hope the king would ever let any of his sons, let alone the heir, associate with a Forester.

"I'll be careful."

Her dad hugged her and then left.

Rider stared at herself in the mirror. It was just a dress and she'd seen her own reflection countless times, but she couldn't get over how different it made her look and feel. The red brought out the colour in her cheeks. She swished the skirt around her legs again. Would Prince Teo like it? She stuck out her tongue. What did it matter? He'd never find her in the crowded ballroom with a mask on.

Rider changed out of the gown and hung it in the closet. A lightness filled her chest as she anticipated wearing it. She wouldn't admit it aloud, but she couldn't wait for the ball.

When Saturday evening arrived, butterflies took residence inside Rider's stomach. Alone in her room, she smoothed her hand over her abdomen. The sparkly clips Granny had given her for her sixteenth birthday secured her long, dark locks in an up-do. The card had read "Every girl needs a little sparkle." Rider had tucked both away in a drawer at the time, not having a place to wear them. Tonight, they were the perfect accessory.

Rider had found a piece of black velvet at the general store, which she used to make her mask, trimming it with red lace. Gingerly, she slid the elastic over her head. The elastic hurt if you let it slip, which she'd found that out the hard way while making the mask. After stepping into her shoes, she surveyed her work in the mirror. Satisfied, she carefully placed one high-heeled foot in front of the other until she had managed to make her way to her father in the front room.

He grasped her hands in both of his. "You're so grown-up and beautiful." He kissed her forehead. "Your mom would be very proud. Have a good time."

Rider squeezed her dad around the waist, careful not to crush her dress. "Thank you, Dad." She grabbed her sneakers and held them up.

"I'm wearing these walking to the ball, and then I'll put mom's shoes on. No point breaking my neck before I have to." After slipping her cloak over her shoulders, Rider put the heels in the bag and stepped into her sneakers. She did an awkward curtsy for her father, who chuckled and waved her off. The moon was full, casting a spotlight on the earth. Stars sparkled like diamonds, adding glitter to a dark sky. Rider inhaled the cold, clean air.

Ethan, his parents, and sister stood waiting on the road. She waved and hurried forward, glad for the company on the walk into the city.

"You look dashing tonight." She eyed Ethan's suit, so different from his usual uniform of jeans, T-shirt, and jacket. He had on a white mask with black markings along the edges that covered the top portion of his face.

He playfully bowed. "Thank you. You… I, uh, like your dress."

"Thanks." Why was he all tongue-tied? She removed the mask, as did Ethan. "I want to be able to see. These are terrible if you have to walk more than fifty metres."

"But they are good at hiding your identity." He twirled the mask by the elastic. "I'm glad you decided to come this year. Duko doesn't care one iota about us, but the food is good, the music tolerable, and it's a night out on the king's dime."

"Wow, how cynical of you." Rider stepped carefully around a puddle of dead leaves. All she needed was to get her dress dirty.

"Why didn't your parents ever take you?"

Rider scrunched her nose up. "I don't know. I think they might have if Mom had lived. They used to go before I was born."

"You're going to have fun. At the very least, we can make fun of the royals as they try to fit in with the common folk." Ethan finger quoted the word *common*. "It only lasts for about an hour; then they find their cliques, and that's that."

Rider kicked a pebble out of the way, ignoring the tightening in her chest. Ethan didn't need to know she was attending the ball because a royal had asked her. Up ahead, the lights from the city twinkled in the dark night. The tops of the palace towers were lit up like a birthday cake with candles. The guards at the gate barely scanned their papers, probably in a rush to get to the party themselves.

The closer they got to the palace, the more the butterflies in Rider's stomach dive bombed. Because she'd never been to a ball, not because of a certain handsome prince.

People in formal dress crowded the streets. Women in blue, purple, pink, green, and yellow gowns paraded before Rider's eyes. Men wore dark tuxes or, as in the case of most Foresters, dark suits and ties. Tuxes were a luxury that most didn't need or could afford. The women usually wore their dresses again the next year, Rider guessed. No one would remember from year to year that it was the same dress.

The scene outside the palace reminded Rider of a moving kaleidoscope. The masks covering everyone's faces lent an elegantly eerie feel to the evening. A shiver ran over Rider's scalp, and she stepped closer to Ethan and his family. How would she know who was who? Who could be trusted?

They put their masks on and strolled up to one of the three entrances that welcomed guests to the ball. Rider's party entered by way of the middle one. Once inside, a moving sea of people swept along to the area where they left their coats with valets. Rider changed shoes and handed over her cloak and the bag in which she'd stowed her running shoes. She shoved her coat ticket in a small pocket, hidden in her dress. As she waited for Ethan and his family, she gaped at the posh room around her.

Large crystal chandeliers hung from the high, vaulted ceilings, casting soft light on all the party-goers. The plum-coloured carpet under her feet was plush, her heels sinking slightly. The urge to remove her shoes and walk around barefoot overwhelmed her. The cream and gold papered walls added warmth. An elderly couple she recognized from the forest passed by. The patches on the elbows of the man's jacket and the old-fashioned dress the woman wore did not dim their smiles. Rider waved, but her smile wobbled. Duko lived in outrageous wealth while he kept the Foresters taxed and under his thumb. Now he was threatening to take away their jobs. She flexed her fingers.

"You ready to put your dancing shoes on?"

Rider startled at Ethan's voice. He'd snuck up while she was fuming. She forced a chuckle and hefted her skirts. "They're already on, but

I'm warning you Ethan, I'm a terrible dancer, and these shoes could kill. I think it's better if I observe."

He offered his elbow. "I'm not taking no for an answer. You'll be fine." He side-eyed her. "I don't think your dance card will stay empty for long."

What did he mean by that? Would guys want to dance with her? Not sure how she felt about that, Rider grasped Ethan's elbow and managed not to trip as they followed the crowd into the grand ballroom. She'd been so focused on Teo and listening in on the gossip that she hadn't considered she might have to dance with strangers. She chewed her lip as they walked through the large double doors.

Inside the ballroom, more crystal chandeliers hung from a gold ceiling. Was that real gold? Surely they didn't waste gold on a ceiling. She shuffled with the others towards the centre of the room, the grandeur continuing to unfold. The hardwood floor shone, ready for dancing. Tables laden with decadent food lined the far side; loveseats and chairs sat waiting for weary dancers in various groupings throughout the space. Wait staff wove gracefully throughout the room with their trays of colourful drinks.

Rider's head spun from the sensory overload. She tightened her grip on Ethan's arm, glad for his steady support and company. She could always depend on her friend.

The butterflies in her stomach took flight again as she peered around the room. *Was he here?* The masks and finery made it challenging to distinguish anyone's identity. Relinquishing Ethan's arm, she picked up a glass filled with pink liquid from a table lined with drinks. She swallowed a mouthful of the sweet fruity liquid.

"You might want to slow down there," Ethan warned, as she drained her glass. "I know it's only punch, but the sugar rush will kill you."

Rider clutched the stem of her flute. "Thirsty from the walk."

Ethan gestured with his hands, palms up. "What do you think? Too showy? Decadent? Love it?"

"I can't even find the words." It was disgustingly decadent and beautiful at the same time.

"Yep, our generous King Duko goes all out for his kingdom." He pressed a hand over his heart.

Rider pinched his upper arm. "Shh. We don't want unwanted attention."

Ethan stared past her left shoulder. "Too late."

Chapter Seventeen

Teo

THE MASK DUG INTO Teo's temples, blocking his peripheral vision so he had to crank his neck to search the room. The desire to rip it off was all-consuming, so he clasped his hands behind his back.

"Looking for someone?" Teo couldn't see Bleddyn's face, but he could hear the amusement in his voice, along with... was that a hint of interest?

"Not particularly. The masks make it difficult to tell who's who. Not that it matters—since most of them are Foresters."

"Indeed." Bleddyn shoved his own plain black mask up his nose with one hand while he grabbed a flute of foamy, pale pink liquid from a tray carried by a server with his other hand. He sniffed it warily, then sipped. "Not bad—a little on the sweet side." Lifting his glass in the direction of the refreshment tables, Bleddyn said, "Since you aren't keeping an eye out for a gorgeous beauty from the forest, I won't tell you about the woman in red."

Teo's eyes snapped to his brother.

"Ah, so you *are* looking for someone."

Teo let out a low growl. "Don't toy with me."

Bleddyn smiled at a woman in a flowing green dress as she passed. The guy never missed a flirting opportunity.

"You're no fun. She's at your nine o'clock in the crimson dress, black mask with red trim." He paused while Teo searched the area his brother had indicated. "Don't forget who she is, big brother."

Teo ignored Bleddyn, his gaze landing on Jenna. Only the stunner in the red dress wasn't the Jenna Hood he'd met previously. No, this evening, she shone like a star in a dress that fit her curves, the dark curls that framed her porcelain face caught in an up-do that exposed a graceful curve of neck. The shade of her dress reminded him of her hoodie. *I definitely like the dress better.*

Bleddyn cleared his throat. "I know we're wearing masks, but you might want to stop staring and shut your gaping mouth."

Clamping his jaw shut, Teo reached out with one hand, gently shoving his laughing brother. Teo felt like throwing him to the ground, but that kind of behaviour at a ball was frowned upon.

The revellers faded as his focus narrowed in on the girl. Weaving in and out of the maze of people and tables, Teo got to within a few yards of her before he noticed the guy standing beside her. The other courier. His heart stuttered. Who had invited him? Technically his father did, but when Teo asked Jenna to come, he hadn't pictured her bringing someone else. They stood close together; she was laughing, probably at something the guy had said. Teo frowned and then shook himself. *You're the heir to Wolf kingdom. Does it matter if she's with him?*

Thrusting his shoulders back, Teo closed the distance between them. He cleared his throat, waiting for her to acknowledge him. When she faced him, the mask on her face couldn't hide her beauty. He caught his breath.

"I told you I'd find you." He bowed slightly. "You're beautiful."

That long, elegant neck turned a pretty shade of pink. It clashed with her dress, but Teo thought it was the best colour combination he'd ever seen. Although his heart raced, he schooled his features into his best charming smile. That he had that effect on her made him ridiculously happy, even though it shouldn't. He snuck a glance at his father across the room, chatting with friends. Who cared what his father thought? The only person on his mind at the moment was the girl who stood in front of him.

"Are you sure you have the right person?" she teased.

Was she flirting? He could get on board with that. Lifting up his hands, he turned in a circle. "Who else would wear a red dress but the Red Hood?"

The other courier stepped between them. "I'm sorry, who are you?"

Teo drew himself to his full height, which was slightly taller than the guy. He levelled a stare at him, resisting the urge to shove him out of the way. "A friend. And you?" he growled.

"Ethan. Childhood friends." He stood his ground. Impressive for a Forester.

As though sensing the tension between the two, Jenna threaded her hand through Ethan's arm. If she had hoped to ease her friend's concerns it clearly didn't work; Ethan's thin-lipped smile never reached his eyes. "I take it you're not from the forest?"

"No, I'm not. More a friend *of* the forest. I'm Teo." The words were out before he could rein them in. *Friend of the Forest? Yeah, right.* He cleared his throat, scanning the room. Although cavorting with the Foresters tonight was considered politically correct, he didn't need his brothers or father giving him grief. Or asking questions. Yeah, they were no friends of the forest. He slid his gaze to Jenna, locking on those eyes. But he might *want* to be a friend.

Ethan scoffed, but Teo ignored him, bowing to Jenna. "May I have this dance?"

She smiled as she let go of Ethan and took Teo's arm, following him to the dance floor. Teo had never been so thankful for a masquerade ball. His father wouldn't be able to tell who he was dancing with. And if he did? Teo would argue he was being an obedient son. The king encouraged all Wolves to mix with the Foresters for this one night. Make the Forest clan feel seen, the king had ordered. It was quite the performance, his father usually winning best actor. His brothers and himself not far behind. How many times had he charmed young Foresters only to forget them the next day?

Only you're not acting.

Or following orders. Tonight, Teo was doing what *he* wanted. And Prince Teowulf wanted to dance with Jenna Hood. Forester or not. A lightness filled him as he drew her close, tucking her small hand close to his heart while his other hand rested on her waist. They fit together like two puzzle pieces, and he enjoyed the sensation of holding her. Warning bells pealed in his head. How could they fit together when they were forbidden? Her fingers glided over his shoulder, brushing against his neck. A shiver went through him. He wasn't going to think about all the negatives tonight.

Spinning and gliding across the floor, they danced until the band took a break. The temptation to whisk her away, remove that darn mask, and kiss her like she'd never been kissed threatened to overtake his good sense. He let her go, putting space between them as the music faded, gathering his wits. Gesturing around him, he asked, "Are you enjoying yourself?"

"It's a wonderful party. I've never been before."

"Really?"

She tucked her hands in the folds of her skirt. "No, my parents didn't attend after I was born. I guess they weren't interested in it, and neither was I."

"And this year?"

She raised her eyebrow. "You asked me to come."

He rested a hand on her waist and leaned close to her ear. "I'm happy you did." A waft of honeysuckle teased his nose and he wanted to inhale deeply, but a firm tap on his shoulder jolted him back to his surroundings.

Bleddyn held out his hand, a huge grin on his face. "May I?"

What if Teo refused his brother? Creating a scene would spoil everything, which was likely what Bleddyn was counting on. Teo glared at his brother, but reluctantly released Jenna into his arms. "One dance," Teo snarled.

His brother swept Jenna away, that smug grin still on his face. Teo stalked to the punch bowl and poured himself a cup of the fruity drink, pretending he wasn't watching his brother and Jenna. Grimacing as the sweetness hit his throat, he hastily set the cup on the table. As he swiped his mouth with a napkin, he noticed Ethan monitoring the dancing couple's movement around the room. Was he a friend or more? If Teo was reading body language right, he guessed Ethan wanted more, but Jenna didn't seem that into him. Warmth spread through him at the realization, and Teo nodded to himself as he tossed the napkin into a tiny silver bucket on the floor. Not that it mattered, since nothing could happen between him and Jenna, but Teo planned on enjoying tonight.

After the music stopped, Teo picked his way around dancers toward Jenna, halting mid-step as Seth appeared out of nowhere, next to Bleddyn. *No, no, no.* He felt as though he was playing musical chairs with Jenna and his brothers. What was Seth doing, asking her to dance? Had Bleddyn told their youngest brother about her? His father and mother sat on the dais, laughing, drinking champagne, and chatting with other party-goers. They had the best seats in the house—they could see everyone from there, which was no accident if Teo knew his dad. As if on cue, the king glanced over to where Seth and Bleddyn stood with Jenna, and his eyes narrowed.

Panic crawled up Teo's throat. What should he do? If he went over to Jenna now, his father would become even more suspicious. If his father had noticed Teo dancing with her earlier, then there was going to be trouble.

Teo frantically cast about for a diversion. Spotting his father's best friend, Hammond, near the food table along with his daughter, Teo hurried over to them. The man had silver hair, but the muscles he sported through his tux belied the fact that he was the parent of young adults.

"Hello, Hammond." Teo held out his hand to the gentleman. "Regina." He nodded at the young woman, whose eyes had widened upon his arrival. Inwardly, Teo groaned. Regina had been crushing on him since they were ten and got tongue-tied anytime he was near her. It made him feel awkward, and he'd really hoped she had outgrown it. He focused on her father.

"Teo, so good to see you." The man placed two beef skewers on a plate. He picked up a third, waving it slightly. "Great party, as always. This is my favourite night of the year."

"Credit goes to my mother." There was no time for small talk. "Hammond, my father was looking forward to seeing you tonight. I see he's got a free moment." Teo gestured to his father.

"Oh? I guess we better not keep him waiting." He abandoned the plate on the table. "Come along, Regina, let's go speak with the king. Take care, Teo."

Hammond and his daughter approached the dais just as the king stood, appearing to search the room.

Hammond joked, "Looking for us, Duko?" He bowed and Regina curtsied. The king waved them up onto the platform, seeming to have forgotten what had caught his attention. One could only hope.

Teo raised his eyes to the ceiling, mouthing *thank you* as his shoulders loosened. He spotted Seth waltzing Jenna around the floor with ease. Bleddyn was attached to a curvy blonde in a royal-blue dress that left little to the imagination. *Figures.* Teo tugged on his mask, pulling it slightly away from his face, then let it snap back. Ethan stood stiffly with a girl dressed in head to toe white. She was talking, but Ethan didn't appear to be listening; instead, he, too, kept an eye on Jenna and Seth. His frown told Teo all he needed to know. Their eyes met, and Ethan excused himself from the girl.

"Don't you think you have a conflict of interest with Rider, *Prince Teowulf?*" he said, squaring his shoulders.

What was with this guy? Teo smirked. "Rider?" What kind of terrible nickname was that? "Are you her guard dog?"

"I'm concerned she's gotten herself tangled with a Wolf in prince's clothing." Ethan shoved his hands into his pants' pockets. "Are you spying on the Hoods for your father? How do you even know her?"

Before Teo could escalate the conversation further, Jenna and Seth whirled to a stop beside them. "Thank you for the dance." Seth bowed.

"Thank *you*." Jenna's voice was slightly breathless. Her glance slid between Teo and Ethan. "What's going on, Ethan?"

"Just getting to know Teo here since he's a... friend." Ethan stepped between Teo and Jenna, blocking Teo off. "Is your dance card full, or may I have this dance?"

Jenna hesitated before nodding. As Ethan escorted her to the dance floor, she glanced over her shoulder at Teo.

Teo growled to himself. He didn't like Ethan. Why? Maybe because Teo wished he could whisk Jenna—who'd suddenly become the belle of the ball—away from everyone. He straightened his jacket.

Seth stood beside him, contemplating the dance floor. "A popular girl. I was hoping to find out who she was. She drew you and Bleddyn like bees to honey." He ran his thumb over his chin. "Who is she?"

"A girl I met in passing." Enough truth that Seth might buy it. Teo ran his finger between his mask and temple, wiping away the sweat that had pooled there. The room was warm and his brothers' actions made Teo's internal temperature rise.

"You're a pathetic liar. Were you switched at birth?" Seth mused. "She's *someone*, because the whole time we danced, she fished for information about you and the trade deal. Now, I may be the youngest Howell, but I am not an idiot. I'm guessing she's Jenna Hood." Seth tugged on his bow tie. "Has Father asked you to keep an eye on the Hoods?"

Duko would only trust an assignment like that to Seth, not Teo. Was Seth spying on his own brother? They were supposed to have each other's backs. "No, I'm not spying."

"Then why are you interested in her?"

If he lied, this interminable conversation might end. "I'm not interested in her. I'm doing what we're supposed to be doing, mixing with the Foresters on this one night—farce that it is."

Seth crossed his arms. "Bleddyn said you had a crush. He didn't mention she was a Forester, and a Hood to boot."

"Bleddyn doesn't know what he's talking about," hissed Teo. Bleddyn had a big mouth. Teo should have lied and said he was spying. He was done with this conversation and Seth's questions.

"Really? Your jealousy of her friend," Seth tilted his head to the dancing couple, "seems to indicate otherwise." A sly smile crossed his lips. "She is gorgeous and she smells delicious. But delectable enough to risk father's wrath?"

Teo glared at his brother through the mask's eye holes, afraid he'd give himself away if he said anything more. He didn't need Seth running to their dad to report that his heir was infatuated with a Forester. Teo rubbed his chest where a small pain had ignited. His brother wouldn't do that. Would he?

"Even if Father allowed you to find your own bride, do you really believe he would ever agree to you marrying an outsider?" He flicked imaginary lint off Teo's shoulder. "Don't be a fool, big brother."

Was that a warning? Before Teo could respond, Seth faded into the crowd. Sweat trickled between Teo's shoulder blades. The sweet scent of perfume combined with the aroma of meat soured Teo's stomach. Had his dad turned Seth on him? And why mention a bride? Who said anything about marriage? Seth was nuts.

I want to get to know her. That thought surprised him. He sat down at one of the tables, both his father and Jenna still in full view. She moved gracefully across the floor in Ethan's arms. He rubbed his chest. Yes, he wanted to get to know her. What else made her feisty, besides himself? Why did she wear red all the time? What did she like to do in her spare time? But those questions would have to wait until he could get her away from his brothers and her idiotic friend. He frowned.

The king was still engrossed in conversation with Hammond on the dais. Good. Hammond had unwittingly done what Teo wanted him to—distract the king. Teo quickly maneuvered his way to where Ethan and Jenna danced. After tapping Ethan's shoulder, Teo was rewarded with a glare from the guy, but Ethan relented his position. Teo smiled smugly. *Don't mess with a prince.*

He held out his arms to Jenna. "You're the prettiest girl in the room. A guy can barely get a dance." He maneuvered them through the crowded dance floor until the music died. Jenna was graceful on her feet, which made her a perfect partner. Teo enjoyed sweeping her around the room, the smile on her lips. They turned a few heads, making Teo nervous. They didn't need any extra attention. "It's warm in here. Would you like to get some air?"

She slid out of his arms, and he resisted the urge to draw her close again.

Jenna fanned her face. "That would be great."

"You've been dancing non-stop since you got here."

She raised her eyebrow. "Keeping count?"

He suppressed a smile, lifting a shoulder as though he didn't really care. No need for her to know that, indeed, he'd counted. They strolled out into the fresh evening air. The stars twinkled as they made their way to the far end of the enormous balcony. Casting a furtive glance over his shoulder, Teo made sure no one was following them. He leaned a hip against the railing, promising himself he'd socialize with the other guests later. For the moment, all he cared about was learning more about Jenna Hood.

Chapter Eighteen

Rider

COOL AIR CARESSED HER warm cheeks as Rider gripped the balcony railing with both hands, staring at the stars. Potted shrubs placed here and there were strung with small white lights, creating a romantic atmosphere that even Rider couldn't resist. She closed her eyes. Her head was spinning from all the dancing and attention. Much to her surprise, she'd danced with all three princes. *And learned nothing about the king's plans or the trade deal.* Although she'd asked questions and pretended to be clueless, she'd still come away with no answers. If the king's sons knew anything, they were master liars. Why did that surprise her? *Never trust a Wolf.*

The crown prince removed his mask, and she couldn't help but admire his strong jaw and nose. The word *handsome* didn't do him justice. He was a masterpiece. She shook her head. Had she totally lost it? Clouds drifted over the moon, casting shadows on the balcony. Hopefully they hid her reddening face.

"What are you thinking about?" Teo tossed his mask on a nearby bench. "Would you like to sit?"

She lowered herself onto the bench, sighing from the relief of taking the weight off those ridiculous heels. Teo sat beside her, his thigh brushing against her leg. His closeness, as well as the smell of his cologne, tilted her world. All thoughts of enemies and princely brothers fled her mind. She unfastened her mask and let the cool air seep over her eyes and nose. "Wow, those masks are hot."

His gaze lingered on her face. "You shouldn't hide behind a mask or a hood." His voice was low, soft.

Her heart raced, despite her warning to herself. She had a job to do. Compliments and flattery were not going to wear her down. "I like my hood; the mask, not so much. Besides being hot, it's hard to see." She smoothed her skirt, the softness of the material soothing her frayed nerves. "I think your father would disagree with you. He'd like to hide all the Foresters."

Teo stiffened. Did he feel the same? Had she gone too far with her observation? She clutched her mask. She didn't want to scare him away. And it wasn't solely because she wanted to find out what he knew.

Teo ran his hand along his pant leg. "My father isn't always right. He makes mistakes too."

"A mistake is trying your best to do the right thing but messing it up. Oppressing people because you don't like them and then taking away their jobs is prejudiced and cruel."

Teo clasped his hands between his legs. "He has his reasons."

Rider raised her eyebrows. "And that makes it right?"

His jaw tightened. "Didn't I say he isn't always right?" A frostiness edged his words. They stared intently at one another until he sighed. "Can we not talk about my dad tonight?"

No point arguing with a person who wasn't ready to hear the truth. Although he *had* admitted his father might be wrong. That was a victory for Foresters everywhere, right? Rider relaxed in her seat, taking a deep breath. She didn't want to argue with him—fighting would ruin the beautiful night. A breeze ruffled across the balcony, making the lights on the branches of the bushy shrubs dance. Rider rubbed her arms. Teo shrugged out of his jacket and then wrapped it around her. His body heat had warmed the material, and she snuggled into it. They sat in silence for a few minutes. Why was this boy, this Wolf, being so kind to her, a Forester? Maybe change wasn't as far off as she'd feared.

"I hope you aren't col—" The words died on her lips, forgotten. He was closer now, and she noticed his long lashes framing his eyes. His gaze dropped to her lips, his breath mingling with hers. Was he...?

"Teowulf!" The shout echoed through the night like a gunshot.

She gasped as they jerked apart, her thumping heart threatening to break ribs.

Teo cleared his throat as he jumped to his feet. "It's my uncle. I'm sorry, I need to go."

Rider stripped off his jacket and handed it to him, then put her mask on, afraid his uncle would suddenly appear and identify her. Teo slung his jacket over his arm, shoving his mask into his pants pocket. "I'm so sorry," he mumbled as he hurried away, leaving her standing alone.

What just happened? Had he been about to kiss her? No. She must have misread the moment. No way would the heir to the throne kiss a Forester. Laugher erupted nearby, and Rider spotted a group of women in gowns of rich jewel tones coming her way. It felt as though their laughter was meant for Rider. How stupid of her for thinking Prince Teowulf wanted to kiss her. Rider hurried back to the ballroom. Where had Teo vanished to like a puff of smoke? His uncle must hold a lot of sway, since Teo had bolted as soon as he'd called. Or had he been ashamed to be seen with her? Rider stared at the floor. No, he'd danced with her in front of everyone.

It didn't matter. She'd forgotten her focus for the evening, which was to gather information. Rider pushed her shoulders back, gazing around the ballroom. Her steps faltered as she locked eyes with the king. Quickly she dropped her gaze and ducked behind a chatting group of people. Her stomach was like a lead balloon. Had Teo been summoned by his father because he knew his son was with the Hood girl?

Determined to find out, Rider circled the room. Off to the far side, Teo and his uncle disappeared through an exit. She hurried toward it, but Ethan blocked her path, gently catching her wrist.

"I've been looking all over for you. I saw the prince come inside. Alone. Are you okay? Did he hurt you?" Ethan's eyes roamed over her as though he was assessing her for injury.

Rider tracked where Teo had gone. She couldn't lose him. She tugged her hand free. "No, he didn't hurt me. I'm fine. Getting air." She fanned her face. When she made a move to step around him, he stuck out his arm again, stopping her.

"What's going on, and where are you trying to hurry off to?"

Rider huffed out a breath. "Nothing is going on."

"Really? One Wolf Prince can't take his eyes off you, and then the other two show up, each vying for your attention. You're a Hood; King Duko just took away your livelihood. None of this seems coincidental to me. Things aren't adding up."

By now, Teo was long gone. Rider sighed. "Okay. I've run into Prince Teo a couple of times here in the city. His brother questioned me at the gates, and Teo intervened. I'd never met the youngest brother before tonight. I have no idea why they sought me out, other than Prince Teo asked if I was coming tonight when I saw him last."

"So that's why you came?" What looked like hurt filled Ethan's eyes.

"I, uh… partially." She avoided looking at her friend.

"Oh." All the air sucked from the room with that one word.

"I'm sorry, Ethan. I was curious about the Howells, but I'm glad I got to spend time with you, too."

"You're playing with fire." He tilted his head toward the exit where Teo had disappeared, frowning. "He's the crown prince of *Wolf* kingdom. We don't trust Wolves."

Rider crossed her arms over her chest. "I know exactly who he is, but I thought maybe I could find out what the king has planned for the Forest, now that he's taken some of our occupations away. Discover more about ChemTech's medicine. If I happened to have to dance with a couple of princes to find out, so be it. That's all." But maybe they could trust this Wolf. Perhaps?

"This isn't a game, Rider."

"I know that," she snapped. Why was he being so stubborn? "I'm sorry. Please stop worrying. It was all very shallow and flirty. Nothing to get excited over." She stole a glance to where she'd last seen Teo, but he hadn't returned to the ballroom.

"That's what I'm afraid of. Be careful."

"I always am."

Ethan snorted. "Riight. That's why you have several scars from going too fast on your bike." He blew out a breath, seeming resigned. Gesturing to the dance floor, he asked, "Maybe you'd like to dance once more?"

"I'd love to." Perhaps dancing with Ethan would get him off her case, as well as allow time for Teo to show his face again. Ethan led her out onto the floor, a smile curving his lips. Rider's chest tightened. She should give Ethan all her attention, but her mind wandered, as did her eyes. Had Teo not wanted his uncle to see them together? Rider stepped on Ethan's toe and they stumbled. He winced.

"Sorry," she whispered.

"It's okay, but maybe try not to space out," Ethan grumbled. Rider managed not to cripple him. As soon as the music ended, they strolled over to the punch table. Ethan held out a glass, but Rider shook her head.

"Ethan, it's getting late. I'm ready to go."

"Okay, I'll walk you home. My parents and sister left an hour ago. I'll find our coats." He set down the punch.

"Thanks." Rider handed him her ticket. Humiliation and curiosity warred for her attention. What was that Wolf up to? Why had he run off? Was it her or something else? Sighing, she followed Ethan out of the palace.

Chapter Nineteen

Teo

Teo stood in the king's study, observing his father beneath hooded eyes. Dark paneling, heavy drapes, and paintings of frowning relatives made the room extremely foreboding. This had never been a room Teo could tolerate for more than a few minutes.

His father ordered Teo to sit, so he stood, his spine ramrod straight. Bleddyn sat sprawled on a large leather chair to Teo's right, and Seth had settled, ankles crossed, in a chair to his left. Uncle Alarick leaned against the wall behind Duko, observing everything, saying nothing. They could have been posing for a cover of a men's magazine but for his father's scowl. A vein throbbed along the king's temple. *That's never a good sign.*

"I'll ask for the last time, who is the girl in the red dress? All three of you swarmed her, so she must be someone of interest."

"I don't know who she is; I only went over to her because Bleddyn was dancing with her." Seth covered his mouth as he yawned.

Bleddyn snorted. "Try more like all you saw was a gorgeous face under that mask. Which is why I was there. Just another pretty girl. I thought you didn't care who we danced with?" He casually flicked non-existent lint from his sleeve.

"When all three of you approach her within a short time frame, it begs curiosity from everyone. Am I to believe then, that not one of you got her name?" Sarcasm dripped from the king's every word.

"It's a masquerade ball for all the kingdom, including Foresters, whom we are forbidden from interacting with outside this night, so why would we ask for a name?"

Teo winced at Bleddyn's tone. Was he trying to irritate their father further?

"Did she know that all three Wolf princes were vying for her attention?"

Seth stretched out his long legs. "It's no secret. We stick out like sore thumbs. I think the media sends out details of our costumes beforehand. I had at least three women approach me not five minutes after the ball began. They knew exactly who I was, so I'm sure the girl did too."

Teo eyed his youngest brother with interest. Was Seth deflecting attention from him? Maybe he wasn't their father's yes man like Teo thought.

"It must have been very heady for her to have all three of you fighting for her attention." The king frowned. "Teo? You've been quiet."

The desire to avert his eyes overwhelmed him, but Teo met his father's stare. Shrugging as if he was bored with the conversation, he said, "Bleddyn's right, just a pretty face."

Duko held his hands together as though he was praying. His eyes flicked from one son to another. Perspiration broke across Teo's upper back. His heart raced, but he schooled his features into blankness.

Finally, his father nodded. "Very well then. You may go."

Bleddyn and Seth jumped to their feet and headed to the exit before their father could change his mind. All Teo wanted was to get as far away as possible from the king. He started to follow his brothers out. Seth was making a beeline for his suite. Bleddyn waited outside the office, but out of sight.

As Teo passed the threshold, his father said, "The forest is a dangerous place. Stay away from it, and stay away from the Hood girl."

Teo halted, glanced over his shoulder.

His father's eyes glittered. "Don't play me the fool, Teo. There's only one person who wears that colour of red, which was created by Ruby Hood, who, by the way, wore that dress when she was a little older than her daughter is now." He smirked. "That's Foresters for you—recyclers to the core." His eyes met Teo's, but there was no mirth in them, only steel. "Any girl who can't buy a new dress for a ball is not fit for a son of mine, let alone the crown prince. Stay away from her." Duko turned to Alarick, who was probably going to get a piece of the king's mind too. Teo was dismissed.

Teo shoved trembling hands into his pockets as he stepped into the hallway. The suite doors closed behind him. Bleddyn came alongside Teo, his eyes wide. "How does he do that?"

A shiver ran down Teo's spine. "I guess we underestimated our father's spies. What do you think he knows?"

"I'd bet my money on everything. I'm pretty sure he didn't buy the pretty face dog and pony show. I'm assuming Ruby Hood is Jenna's mother."

"I don't know. But from what Father said, yes, I would guess so."

"He knew her mother? Because that's what it sounded like. He recognized the dress." Bleddyn snapped his fingers. "That's how he knew her, not his spies. Ruby must have made an impression if he still remembers the dress."

"Yeah." The Hood women do that—make an impression. "Thanks for having my back in there. At least all our stories were on the same page."

"That's what I'm here for. Wing man and co-conspirator." Bleddyn saluted. "I was as surprised as you when Seth showed up to ask Jenna to dance. I'm not sure why he came over."

"Maybe he really did think she was another pretty face."

Bleddyn side-eyed him. "None of us are blind, Teo. She's gorgeous. Even with a mask on." He chuckled softly. "But really, a red dress? You could have emphasized inconspicuous. It's bad luck that Father recognized it."

Not only bad luck but dangerous. Had Jenna left the castle? Teo hoped she'd gotten home okay. Surely his father wouldn't detain her. She hadn't done anything wrong.

As if reading his mind, Bleddyn said, "I'm pretty sure Father was too busy with us to bother with her. At least for tonight."

"You're probably right." Teo rolled his shoulders. "But that dress was something." He couldn't keep his lips from tugging up at the memory of Jenna Hood standing there, looking like a goddess.

Bleddyn pointed his finger at Teo. "You've got it bad."

He shoved his brother's finger away. "I don't have it bad. I don't have it at all. Like you said, she's a pretty girl. No law against appreciating beauty, is there?"

Bleddyn's suites were just ahead. He turned to Teo, all the joking gone from his face. "If it belongs to the forest, you know there is. Be careful. We don't know what she's up to, and now Father's suspicious. You need to be extremely cautious."

"Stop worrying—it's not like you. Besides, I've got it under control."

"Do you?" Bleddyn swiped a hand down his face. "I hope so." He unlocked his door and waved good night before disappearing into his room.

Teo wandered in the other direction, turning the conversation over in his mind. Bleddyn was right. He had no idea what Jenna Hood was up to. Was she using him to get information? His dad would have a coronary if he knew any connection between Teo and Ruby Rider's daughter went beyond tonight.

Teo was in big trouble and now, so was she.

⸻◆⸻

A week after the ball, Teo was patrolling along the wall of the city when he spied through his binoculars a familiar red hood in the woods, bobbing amongst the shrubs and trees near the edge of the forest. He focused his lens. *What's she doing?* She squatted and picked up a green leaf and then dropped it in the basket she carried. Memories of her helping Seth long ago flooded his mind. She'd grown up, but he had a feeling that she'd help again if the need arose. She continued to gather green plants. He scanned the area again with his binoculars. Why bother to harvest when Hood Medicine wasn't trading with Wolf City anymore? Or anyone else in the Wolf Empire, for that matter. *Maybe personal use. I hope that's all it is.*

He'd kept his distance after the ball. His father's watchful eye was all the motivation Teo needed to stay away. Jenna didn't deserve any unnecessary attention from the palace. Being seen anywhere near his family, including himself, would only bring her trouble.

Yet here she is. It was as though fate was dropping her in his lap. Teo tore the binoculars from his eyes and studied the crowd of people lined up to get into the city. He rubbed the back of his neck. The girl was maddening. She was like a bull's eye in that hoodie, gathering plants in full view of the wall and the guards. He pivoted to head in the opposite direction, not wanting to arouse his co-workers' attention in either himself or her. They'd run straight to his father's spies. The message to stay away rang loud and clear in Teo's ears.

He avoided looking in her direction again, assessing every other area but the one where Jenna worked. Finally, Teo finished his watch and headed into the guard offices on the ground level.

"Teo, I need you to work an extra shift today," his commanding officer called out to him as he passed his boss's private office.

Teo stopped and leaned against the door frame. "Okay, what's up?"

"Greyson's sick and Phil's home too, so I'm short-staffed. Can you stay?"

"Sure, I can pull a double." Teo loosened the top button of his coat. "Is there a bug going around?"

Commander Silver frowned. "Must be. Anyway, I appreciate you sticking around. Thanks."

The staff room was nothing fancy. Wooden chairs and tables filled the room, along with a table that held a large pot of coffee. Teo made his way over to it to grab a mug. The larger the cup, the better if he was going to pull a double shift. The fragrant black liquid steamed as he filled the mug. After taking a fortifying sip, which burned his tongue, Teo dropped into a chair at the table, near the window. The hot liquid slid down his throat and warmed his insides, momentarily quelling the chill on his skin.

Seth dropped onto the chair beside him, a cup of tea in his hand. What was he, a granny in disguise? He set the cup on the table. "So, big brother, would you care to fill me in?"

"Commander Silver asked me to work a double." Teo rested his feet on the chair across the table.

"Don't play dumb; it doesn't suit you. The ball, Dad, the red dress... the fact you spent too much time staring at the forest today through your binoculars—care to expand on any of it?"

"Nope." Teo drained his cup and set it on the table with a thud. Maybe if he ignored his youngest brother long enough, he'd leave. He'd been avoiding Seth the last week precisely because he didn't want to answer any questions. He wasn't sure he would like the answers himself. Sure, Teo might be slightly attracted to Jenna Hood, but it was nothing more than harmless flirting, a little chemistry. He could ignore chemistry, right? He'd almost failed that class. An image of Jenna in the red dress flickered. *Keep telling yourself that.* He blinked twice, trying to wipe his mind clean. He needed to stay focused because his father was of even more concern than Seth. What did the king know about Jenna? Could she actually be in danger?

He slid a sideways glance at his brother. Was he on a spying mission for the king? He wouldn't put it past either of them. If Seth thought Teo was jeopardizing the Wolf Empire in any way, he wouldn't hesitate to go to the king. How many times in the past had Seth tattled on both Bleddyn and Teo? He sipped his coffee, giving himself some time. Seth could ask all the questions he wanted, but Teo wasn't giving him any answers.

When he couldn't stand his brother's silent appraisal any longer, Teo shifted on his chair. "If anything *was* going on, it still wouldn't concern you. We're brothers and apparently have similar tastes in women. I assure you it was a coincidence that we all ended up dancing with the girl." Teo lowered his feet to the floor and crossed his ankles.

"I know you think I'm spying for Father." Seth's words settled over Teo like a wet blanket. He met Seth's clear eyes. If his brother was hiding something, he was awfully good at it. "Maybe I used to do that, but I'm not... I see what's going on. What Dad's doing. I'm on your side, Teo. You can trust me."

Teo finished his drink, mulling over his brother's words. Could he trust Seth? He stood. "Thanks for clarifying that. I'm not sure what side you're referring to though. There's no battle going on between me and Father. I've got to get to work."

Seth stood too. His youngest brother was almost as tall as Teo. When had that happened? "I mean it. You can trust me." Seth picked up his own cup.

Teo hoped Seth was right, but, at the moment, Teo couldn't afford to trust anyone.

Chapter Twenty

Rider

R IDER'S TRIP TO HARVEST herbs growing near the city had been successful. Thankfully, frost hadn't killed them off. Her basket was full and her dad would be pleased. The autumn sun was unusually strong today, and she enjoyed its warmth as she strolled along the forest path. Squirrels darted around, their cheeks bulging with nuts.

She'd wanted to continue on into the city; instead, she'd turned the opposite direction and headed home. It'd been a week since the ball, and, although she'd been to the city a couple of times, she hadn't seen Teo. Where had he gone that night? *Forest and Wolves don't mix.* She'd be wise to pay attention to those age-old warnings, but they didn't sit well with her any longer. Maybe Granny was right.

If she wanted to be friends with a Wolf prince, why couldn't she? If she wanted to go on a date with a Wolf— *Stop right there.* The crown prince was definitely gorgeous and he made her heart stutter, but friendship was what she was after. They needed an ally in the city. And a royal ally would be a huge bonus. But that was all. Definitely. Besides, he was arrogant, Wolf or not.

And Rider couldn't get past the thought that perhaps the prince was only using her as a diversion until he tired of her. *Like you used him to get information?* Yeah, maybe they were both guilty of ulterior motives. However, if she was honest with herself, she'd looked forward to seeing him at the ball. Had he wanted to see her too?

Running her fingers through her tangled hair, she slowed her pace, hunching her shoulders. Why were things so complicated? Crazily, she'd thought she could convince him that Foresters and Wolves were equals, and they could have a great partnership. And maybe turn his head at the same time.

She was an idiot for even going there. He was next in line to rule. Maybe she could convince him to listen to their side of the situation, but he'd never do more than flirt. Even if he didn't agree with his father, Teo would not go against the king's orders. Would he? He did have a reputation for being a rebel.

No, he wouldn't. She kicked a pebble along the path. Scenes from the ball were stuck on replay in her mind. Was he in trouble with his father? Maybe that's why he had disappeared, and it had nothing to do with her at all. She'd noticed the king keeping an eye on his sons throughout the evening. It had made her slightly uncomfortable, but it wasn't as though Duko would recognize her. She'd never met him.

However, it was no secret that Prince Teowulf didn't have the best relationship with his father. Maybe something had happened during the ball to precipitate some kind of fallout. Her house came into view, and Rider ran the rest of the way.

Once inside, she threw the plants into the large ceramic kitchen sink. After turning on the faucet, she let it run cold. Once the sink was half full, she turned it off. Her father walked in, carrying the newspaper.

"Hey, how did the foraging go?"

"Got what you needed."

"Wonderful." He poked a finger at the soaking plants. "Something up?"

Rider shrugged. "I don't get boys."

"Does this have anything to do with Ethan or the ball? You've been quiet since that night." He dried his fingers on the towel hanging over the handle of the stove. "Did something happen?"

Rider swished the plants through the water. "Ethan? No, we're just friends, nothing going on there. It's... someone else. Someone I met recently who attended the ball. I don't understand him."

Her father chuckled. "I think that's an age-old problem between males and females. What did he do?"

Shaking water from her hands, she chewed her bottom lip. "We were talking and he got called away by his uncle. He left so quickly it was obvious he didn't want his uncle to see me with him. I'm not sure if he was embarrassed or what. And I haven't talked to him since. I think he's brushing me off."

"I can't image he was embarrassed to be with you. If he was, he's an idiot and you should forget him. He's not worth your time." Her father frowned.

"I know. But he didn't seem to be that type of guy. I just hate being in this limbo. I'd like answers."

"Then go get them. Communication works wonders, Jenna-girl. Why not start there?"

Rider stared at the watery plants. Her dad was right. She needed to talk to Teo. She picked up a leafy plant and swirled it around in the cold water, the dirt falling away to the bottom of the sink. Maybe she'd not only get answers to why he ignored her but she'd find out how to help her dad. First, though, she had to figure out how to contact Teo, being the crown prince and all.

◆◇◆

Rider slowed the bike as she approached the city gates. Guards roamed the area, either checking papers or patrolling along the wall. She searched every guard's face, but no Teo. Would he talk to her if he was here?

Rider was picking up a grocery order in the city for her dad, which was a good excuse to look for Teo. Trying to figure out how to contact a crown prince had proved to be a challenge, as she'd anticipated. Spotting him at the gates was the only solution she'd been able to come up with. And the opportunity to do so was dwindling quickly. Although forest people were allowed in the city for legitimate reasons, like buying Wolf products, Rider wasn't sure if that included Hoods. A shiver ran down her spine as guards, their faces stern, questioned people. Maybe this wasn't such a good idea. It was stupid and dangerous to come into the city alone. Should she have asked Ethan to come with her? She shook her head. *I can take care of myself.*

Her father's warning to keep her head down and avoid drawing attention rang in her ears. The red hoodie had been left at home in favour of a boring grey one that blended in. She could make safe choices without giving in to fear. After showing her papers, Rider passed through the entry and walked her bike toward the road that led to the market.

Blue eyes in the crowd locked with hers. Although her body was still, her heart jump-started. As Rider managed to get her feet working and step toward Teo, he abruptly pivoted and headed in the opposite direction. He may as well have slapped her. Eyes burning, Rider blinked several times. Arrogant Wolf. No way would she give him the satisfaction that he had *any* effect on her.

Chapter Twenty-One

Teo

WHY IS SHE HERE?

Did she have a death wish? Teo clenched then flexed his fingers as he stared from the safety of the office after Jenna's retreating figure. Panic crawled up his throat as he'd watched her ride up to the gates from his post at the entrance. After his father's inquisition the night of the ball, Teo had reluctantly stayed away from her. But was this stubborn girl exercising caution? Nope. Here she was entering the city like it was no big deal. He wanted to wring her neck, but he also wanted to protect her. His father wouldn't think twice about arresting her if he caught wind that Teo or one of his brothers had been seen with her. As a result, Teo had acted like a jerk a few minutes ago, glaring at her and then walking away. Would she get the message to stay away from the city, from him? Did he even want that? It would mean not seeing her. His heart stuttered at the thought.

It was too risky being seen together. Especially now when his father was paying attention. His spies would report Teo. He glanced around the small room, eyeing his co-workers. Some were on the king's payroll, Teo would bet his paycheck on it. It was better, no, safer, to keep his distance.

Teo scrubbed his eyes, exhaustion hitting him like a rogue wave. Why did it have to be complicated? He lowered his hands and watched a young couple show their papers to the guard. What would it be like to be normal? Everyone had problems; Teo understood that, but his particular brand of royal issues was a vexation. Teo turned from the window, grabbed an apple from a basket. He bit it, the juice dripping down his chin. Using the back of his hand, Teo swiped it away. The couple he'd seen from the window lived a fairy tale to Teo, which was ironic, since he was the prince. He finished the fruit, tossing the core into the garbage. Once more he glanced out the window, sighing. It was the regular people who had the life Teo ached for.

Chapter Twenty-Two

Rider

THE CITY WAS BUSTLING and Rider let herself get lost in its busyiness, trying to erase the memory of Teo rejecting her. When she'd drawn close to the gate, he'd walked in the other direction instead of greeting her. Was she mad or sad? Maybe a little of both. How dare he? Did he think because she was a Forester he could treat her like dirt? Even if his actions so far indicated the opposite, it still didn't take the sting out of his brushoff. Any hope of an ally in Teo lay trampled at the city gates.

The small grocery where Rider and her dad shopped for goods that they couldn't get in the forest came into view next to Dr. Lupine's office. A warmth spread through her chest as she remembered the doctor's kindness toward her father. She locked her bike to a nearby pole. After grabbing her canvas grocery bag, she hurried toward the small shop.

"Rider."

She halted, casting about for the source of the voice. A shadow moved in the shade of the canopy over the office door. A family wandered by, the kids playing tag around the adults; another couple, holding hands, studied a shop window. At least she wasn't alone on a deserted street. She studied the entrance to the office, her shoulders dropping as Dr. Lupine stepped out into the light, motioning her over.

"I thought that was you. I saw you from our windows. I need you to get a message to your father." He cast a furtive glance up and down the street.

"Uh, okay." A prickle skipped over her scalp at his unease.

He motioned her under the canopy. "I wanted to give your father a heads-up. In the last week, I've seen a number of patients with a strange illness. I've made a list of symptoms." He handed her an envelope. "Give this to your dad. I've included a note for him too." His bushy eyebrows furrowed. "Be careful. This sickness is very contagious."

Rider shoved the paper into the bottom of her boot. "I'll see that my dad gets it. Are you okay?"

"We're fine. The office tries to be preventative, and we have safety protocols in place. An added bonus is the Wolf Pack doesn't show up anymore. Is anyone ill in the forest?"

"Nothing unusual that I've seen or heard."

"Good. Take care." The doctor vanished into his office.

Rider peered into the street, her stomach in knots. Forgetting the groceries, she quickly unlocked her bike and rode toward home. She passed inspection at the gate with no problem. Teo was nowhere in sight but she didn't care. She wasn't about to let a Wolf dictate her life. Besides, the note in her boot burned. Her dad needed to read what Dr. Lupine had written.

Arriving home slightly out of breath after her hard ride, Rider ran to her father's office.

"Dad."

He looked up from his desk. "What's wrong?"

Rider yanked her foot from her boot, felt around for the note, and pulled it out. "I saw Dr. Lupine and he wanted me to give you a message. There's a mystery illness infecting people. It's very contagious, he said." Rider shoved the envelope at her father.

Her father opened it, scanning the contents. Rider bent over, breathing deeply. After she could draw in enough air, she asked, "Is anyone sick in the forest?"

"A few runny noses and sniffles. Nothing unusual."

Her dad tapped the pages against his palm. "I need to research a few things," he mumbled, more to himself than her, as he starting thumbing through texts on his bookshelf.

Rider wrung her hands. Could life get any more complicated?

—◆○◆—

A day later, Rider and Ethan stared at the playing cards in their hands, neither focused on their game.

"What're the symptoms again?" Ethan tapped his cards lightly on the table.

"Fever that leaves you so fatigued you're bedridden. The weird factor is the hallucinations. Seeing things that aren't there, hearing voices. Then the bleeding starts from your ears and nose."

Ethan shuddered. "That's bad."

"Yeah. There have been one death and fifty documented cases as of yesterday. Two are in critical condition in the hospital. Since Dr. Lupine sent his message to Dad, it's blown up."

"All Wolves? No Foresters?"

"Nope, only Wolves. Most of the doctors have been keeping track. I guess they noticed a pattern, but that could change." Rider ran her sweaty palms along her thighs. Was Teo sick?

Ethan set his cards face down on the table. "How long has this been going on?"

"It started about a month ago. A case here and there. None of the doctors has seen anything like it before. But Dr. Lupine didn't like what he was seeing, and the palace is ignoring the doctors' pleas. He sent Dad a message yesterday."

"Why aren't they calling this an epidemic and quarantining people?"

"I think they're trying to avoid panic because they don't know what it is, or how to treat it. From what Dad said, Duko and his officials are barely acknowledging there's a problem. They insist ChemTech is working on it and will have something to treat it soon." Rider rolled her eyes. "Not sure how they could come up with a treatment that quickly."

And if the complaints about the effectiveness of Chemtech's pain meds were any indication, there was the question how reliable the drugs would be.

"What's your dad saying?"

Rider traced the top edges of her cards with one finger. "Not much. He's out running an errand and trying to find out what anyone knows here in the forest." She threw her hand on the table. "I can't concentrate. Do you want tea?"

"Make it healthy, please; I don't want any weird hallucinations or bleeding."

"It's only Wolves contracting it."

"You can never be too careful. I mean, what if the germs mutate?" Ethan's face paled.

"Don't be a hypochondriac." Rider shoved his shoulder. She put the kettle on to boil and then leaned her forehead against the window. Grey clouds rolled in and she hoped her dad returned before the storm.

⊸◦⊷

Dr. Hood arrived as the first large raindrops fell. Shaking his arms out of his jacket, he sniffed. "Smells good in here." He dropped his bag on the floor. "Hey, Ethan, how are you?"

"I'm good, sir."

"I made tea." Rider poured three cups. "It's peppermint to keep away the germs."

Her father wrapped his arms around Rider and gave her a squeeze. "Since when have you ever been a germaphobe?"

"I'm not, but I believe in preventative care." Balancing a tea tray, she followed him into the living room, Ethan behind her.

Her dad dropped into his favourite rocking chair, the one that had been in the house since Rider could remember. It creaked as he rocked.

"Any more news on the sickness?"

"Do you think it will mutate?" Ethan asked at the same time.

Dr. Hood scratched his chin. "Ethan, that's a good question but something you don't have to worry about. Only Wolves are getting sick. As a precaution, make sure you wash your hands frequently and don't share spit with anyone." Her dad waggled his eyebrows. Ethan's pale face turned beet red. Rider hid a smile behind her mug. Her dad liked to tease her friend; Ethan's gullibility only made it more fun.

"To answer your question, Jenna-girl, I have no new information."

"Workers talk at the mushroom farm. They overheard guards at the city gates saying one of their mates was ill." Ethan stacked the cards from earlier into a pile.

"Other than Dr. Lupine, I have no ties to any of the doctors or hospitals anymore. The king made sure to cut us off completely when the trade deal ended. So, I don't know anything more."

"Is there anything we can do?" Rider hugged a pillow to her chest. The handsome face of a certain prince came to mind. Granny's words about getting along with Wolves echoed. If Rider truly wanted unity and equality, maybe she had to change her attitude first. And she didn't want anyone to get sick. Even Wolves. Or Teo.

Dr. Hood sipped his tea. "I don't know. I'd like to see the disease firsthand."

Ethan faked a gag at her father's words. The guy really was a germaphobe.

"Do you trust ChemTech? From what the doctors have said, their drugs for ordinary aches and pains have very little potency." Rider pulled her legs under her, curling into the couch's corner.

"I have to give them the benefit of the doubt. Hopefully they figure it out. But you don't need to worry, since it does seem to be only hitting the Wolves."

But I am worried. "I don't want anyone to get sick, even Wolves." Rider was surprised to find she meant it. Maybe Granny was onto something. "And I think this might be an opportunity for you to prove the Wolves need you. You could figure this out if they'd let you help."

Her dad tilted his head. "Thanks for your vote of confidence, honey. It would be nice if I could speak to a doctor who has personally seen this."

"Dr. Lupine might speak to you. He gave you the heads up."

"He might, but he's got to come to me first. I don't want to endanger him or his patients by approaching them. If the king ever found out, they could be put in jail or worse." He drained the last of his tea. "I'll take care of it. I want you two to mind your own business and stay out of the city until we know what we're dealing with."

"No problem there," Ethan enthusiastically agreed.

"Jenna-girl?"

"I'll be careful, but I'm not letting a few germs stop me from doing what needs to be done."

Her dad frowned but he let it go. "Thanks for the tea. I need to go to work." He withdrew to his office.

Ethan set his mug on the table. "Rider, promise me you won't do anything stupid. Especially with the Wolf."

"I won't." She wasn't lying. Anything to do with saving Teo was not stupid.

Ethan removed his glasses, rubbed his eyes. "Why don't I believe you?"

Chapter Twenty-Three

Teo

TEO POSITIONED THE SCARF up over his nose and mouth, hoping this meagre measure would provide protection from this heinous disease. He cursed his father for prohibiting the Wolf Pack from wearing medical masks to protect themselves. The members of the Pack who guarded the gate were exposed to all kinds of people every day; they needed a defense. Ten people were out sick, one of whom wouldn't be returning. Teo's stomach churned at the thought of the older guard, Geo. He'd had kids and a wife. Now they were without a dad. This was serious, and Teo's own father acted like it was nothing more than an annoying bug. Teo cussed to himself as he walked to the officer's building. He spied Bleddyn through the window; his brother didn't look too good.

Teo pushed past people, entering the building at a jog. *No. No. No.* He rushed into the staff room, but no Bleddyn. Seth stood near the kettle, pouring himself a large cup.

Teo locked eyes with Seth. "Where'd Bleddyn go?"

"What?" Seth craned his head left and right. "Ah, he was just here. Why are you looking for him?"

"I saw him through the window and he didn't look good—like he was injured or sick."

Seth lifted his cup toward the exit to an area where they took their breaks on nice days. "Check outside. Maybe he's getting fresh air. He's on break."

Teo slowed his breathing. "He looked sick," he repeated.

"I'll come with you." Seth set his mug on the counter and followed Teo outside where they found Bleddyn slumped against the wall. As they neared him, he held his hand up. "Don't come any closer. I think I'm sick." His voice rasped and he swayed slightly.

"We need to get you home and under medical care." Seth stepped closer.

"Stop. It could be this sickness. I don't want you to catch it."

Teo grabbed Seth's elbow, squeezed it. They needed to get Bleddyn help now.

"Wait. Put these on." Seth yanked out two medical masks from his pocket and handed one to Teo.

Teo raised his brows. "Where'd you get those?"

"One of the doctors gave them to me when I patrolled by their office this morning. He said we shouldn't risk the crown. I was going to give them to you as soon as I saw you both. Put it on."

Teo slid the mask over his nose and mouth. "See, Bleddyn? We're protected from your germs." Bleddyn's bleary eyes flicked to them. Teo and Seth rushed to him.

"I need a mask."

Seth handed one to Bleddyn, who fumbled with it but got it on.

"We're taking you home." Seth slid his arm around Bleddyn, while Teo did the same on the other side. Their brother sagged between them. Another officer came outside, a newspaper and coffee cup in his hand, but stopped when he saw the brothers.

"Go back." Teo yelled. "Tell the Commander that we're taking Bleddyn home. He's sick." The guy nodded, rushing inside.

"Let's go the back paths to the palace," Seth suggested. "We'll take one of the carts we use for supplies. It'll be faster." They half-dragged Bleddyn over to the vehicle. Teo hefted him into the back and then climbed in beside him, wrapping his arm around Bleddyn to keep him steady. Seth jumped into the driver's seat.

"Let's go." Teo smacked the top of seat with his free hand. The cart jolted forward. Bleddyn moaned. A knot formed in Teo's gut, tightening as they drove to the palace. Bleddyn's eyes rolled up before his eyelids flickered closed. Had he passed out? "Stay with me, brother," whispered Teo.

———❖———

This sickness was unlike anything Teo had seen. He swallowed down both the revulsion and the panic that threatened to spew out of him. Bleddyn lay still, sweat trickling along his temples and dotting his upper lip, his face whiter than the sheets he lay upon. His brother's bedroom was eerily quiet, not the usual jovial space where Teo had spent hours laughing, playing pranks, and talking about girls. Teo inhaled, grimacing. The sour scent of sickness filled the air, turning Teo's stomach. The doctor said Bleddyn's temperature was danger-ously high. His brother mumbled incoherently. *Hallucinations, the next phase of the disease.*

Teo slipped out of the room that reeked of death into an empty hallway. After ripping off his mask, he stilled, letting cool air wash over his heated skin. Fingering the papery material, he bit the inside of his cheek. His father had relented on the use of them, at least in the palace, but still maintained this illness was nothing serious. "A flu bug, just a flu bug," was his mantra. The city had taken to calling it the Lupine flu because Dr. Lupine had figured out it was a new bug.

Teo wandered aimlessly along the hall, not knowing what to do with himself and not wanting to leave Bleddyn for long. Including Geo's, five families that he knew of had lost loved ones to this illness in the last few days. His father's voice drifted down the hall along with a second man's voice. Teo ducked into an alcove behind a topiary tree.

"Your Majesty, with all due respect, the drugs ChemTech sent over aren't working." His father and Dr Lupine came into view through the branches of the tree. The doctor's urgent tones raised the hairs on Teo's neck, and he pressed himself against the scratchy bark.

"We need to try something else." The doctor waved his hands as he spoke.

"No, ChemTech is working around the clock on this. They need more time. They'll come through for us."

"Respectfully, sir, I don't know how much more time we can give. Bleddyn—it's a bad case."

The pair moved away toward his brother's room, their voices fading but the meaning behind Dr. Lupine's words ringing in Teo's ears. Bleddyn was going to die if they didn't do something different and soon. *I've got to make Father listen.* And not only for Bleddyn but for all the people who might get sick and die. Teo ground his teeth together. The king hadn't listened when Teo had gone to him about the pain killers not working, why would he listen now? Was getting revenge on the forest—the Hoods—worth risking Bleddyn's life? Was his father that far gone? A chill pricked his spine as he realized he didn't know the answer. He inhaled sharply. Who could help him?

Uncle Alarick. Teo raced towards his uncle's suite.

—◆—

Uncle Alarick's rooms were simple by the palace's standards. A typical bachelor pad with hues of blue and grey, the scent of polished leather and lemon inviting friends and family to come in and stay a while. Teo found his uncle staring out the floor-to-ceiling windows in his study into the courtyard beyond.

Teo rapped lightly on the partially opened door. "Uncle Alarick?"

The man turned. "Teo, come in. Do you have news of your brother?" There was no mistaking the anxious tone in his uncle's voice.

"He's the same. High fever and a lot of pain. He's dreaming, but he's not conscious." He swallowed over the lump that had suddenly appeared in his throat.

His uncle's face was drawn tight, his usual happy countenance gone. "What can I do for you?"

"Father is wasting time, waiting for ChemTech to figure out a drug that works or cures the illness. I overheard him speaking with Dr. Lupine, who told him the drugs aren't working and there's no more time. I went to Father a few weeks ago, told him ChemTech's pain killers didn't work on my migraine but he wouldn't listen. I had taken some of Dr. Hood's pain elixir four hours after taking ChemTech's pills. Dr. Hood's medicine worked. Father didn't believe me, said it took time for ChemTech's drugs to work. It's not true. Hood's medicine is what did the trick." Teo scrubbed his eyes. "He's risking Bleddyn's life. I can't believe I'm saying those words. What kind of a father plays around with his son's life? Is revenge worth that kind of price?"

His uncle returned to staring out the window. A minute passed. Had his uncle heard him? Teo opened his mouth, but his uncle's voice, low and steady, cut him off. "Your father has a meeting in Greystoke City this afternoon. As soon as it's clear, we need to get your brother to the forest to see Dr. Hood."

"It's treason if we get caught." Teo wiped a hand over his mouth. Both panic and relief surged through him. Panic at the thought of his father finding out and relief that Uncle Alarick was going to help them.

"Hate is an awful curse, Teo. Worse than treason." His uncle went to his desk and withdrew a file. "I'm writing a letter to the king, taking full responsibility if this goes south."

Could they trust Dr. Hood? Did they have a choice? Bleddyn could not die. Teo would do anything to save his brother, even if it meant trusting someone who was supposed to be his enemy.

"I'll send word to Dr. Hood that we are sneaking Bleddyn to him this afternoon. I'm not sure he'll be able to help him, but if Dr. Hood is half the pharmacist I suspect he is, then he's already working on finding a drug to help." He sat at his desk and started to write. "Find Seth and we'll figure out how to make this work so we don't end up looking at an executioner." His uncle likely meant it as a joke, but Teo knew that if the king found out, there was truth in the statement. He turned and ran to find Seth.

Chapter Twenty-Four

Rider

THUMP. THUMP. RIDER FOLDED over the corner of the page of her book before hurrying to the front door. Ethan waved the paper in his hand as he staggered over the threshold.

"For... your dad," he huffed out.

Her father peeked around the corner of his office door. Clearly catching Ethan's words, he came into the main room.

"Take deep breaths," Rider instructed as she took the paper from Ethan, who was bent over at the waist, gulping air.

Her dad scanned the paper.

"Who is it from?" Rider peered over her dad's shoulder.

"Alarick. One of the princes has taken ill. They're on their way here." He hurried to his office. Rider stood gaping after her father a moment before whirling to face Ethan.

"Who gave you the message?" Rider forced her stiff lips to move.

"One of the valets from the palace. I was delivering truffles to the kitchen when he slipped it to me, telling me to get here like yesterday. I hustled as fast as I could. Thankfully, they didn't stop me at the gates. The Wolves don't seem too interested in getting near each other, or anyone else for that matter."

"You don't know which prince is sick?" Her voice rose an octave.

"No." Ethan met her eyes but refrained from saying anything else.

Her dad barrelled out of the office waving another piece of paper. He had been working night and day on finding a drug for the Lupine flu since the news broke about the epidemic. Although he wasn't commissioned to do it, her father had set out to find a treatment or cure because he was worried about a worst-case scenario. Every day that ChemTech failed to produce drugs that worked sentenced the Wolves to sickness and death.

"Jenna, I need you to go gather these herbs and do it quickly." He handed her the scrap of paper. "Go now."

She ran to the root cellar where they stored dried herbs and plants. *Who was sick?* The question urged her to work fast, even though her hands trembled. Soon she'd have an answer.

Taking the stairs two at a time, Rider rushed back to the kitchen, dropping the herbs into a bowl.

Her father called from his office. "Boil water and start diffusing oregano oil, please."

"Did Ethan leave?" She'd totally forgotten him.

"Yes, he needed to finish his deliveries." Silence, then, "I don't think he wanted to stick around, either. The boy has a weak stomach."

Wasn't that the truth? Ethan turned pale at the mention of illness or bodily fluids. She chuckled to herself at the memory of him going green when she'd fallen off the swing and busted her lip when they were ten years old. The sight of the blood had been traumatic for him, and he wouldn't go on the swings for months after. The memory calmed her racing heart.

She filled the kettle, settled it on the stove, and struck a match. Flames leapt around the bottom of the coils. Next she ground the herbs with a pestle until they were almost a fine dust. Finally, she set up the diffuser, breathing in the spicy smell of the oregano.

Her dad came out to the kitchen and sifted through the finely ground plants.

Rider eyed him. "Can you help the prince?" *Please say yes.*

"I'm going to try. I've been studying the research from that previous flu that went through years ago. I thought there might be a connection, since that flu affected the Wolves worse than the rest of us. Turns out there is some overlap in the symptoms. I'm going to try using a stronger version of the drug used then with a few modifications." He scooped up the bowl of herbs. "Thank you. Now you need to leave. It's safer."

"No... I can help." Rider wasn't leaving. If it wasn't safe for her to remain in the house, then what about her dad? "I'll stay out of the way. I'll cover my mouth and nose."

"It's not the flu I'm worried about. The less you know, the better. If we get caught... the consequences will be severe. If you're not here, then you don't know anything."

A commotion out front made Rider jump. Her dad frowned. "Go, Jenna-girl. Now." He opened the back door with one hand while balancing the bowl in his other hand.

Rider planted her feet. "Let me help."

"It's too dangerous." His jaw hardened.

Rider opened her mouth to protest as an older man burst into the kitchen from the living room. "Dr. Hood!"

Rider took advantage of the distraction to move farther into the room. The man Rider recognized as Teo's uncle.

"Bring the boy to my office." Her father pointed down the hall and then turned to Rider. "Pour the boiled water into a basin and bring it to me in the office along with some cloths. I already have a dose of the drug made up, but I may need to make more." He blew out a breath. "Cover your mouth and nose."

Rider nodded, but her eyes stayed glued to the living room and the three men coming in through the front door. She grabbed the counter to steady herself, her knees weakening. Teo and Seth half-carried, half-dragged their brother Bleddyn, who was pale and sweaty, between them. A sour odor wafted by. Teo's haunted eyes met hers briefly before he entered her father's office.

He's okay. All her anger about his ghosting her drained away. Clan struggles didn't matter when it was life and death. *He's okay.* Guilt chased the relief because his brother was obviously extremely ill. Noting they all wore masks, Rider breathed a little easier. She tied a handkerchief around her own nose and mouth, then poured the boiled water into a basin, grabbed a clean towel, and carried it all on a wooden tray to her dad's office.

The three Wolves stood off to the side, their eyes glued to the examination table while her father checked a nearly unconscious Bleddyn. Only Teo turned his head her way as she entered the room. She nodded slightly. *It's okay—it's gonna be okay*. He visibly relaxed, his shoulders drooping.

As Bleddyn began to writhe on the table, mumbling incoherent words, her dad spoke, his eyes never leaving the sick prince. "Take the others out to the kitchen, get them to wash up, then give them a teaspoon of that elixir there on my desk."

The brown bottle was tiny and fit in the palm of her hand. Rider cradled it as if it were a treasure. Tilting her head in the direction of the kitchen, she motioned the men forward. The youngest brother hesitated, but Teo grasped his arm. "We can trust Dr. Hood," he muttered to his brother. The words were like a balm to Rider's heart.

After they had washed, Rider handed each a teaspoon of elixir.

"What's this?" asked Seth. He didn't look quite as polished as he had at the ball. He seemed more ordinary.

"It's an immunity booster. It will hopefully help you fight off any infection." She forced her lips up. "Better than you'll get from ChemTech." She couldn't help the snark. When he didn't remove his mask, she shrugged. "It's your choice. No one's forcing you to take it."

Teo growled, "Take it, Seth."

The younger prince removed his mask and swallowed the medicine, grimacing. He glared at his brother as he readjusted the mask over his mouth.

Alarick and then Teo swallowed the medicine before dropping their spoons in a bowl of boiling water. Avoiding Teo's eyes, Rider swiped the counter with a soapy cloth, hoping they'd go into another room. Now that she knew he was okay, his rude behaviour lately stung. All of sudden, the desire to smack him was overwhelming. Probably not a good idea to assault the crown prince. Again. What was wrong with her? At the sight of him with his sick brother she was ready to forgive, but now she was mad? Her emotions were veering from one extreme to another.

"Thank you." His voice was low and husky behind her. She whirled, her eyes locking on his, which were lined with worry and dark circles but also something else. Perhaps gratitude? The fury drained out of her.

"You can wait out here until my father is finished examining your brother."

"We're staying with my brother." Seth stalked to the office.

Teo grasped her elbow, his fingers warm through her shirt. Sparks ignited where he touched her.

"I'm sorry about Seth. He's worried and forgetting his manners."

"It's fine." Not really—her dad didn't have to help them, but maybe she could look at it from the prince's perspective. Seeking help from your life-long enemy couldn't be easy. The guy was obviously scared for his brother. Teo's fingers lingered a minute longer, the sparks turning to lightning bolts on her arm, then he followed his brother to her dad's office.

Alarick remained in the kitchen, observing his nephews. Uh oh. Rider had forgotten he was there. Had Teo? Hadn't he run from her when his uncle called him at the ball? Rider wrung the cloth out in the sink.

"Thank you." He studied her a minute more before striding after his nephews. Rider threw the cloth onto the counter and sagged a hip against it, hoping Alarick hadn't noticed the current zapping between her and Teo. If he had, at least he'd kept quiet.

She finished sterilizing the spoons, sink, and counter, then Rider stole a glance into the office. Her dad's hands ran along Bleddyn's throat. The other three stood silently off to the side. *Please let this work*. Bleddyn had to get better, and Teo couldn't get sick. No other outcome would do.

⸺◆⸺

Rider halted her pacing, glaring at the clock. Its hands had only moved five minutes from the last time she looked. The door to her father's office remained tightly closed. She sighed, throwing herself onto the couch.

After what seemed an eternity, Teo and Seth appeared, carrying Bleddyn on a stretcher. He was still deathly pale, but at least he wasn't thrashing around. The older gentleman clutched a brown paper bag, which he stuffed into his coat pocket. Rider suspected it held the experimental drug Dr. Hood had made, as well as more of the immunity booster. Would the new drug work? Were the princes' allies or would they betray her dad by telling the king who helped them? Time would tell. Rider rubbed her upper arms, suddenly chilled.

Alarick shook her dad's hand. "Thank you, Dr. Hood. We are extremely grateful."

Her father checked the front window. "Looks like the coast is clear."

The somber party left, leaving silence in their wake. Rider slit the curtain with two fingers. Teo, his uncle, and brother laid the stretcher in the back of a cart used by the Wolf Pack at the gates. She stayed rooted there until they had vanished into the forest.

In the kitchen, she found her dad washing up. "They took an enormous risk coming here. I can't predict the outcome. He's very sick and I'm not sure I have the drug exactly right yet. It could go either way. But I am positive the drugs from ChemTech aren't working at all. Bleddyn's pain had already diminished from the one pain killer I gave him. So, that's something, at least. I'm hoping that the pain killer combined with this experimental drug will bring not only relief from the symptoms but healing. It must be terrible to see him thrash around."

Questions whirled around her brain. "Will he die? Are the others showing any signs of sickness?"

"I hope it's given him a fighting chance. They have to give him another dose in forty-eight hours. It's a waiting game now. The others didn't show any symptoms, which is a miracle." After drying his hands, he folded the towel. "I can't believe they took that kind of risk. If Duko finds out..."

Rider slid her arms around her father's waist. "I know why. You're the best pharmacist in this kingdom. You've always cared for anyone who was sick, Forester or not." She laid her cheek against his chest, his warmth and the woodsy smell of him comforting her. "How contagious is it?"

"From my research, the germs spread through saliva, so as long as they don't touch anything his saliva has touched, they should be fine. That immunity booster will hopefully help them fight off the germs."

"What about Duko? What if they betray us?"

"Alarick is no fool. He's not like his brother. He knows Bleddyn's health depends on Duko not finding out." He squeezed her. "Maybe we've found ourselves an ally."

"Do you think so?" Doubt filled her voice.

"I have hope." He ran his hand over her hair. "Perhaps I've been wrong. Alarick and the princes didn't let prejudice get in the way of bringing Bleddyn here. We can trust them. But *Duko* can't be trusted. He's hated us almost his whole life." Sadness crossed her dad's face.

There was more to the story, and her dad clearly knew what it was. Astonished by this revelation, Rider tipped her head to the side. "What happened?"

"Duko's youngest brother died when they were kids. I was ten at the time. The youngest prince adored Duko. He fell down a ravine, here in the forest, after it had rained, and he hit his head. Duko ran to my father's place for help but, unfortunately, my dad let his own prejudice get in the way. He wouldn't listen—he told me later he thought the princes were trying to get him in trouble with the king, as the two of them didn't get along. My father had wanted to expand his medicines into other kingdoms, but the king blocked it. My stubborn old man tried to do it anyway, and the king threw him in jail for a week. One of Dad's friends died the week he was incarcerated. An infection from a cut that, had it been treated, would not have been fatal. Things got worse from there. Anyway, after Duko's youngest brother died, the king blamed both my father and young Duko, who was just a kid himself. I believe the whole experience scarred Duko. He blamed the forest and my father. It's part of the reason for all the hate today."

"I get why he'd blame Grandpa, but why the forest?" Maybe there was more to Duko than being an arrogant Wolf. He had real wounds and scars. And her own grandpa had contributed to them. Her stomach soured. It made her sick to admit it, but it was possible all the blame wasn't on the Wolves.

"Duko's dad felt it was unsafe. The apple doesn't fall far from the tree. He was as paranoid as Duko. The king constructed a wall to make sure Wolves didn't go into the forest after dark or when it rained. After Duko succeeded him, he used it to keep the Foresters out. And since the forest is technically owned by Wolf kingdom, Duko decided to tax us more. It gave Duko the fuel he needed to sow that hate into the Wolf empire." He paused. "And then I fell in love with your mother."

Rider blinked. "What's that got to do with anything?"

"Duko was in love with her too."

"What? But she was a Forester."

"That she was. Forbidden for him, which made her all the more alluring."

Rider's heart pounded against her ribcage. "But Mom chose you. At the dance."

Her dad nodded. "She did. She loved the forest and hated that the Wolves oppressed us. How little they regarded the Foresters. It supplies a large chunk of their food chain, but they take it for granted. She was a much better person than me because she was able to overcome her feelings. She always treated Duko with respect, which I think added to the attraction for him. But me? I was jealous of Duko. He had it all—he was a prince, for crying out loud. After your mother died alone in that city, I became bitter. I've let it shape how I raised you. Your mother would have done better. I'm sorry."

Rider gaped at her dad. She didn't have any words. He patted her arm. "I'd better get to work. Thanks for the help earlier. I know you'll keep this visit to yourself because it would be very bad if it got out that they came here."

Rider clasped her fingers around her father's hand. "You're not a bad person. Here you are helping the princes of the very city that let Mom down. You've always given great care to anyone who was sick—whether Wolves or Foresters. I don't blame you."

His Adam's apple bobbed. "Thanks, sweetie."

Rider stood. "Do you think the king will punish his own blood if he finds out they brought Bleddyn here?" Her stomach clenched at the thought. Would the king be that malicious?

"Hate is a strong emotion. It can make you do things you'd never imagined. Don't ever forget that. Duko doesn't wear humiliation well. We could all be punished if he finds out that it was me, not ChemTech, who helped the boy."

"But if your drug works, how can they keep it a secret? It'll save lives."

"They have a plan and I'm letting them handle it. If they or anyone else comes for help, I'll give it, but I won't put you in danger." Her dad rubbed his eyes, which had dark smudges under them and crows' feet lining the corners. He motioned to his office. "I've got to clean up."

Suddenly, the house was hot and stuffy. Rider stepped outside and unlocked her bike from the post at the side of the house. Her legs itched to move; hopefully the exercise would numb her racing mind. She didn't want to think about all she'd learned or dwell on what would happen to her dad if the king found out Dr. Hood had given an experimental drug to his own flesh and blood.

Chapter Twenty-Five

Teo

THE CLOCK STARED AT Teo, the hands a defiant declaration that it was only early evening, although it felt like midnight. The wooden chair he sat on numbed his butt and hurt his back, but he didn't move.

The events of the day raced through his mind—Dr. Hood treating Bleddyn with care and compassion. His gentle tone and sure hands had eased the worry knotted in Teo's stomach.

But now the knots coiled tight as reality set in. What had they done? Teo cradled his head. His father hated Foresters, but he especially hated Dr. Hood. Yet the man hadn't hesitated to help his brother, even though that act put him in danger. And his daughter. Nothing made sense. Wolves were honorable, not Foresters. Teo had been told that his whole life, yet Dr. Hood had only been kind, helpful... someone Teo would trust if the pharmacist was a Wolf. Teo blinked. No, he trusted Dr. Hood regardless. And maybe his daughter too.

What was the implication of that trust? Teo scrubbed his eyes. Was he wrong about the Foresters? If he was honest, Teo didn't know any Foresters. His only interactions with them were at the gate on duty, where he wielded power and intimidation. He frowned. He was the crown prince and he didn't know the people he would one day rule. What was wr— Bleddyn moaned and Teo jerked his head, his eyes skimming over his brother's prone body.

Bleddyn's pale face was punctuated by dark circles under his eyes, but he rested peacefully, the sweats and thrashing limbs long gone. His chest rose and fell in a reassuring rhythm.

Teo slumped in the hard chair and drummed his fingers on the armrest. An image of Jenna floated before him. She hadn't protested when four Wolves invaded her home. Instead, she'd offered help and compassion too. Although she *had* seemed to enjoy the grimaces on their faces after giving them that foul tasting elixir. Those green eyes had seemed a bit too bright and telltale crinkles at the corners gave her away. She certainly wasn't any vanishing wallflower. He liked that. A lot. Plus, she seemed to have let his bad behavior of late go.

Teo stood, exhaling loudly as he stretched out the kinks in his back. Four hours had passed since they'd returned from the Hood's and still his father had not returned from Greystoke. Uncle Alarick hadn't told either Seth or himself how he'd covered up their clandestine trip to the forest. *If Bleddyn gets better and ChemTech take the credit, how are we going to explain why everyone else is still sick?* The ChemTech drugs that everyone else was taking weren't likely to work.

A soft cough interrupted Teo's thoughts, and he twisted to see his brother staring at him. Rushing to his side, Teo whispered, "Bleddyn." He wanted to take his hand but wasn't sure if that was a good idea. Of course, Dr. Hood had given them the immunity booster and said the flu only passed through saliva. Grabbing his brother's hand, Teo told himself he'd wash after. Bleddyn tried to remove his fingers from Teo's grasp, but he wasn't letting his brother go.

Bleddyn closed his eyes. "You need to leave. I don't want you... sick." Teo strained to hear him better. Memories of Bleddyn's boisterous voice echoing in the halls of the palace as young boys flooded Teo's mind. The maids had always shushed them, which only made his brother laugh louder.

"I'm staying right here. You're going to get better," Teo said forcefully, as if he could will it to happen.

"Love you, Teo," said Bleddyn, his voice weak. His eyes closed.

Teo covered their clasped hands with his other one. "I love you too," he croaked. No more words could get past the lump in his throat.

Bleddyn's soft breathing filled the silent room. After tucking the soft blanket around his brother, Teo washed his hands at the small sink in the room, trying not to think how small and fragile his brother looked.

Soft footsteps echoed in the hall before Seth appeared. "How's he doing?"

"He seems better. The sweating has stopped, so hopefully his fever's broken."

"I hope this works because Uncle Alarick has put us all in a very precarious position with Father."

Teo glared at his youngest brother. "How can you say that?" he hissed. "Father is the one putting *us* in a precarious position. He's risking his son's life. For what? To feed his own hate? To save face? I'm not about to let Bleddyn die. Father can throw me in jail or exile me, I don't care."

Seth's jaw clenched. "Whether Bleddyn gets better or not, if Father knows we went to the forest for help, his wrath will know no bounds. We may as well be dead."

Teo ran his hand roughly over his head, messing up his short hair. "You don't think I'm aware of that? What choice did we have? ChemTech hasn't come up with anything that works. Hood's drugs have never failed us. Look at him." Teo pointed to Bleddyn. "He's doing so much better since we got back from the Hoods'. I'll take Father's anger if Bleddyn recovers." He swallowed. "We've got to convince Father to use Dr. Hood's drugs. They're going to save lives." Teo slammed his fist into his palm.

"Let me take care of that."

The brothers whirled around to see their uncle glaring at them. "You two need to be more careful what you say and where you say it." Alarick walked over to Bleddyn's bedside. He smoothed the bedsheet covering his nephew. "I'll deal with your father; you stay out of it. You never went to the forest this afternoon. Got it?"

"How will you explain it if... when Bleddyn gets better? Father will give ChemTech the credit, but the Wolves taking their drugs will remain sick, even die."

"What if we were seen in the forest? Can Dr. Hood be trusted to keep his mouth shut in the face of a firing squad?" Seth fired questions at their uncle. Apparently Teo wasn't the only one wanting answers.

Uncle Alarick squeezed Seth's shoulder. "No one saw us on those secluded paths, at least no one who would betray us to your father. *When* Bleddyn gets better, I'll figure out how to explain it. One step at a time."

"Eventually, we'll have to tell the truth. Father will extoll the new drug's virtues, taking credit for bringing in ChemTech, but more Wolves will get sick and die. I don't think Dr. Hood is the type of person to let people die, including Wolves, if he has the answer." Teo stared at his sick sibling. How were other families dealing with their sick loved ones? His heart ached at the thought of friends suffering. If they had found the answer, even if it was Dr. Hood's medicine, it was their responsibility to dispense it. They couldn't let more Wolves die.

"I'm planning to switch ChemTech's drugs with Hood's. A few doctors are willing to go along with my proposition. They're desperate for help." Alarick's shoulders sagged. "I've already said too much. Stay out of it for your own safety. Go about your business as usual. We don't need to raise your father's suspicions. Leave it to me." Uncle Alarick turned to Bleddyn, swiping his hand over his forehead. "Get better, son."

The knots coiled tight in Teo's gut. There was too much that could go wrong.

⸺◆⸺

Bleddyn slept peacefully and no other symptoms presented themselves. Dawn was only a few hours away. For the first time since Bleddyn got sick, Teo could breathe, the suffocating feeling loosening its hold. He donned a hoodie, pulling it low over his brow. Jeans and sneakers replaced his military pants and boots. Sneaking out one of the secret passages he and his brothers had discovered as kids, he hurried silently through the tunnel until he emerged into the city. He marvelled that no one had ever sealed the "secret" passages leading out of the palace. Today he was more grateful for that than ever.

Cold air slapped his cheeks, awakening him further. The only people around were guards patrolling the area, a few delivery guys, and city cleaning staff. Teo quickly moved away from them with no particular destination in mind. A short while later, he found himself on the same path they had followed yesterday, which led to a hidden door, cleverly built into the stone wall. One no one would ever see if they didn't know it was there. From there the path led directly into the surrounding wood, skirting the city. It took longer to walk to the Hoods' this way, but Teo didn't mind.

Stars shone brightly and the crescent moon hung like a cut-out in the dark sky. Cresting a hill, he spotted Jenna's house a few hundred yards in front of him. He stood at the edge of the tree line where he'd hid the other day and studied the simple home.

He'd grown up in opulence—polished marble floors, plush carpeting, velvet drapes, and leather sofas. Jenna's house had worn wooden floors, fabric couches that looked as old as her father. Yet peace had filled Teo this afternoon when they brought Bleddyn here. He should have been panicked but he hadn't been. Again, standing here, a quiet calm embraced him like a warm hug, although he'd crept into what should have been his enemy's territory. He scanned the area but not even an animal scurried about. The house was dark. *What are you doing here?* Was he going to knock on their front door in the middle of the night, awaken her father? He shouldn't be here; it was too much of a gamble for him and the Hoods if he got caught.

Teo stepped into the shadows once more, ready to head to the palace, but the memory of Jenna working by the sink, her long curls swept up in a loose ponytail, a few wisps framing her porcelain face, kept his feet glued to the ground. Her hands had moved quickly but confidently. She hadn't been afraid or repulsed. *Brave.* The word took a front seat in Teo's mind. Neither she nor her dad had backed away from them or shown any fear or anger. No snarky comments about Wolves asking for help, even though they were indirectly responsible for putting Dr. Hood out of work. No, she'd been courageous and kind. So had her dad. *Does the king know this? Would it change his mind if he did?* He might as well wish he was a peasant. His father couldn't see past his own hate.

He'd taken a couple of steps toward the city when a light flickered on in one of the upper windows, dimly lighting the landscape. A small silhouette stood at the window. *Jenna.*

The silhouette stood looking out into the night. After shoving off his hood, he moved out of the shadows towards the light.

Chapter Twenty-Six

Rider

RIDER BLEW OUT A breath, lifting the hair that had been stuck to her sweaty face. She kicked off the covers and then ran her hands through her mussed-up hair. After switching on her bedside lamp, she climbed out of bed and stalked to the window, gazing out into the dark night.

Suddenly, a figure came out from the tree line. Her heart leapt to her throat. *Who's out there? Are they keeping our house under surveillance?* She positioned herself to the side of the sill and squinted around the edge of the curtain. The figure was tall and his posture carried a familiar air of authority. Teo.

Grabbing her hoodie and a flashlight, she flew down the stairs, not stopping to think about her actions. Rider skidded to a stop before the front door. What if it wasn't Teo? After a moment, her fingers gripping the knob of the door she'd pulled open a crack, Rider called out softly, "Who's there?"

The shadow took form as he moved closer. "It's Teo. Can we talk?"

Rider stepped out into the night, meeting him on the porch steps. "Is your brother okay?" Why would he be here at this time of night unless something had happened to Bleddyn?

His icy eyes glittered in the dark as his gaze took her in from head to toe. The realization that she had bedhead and was dressed in pink plaid pajama bottoms and her hoodie hit her and she crossed her arms.

"Bleddyn is resting more comfortably, thanks to you and your father. He's not out of the woods, but he seems to be improving."

"That's good news." She inhaled the cool night air. "What are you doing here?" He did not look as if he'd crawled out of bed. Not even a hair was out of place.

"I couldn't sleep. I went for a walk and...ended up here." He ducked his head, shoving his hands in his jean pockets. Was the ultra-confident heir to the throne embarrassed?

Deciding to let it go, Rider nodded. "I couldn't sleep either." She sank onto the bottom step and Teo collapsed beside her. His body heat warmed her side. "The king..."

"Doesn't know anything. He was away at meetings all day in Greystoke. But as far as he's concerned, ChemTech's wonder drugs are working."

Rider turned his words over in her head. "What happens when no one else gets better taking their drugs?"

"Assuming my brother does? That's a good question. Uncle Alarick said he'd take care of it. Seth and I are to stay out of it." He stretched out his long legs, crossing one ankle over the other. "Are you worried about your safety? Because you don't need to be. I won't let anything happen to you or your dad."

Rider studied him. He'd been aloof and rude lately. Would he actually keep them safe? Was he trustworthy? "A little." She brought her knees up to her chest, clasping her hands around her legs. "I don't understand your father. You'd think he'd be grateful if Bleddyn survives."

"You don't know my father. It's not that he doesn't care about Bleddyn. I think he does, but he also cares about his reputation. If his new deal turns out to be a farce, and ChemTech's medicines don't work, it makes him and Wolf Empire look incompetent. He doesn't deal well with humiliation, especially if it comes at the hands of a Forester. His PR people will spin it but..." Teo studied the forest beyond, "...family has never been his priority. Still, I will make sure nothing happens to your family."

"Don't make promises you can't keep."

"I'm not. I do have a little pull with a few of the Wolf Pack guards."

Okay. "But you've ignored me since the ball. Why would I trust you?" There. It was out in the open.

"I'm sorry. I was trying to protect you. If anyone saw us together, my father would go after you. He questioned us about you after the ball."

"What?" The air left Rider's lungs.

"He wanted to know why the three of us were fawning over you. We all said you were pretty and caught our eye." Colour rose up his neck, which was charming. The great crown prince Teo *was* embarrassed. "I didn't need to draw more attention to us."

"I guess that's a good excuse." Rider nudged her shoulder into his. "What happens to you if your father finds out you've gone behind his back?"

"He has his own brand of punishment that he deals out to his sons. Stuff that the public won't notice. Remember the day at the FBC? That was punishment for my poor choices."

"That's why he expired all our papers. Because you were working."

"I knew you were smart."

She cocked her head. "What did you do?"

"I beat up a lecherous idiot."

Oh. He got punished for that? "Well, that punishment doesn't seem too bad."

He eyed her, his gaze lingering. "It could have been worse."

Oh. Goosebumps popped out on her arms. She rubbed them.

"It has been worse."

"That's horrible. Why?"

"I embarrass him. He thinks I'm incompetent and a screw up. It's a long story." He leaned against the step behind him and tilted his head toward the sky. Rider followed his gaze. Clouds had rolled in, turning it a deep indigo. "Do you remember helping us when we were kids and Seth got stung? That was you, wasn't it?"

Her lips curved slightly and she nodded. "Yes. I can't believe you remembered."

"You helped us—how could I not? My father blamed me for letting that happen to Seth. I'm the alpha male and it's my responsibility to take care of my brothers. I failed them. And him."

"But you were a kid. Accidents or, in this case, bee stings, happen."

He shrugged. "Doesn't matter. I'm next in line to the throne—he expects more and I never cease to disappoint. It should be Seth who inherits the throne."

How awful for Teo to feel so unloved. "What makes you say that?"

"Seth's always been Dad's favourite, if you can call it that. At least he has his respect. Seth takes his role as a prince seriously and I don't. Or not as much as Seth."

"I think you have the potential to be a great king." Her words sat there in the silence between them. They surprised her as much as they seemed to startle him.

Turning toward her, he whispered, "You do?" Doubt replaced the usual arrogance.

"Yes. I mean, you're here speaking with me. That's a huge step forward for unifying the clans. You're listening and questioning, from what I'm hearing and seeing. I think you have the potential to bring us together... uh, I mean the Wolves and forest." Her body warmed at her faux pas.

One corner of his lips lifted at her words. He was still way too cocky for his own good, but if she could convince him to move past his prejudice, she believed he could be a good ruler. A great king.

"Maybe..." Teo chewed his bottom lip.

Changing thought patterns and long held beliefs wasn't going to happen overnight, but, with time, maybe she and her dad could show Teo and his family that the Wolves and the Forest clan were equals and could be good partners and allies. At the moment, though, Rider had a more pressing question. "Why would he let Bleddyn suffer?"

"He's convinced himself that ChemTech will find the cure and Bleddyn will get better. It can't happen any other way for him because of the trade deal with the Falls District and ChemTech. If it were to get out that your father came up with a treatment or cure, my father would look like a fool."

Words eluded Rider. That kind of selfish behaviour was beyond anything she'd ever encountered. To risk his own son's health because he might look stupid was unimaginable. Her heart went out to the boy sitting beside her. He lived with abuses and grievances that weren't seen by the public. She'd certainly had her eyes opened since they'd first met.

Echoing her thoughts, he said, "Life in the palace doesn't live up to the glamourization. People think only of the luxuries and prestige when they see us or read about us in the news, but they don't understand the responsibilities that come along with the role. My father's wrong, but, in a small way, I understand the pressure he's under." Lines creased his forehead and a shadow crossed his handsome face.

The desire to comfort him overtook her. "There's a lot riding on his trade deal, I understand that now. Still, if he's wrong... There are times when I've envied the freedom of the Wolves. But you're not really free, are you?"

"Not as much as I'd like. It's not the same as the restrictions and oppressions my father has forced on you, though." He shifted, his hip grazing hers as he leaned closer, facing her. His ice-blue eyes contrasted with the dark night, hypnotizing Rider. Her breath hitched slightly, the sound enough to rouse her from her daze. *He's a Prince and a Wolf. Stay focused.* She shifted her weight slightly, breaking the connection.

"Is there anything we can do to help?"

"You've already done so much." He reached out and tugged a hand from her hoodie pocket, measuring it against his larger one. "You can trust me. My uncle and I will keep you safe." He wrapped his fingers around hers and squeezed them.

Did she trust him? Rider snuck a sideways glance at his rugged features. The square jaw that was stubbled at the moment exuded strength and confidence. Although his eyes could be cold, they could also warm up to a beautiful indigo colour, she'd noticed.

He caught her sneaking a glance. One eyebrow raised as if to say; *you like what you see?* She darted her glance to the trees in the distance. His cockiness was irritatingly attractive. "No screw-up I know would be willing to stand up to their father when it could potentially be costly to themselves. You have a king's heart."

Eyes wide, he wiped his mouth, then shook his head. "You don't know me that well."

"I've seen enough to know it's true, whether you believe it or not."

Teo stood. "I should get going before someone discovers I'm gone and raises an alarm."

Rider wrapped her arms around her stomach. "The more I get to know you, the more I question our differences."

"You might be right. My father, my family, has inflicted much harm on this kingdom."

Rider rose from the step. Changing people's beliefs was going to be a huge undertaking. They were victims of generations of hate. They had been taught it from birth. But as she stood staring at the young prince in front of her, the small hairs on her neck jumped to attention. Maybe things could be different. "You're in a position to change that. Starting with getting the right medicine to the Wolves." She bit her lip. "Will your father let Bleddyn die if he finds out where the medicine came from?"

"Not if I can help it." The line of his jaw hardened. "I should go." He swept a thumb along her cheekbone, leaving a trail of fiery heat. Then he was gone, slipping into the dark night.

"Stay safe," she whispered. She scanned the area and then hurried inside, hoping she'd sleep but doubting she would.

⸺◈⸺

She hid behind the tree, fascinated by the three boys playing wildly in the small meadow. She'd wandered too far from her house and her dad would be upset. The dark clouds and wind signalled a storm. Still, she didn't move. The desire to join the game filled her, but city dwellers didn't come into the forest unaccompanied by an adult. Rider couldn't see any grown-ups, though.

The boys played with sticks and toy swords, battling each other for the right to claim the victory as well as the damsel. Eventually they stopped, and the oldest one said they needed to go to the city. The elder two argued and then suddenly the youngest let out a yowl.

A sting. Rider knew how to fix that. She gathered all her courage and stepped forward.

The sunlight streamed through the window, waking Rider from her dream. Although she was staring at the ceiling, her mind was still lost in her childhood, remembering the boys and the events of that day. *Not a dream.* Teo had confirmed that last night. She'd wondered occasionally about those boys and hadn't put the puzzle pieces together until recently. Those ice blue eyes—that's what finally tipped her off.

Had they met all those years ago for a reason? For such a time as this—to help them defeat this disease? Or, even deeper, to help both the Wolves and the Foresters overcome their prejudice? Although Rider tried to dampen her next thought, perhaps it had been to bring Teo and Rider together? Ridiculous. Never in a million years would it happen. *Teo's not only a Wolf but a prince. Remember that.*

Rider dragged herself out of bed, her brain in overdrive with all the questions. She dressed in her usual uniform of jeans and a long-sleeved T-shirt before heading downstairs to the kitchen to start breakfast.

Her dad strolled in as she poured pancake batter onto the hot frying pan where it sizzled and popped. As he kissed the top of her head, she could smell the clean scent of the soap he'd been using forever.

"Smells like heaven." He poured himself a mug of coffee.

"A minute more." She flipped the discs and pressed them with a spatula. The smell of vanilla and butter made her mouth water. After making up two plates, she sat at the large wooden table with her dad. Amber syrup drenched her pancake, making her dad wince. Rider forked the gooey mess, stuck it into her mouth, and closed her eyes. The sweet goodness slid down her throat. Mmmm.

After several bites, her dad laid his fork on his plate and clasped his hands together. "Your late-night visitor wasn't here to report on his brother, was he?"

Rider coughed, the sweetness choking her. She gulped her water.

"It's a small house, and voices carry in the night. I trust he was a gentleman."

"It's not what you think."

He speared a piece of pancake. "First, I'd like to know how his brother is faring. Has he responded to the medicine?"

Rider wiped her lips with her napkin. "Yes, he's doing better, resting comfortably with no more hallucinations. No bleeding either."

"Good. They need to give him the second dose to fully end it, or it could come back worse than before. No sign of sickness in your friend?"

Rider set her fork on her plate. "So far he's fine." She crossed her fingers.

Her dad grabbed her hand and squeezed it gently. "It has nothing to do with luck. Good science works wonders."

Rider smiled sheepishly. "I know." She shoved away her half-eaten breakfast.

He studied her, concern on his face. "The second thing I want to know is how you know him."

Rider knew she couldn't avoid the question forever. But a little more time would have been nice. "We've run into each other a couple of times in the city. He could have had me arrested for hitting him with my bike, but he didn't."

"Your accident a while back. That was the prince?"

"Yeah."

"Jenna-girl, please be careful. He's a Wolf and the crown prince. Duko is powerful and this is his son, his heir. You know how the king feels about us, and he would never willingly let his son get involved with you. I don't want to see you hurt."

"It's not like that, Dad. We're friends. Although, from what Teo tells me, Duko doesn't care about him."

Her dad used the side of his fork to cut off a piece of the pancake. "Doesn't matter how he feels, there are protocols and traditions. Duko is always about appearances."

Rider stood, her chair scraping the floor. "I'm so sick of Duko's rules. Why do Wolves mistrust us when we've done nothing but provide good care for them over the years?"

"I don't know, honey. I wish I had the answers."

"We need allies, Dad. I think Teo could be one. There must be other Wolves out there who believe in us, who will look at our differences as good things. Surely the doctors will come around to our side if you help them with the Wolf Flu?"

"Many of the doctors recognize the quality of the work we do, and we've earned their respect. Dr. Lupine would certainly be one. But

Duko has spies everywhere. They may side with us in their hearts, but they won't cross the King. It's too risky—not only for them but their families. I'm not sure his son will either. Prince Teowulf's life is not his own. I don't want you to get caught up in a royal family struggle. There's little hope Duko is ever going to reconcile with the forest."

Rider sagged against her chair. "We can't give up. We've got to convince the king that your drugs work and we aren't a threat. We can be equal partners."

"Hate is a strong emotion, Jenna-girl. It makes you stupid and it's learned from one generation to the next. *Both* Foresters and Wolves are guilty of it." Her dad studied his hands. "I'm guilty of teaching you to be suspicious of Wolves. It's a never-ending cycle. Maybe Prince Teo is trustworthy, but I'd hate for you to find out the hard way that he's not. Although I'd love to see the forest and Wolves live in peace, as long as Duko is on the throne, we need to be careful. The Hood name is a black mark to him."

"Teo is not his father. He's not like that, you'll see."

"I hope you're right." He cleared his plate from the table and then dropped a kiss on Rider's head. "Be careful."

Rider stared at her half-eaten pancake. The sugary syrup lay heavy in her stomach now. *Is Teo trustworthy? Can we ever get beyond who we were born to be?*

Chapter Twenty-Seven

Teo

T EO'S EYES FELT AS if he'd been in a sandstorm as he stared at the coffee carafe on the buffet in the family's dining room. The late visit to the forest had wreaked havoc on his body, but there was something about Jenna Hood that kept drawing him like bees to honey. *Pull it together. You've got enough troubles already without crushing on a Forester.* Teo rubbed his eyes. No use denying it any longer—he had a little crush; if he ignored it, it would go away, right? *Not if I keep going to visit her in the dead of night.*

Teo poured a large cup of coffee, holding the steam under his nose to inhale the strong, nutty aroma. After taking a gulp, he sat alone at the dining table, his hands wrapped around the warm mug. The room was chillier than usual.

Seth wandered in and poked around at the buffet, helping himself to coffee before lifting lids off large aluminum pans filled with eggs, meat, and pastries. His brother looked as tired as Teo felt.

"I thought you went with Father today."

Seth heaped eggs on a plate. "Feigned a headache. Can't be too careful these days. Father didn't want to risk making anyone sick." He snorted. "What about me? He was more concerned about the governors' health than mine."

Teo raised one eyebrow. Unusual for Seth to go off about their father. Maybe their relationship wasn't as great as Teo thought. Perhaps Seth had told the truth when he said he was on his brothers' side. His youngest brother had uttered no objections about taking

Bleddyn to the Hoods' either. Not before they went, anyway, even if he'd expressed concerns later about Father finding out.

Seth heaped sausages, bacon, and toast onto his plate. Teo's own stomach rumbled at the sight and the smell of the meat. He rose and piled a plate with eggs and sausages. They sat, Seth across from him, the only sound coming from their utensils scraping against china.

Once satisfied and his plate empty, Teo said, "I stopped by Bleddyn's room on my way here. It might be wishful thinking, but I thought he had more colour in his face."

Seth finished chewing his mouthful. "I saw Uncle last night; he'll give Bleddyn the second dose at lunch while father is out," he said quietly.

"It's a good thing Dad is going to be away today." Teo's voice was low.

Seth lifted his mug in a *cheers* gesture. They sat together in silence drinking coffee, each lost in their own thoughts.

⸻ ◈ ⸻

Teo pushed through the crowded city streets, dodging vendors selling roasted meat on sticks, shoppers with large bags, and bike couriers delivering packages of food from the forest. So far, his father had only halted pharmaceutical deliveries. Teo hoped it would stop there. Jenna's friend Ethan exited a bakery. Teo ducked his head, not wanting to be seen. He had exactly an hour until he had to be at the city gates for his shift, and there was no time to waste. He jogged the rest of the way to the palace, his hoodie low over his face. He'd avoided the tunnels, as he wanted the fresh air. The walk through the city had released all his pent-up energy and stress since he enjoyed observing people in their everyday lives.

Teo nodded to a few of his colleagues patrolling the palace grounds as he hurried to the family entrance. The large clock hanging on the wall chimed the quarter hour. Enough time to slip in and see how Bleddyn was doing before work.

As he approached Bleddyn's suites, raised voices filled the hallway. His father's deep baritone sounded angry. Teo came up short, all the air whooshing out of him. His father. *What's he doing here? He's supposed to be away at a meeting.*

Striding towards the open suite entrance, he found the sitting room empty. Teo tip-toed to Bleddyn's bedroom door. The king and Uncle Alarick faced off with each other, but it was Bleddyn, restless on the bed, sheets tangled around his legs, that captured Teo's attention. *No, no, no.* His eyes flicked to the two men at the foot of the bed, his father's back to Teo.

"Don't do this, Duko! Do you really want to risk your son's life over something that happened decades ago? Is revenge truly worth it? Raffy is long gone. Nothing will bring him back."

"Don't you dare mention Raffy. You've disobeyed and mocked me by bringing Hood's medicine into the palace. ChemTech's medicine is working." Duko pointed behind him to the bed. "Look at him. He was getting better. You've risked everything by giving him Hood's crap."

"You're lying to yourself if you think ChemTech's treatment is effective. It's as potent as a placebo. It's Hood's medicine that was making him better. After one dose, Bleddyn is significantly further along than any patient taking ChemTech medicine. He's living proof that Dr. Hood is on to something. We have more of a chance of saving Bleddyn and the rest of the Wolves with Hood Medicine than we do with that farce of a company." Alarick pressed his hands together as if praying. "Please don't do this. Let me give him the dose. Please, Duko."

Teo's gaze dropped to the syringe in his father's hand. Panic crawled up his throat, constricting his breath. Ducking out of sight, he leaned his forehead against the wall. *Think, think, think.*

"He was getting better until you gave him Hood's drugs. For all I know, Hood is poisoning my son."

Help. Teo needed help. But who could he call? The guard? They were loyal to the king. Teo needed his uncle to stay out of prison. Could he wrestle the syringe out of his father's hand? They were the same height, but his father had a few pounds of muscle on Teo. A moan from the bed forced Teo to move. Saving Bleddyn was the only thing that mattered. He stepped into his uncle's sightline, his hands already fisting and his eyes never leaving Alarick, who pretended he didn't see him. Alarick gave a subtle shake of his head. Teo took a silent step farther into the room, but sunlight glinted off something shiny in his father's other hand. A gun. Teo stopped. Had his father gone insane?

Duko's voice was steel. "Is there any more of this in the palace?" His father held up the needle full of medicine.

"No. But I'm begging you, please, for your son's sake, don't do this."

"I'm arresting you for treason, Alarick. Move away from my son or I will shoot you on the spot." Pocketing the syringe, his father pressed his personal security button, attached to the shoulder of his suit jacket. Backing up quickly, Teo made it to the hallway before his father saw him and then ran for Seth's rooms.

Chapter Twenty-Eight

Rider

R IDER PACED BACK AND forth across the front room, her gaze never leaving the window. The empty path mocked her. *Where is he?* Her father was supposed to be home hours ago, and he was never this late without touching base. She swallowed the scream that begged release. *Please, please, come home.*

Rider hadn't liked the idea of him going to meet Dr. Lupine that morning. Her father wouldn't discuss what the meeting was about, only that the doctor wanted to speak to him privately at the old gatehouse near the entrance to the forest. The Wolves had used it a long time ago as a way to keep an eye on the Foresters. However, since nothing ever happened because the people were peaceful, they'd given up that surveillance before Rider was born. Now, the gatehouse was a useful meeting place.

Rider suspected Dr. Lupine had had enough. More Wolves had died and the numbers were climbing. ChemTech's drugs were garbage. Dr. Lupine was a lot like her dad—he would put his patients first, even at risk to himself. Rider had pieced that much together from the phone call her father had taken that morning. *It's not a set-up.* Because Teo had promised to keep her father safe, and she trusted him to do that.

Then where is he?

Fifteen minutes later, Rider unlocked her bike with trembling fingers. She wheeled it around to the front of the house as Ethan whooshed to a stop beside her. Glasses askew, he sucked in huge gulps of air.

"What's the matter? Is it my dad?" Rider barely choked the words out, her heart thumping against her ribcage.

He nodded vehemently. "The Wolf Pack came to the forest and grabbed him."

Her fingers dug into the handlebars. "*What?* Did you see it happen?"

"I had just passed your dad at the gatehouse when I heard a noise behind me. I'd seen four Wolf Pack guards on the way here but didn't give them much thought. I turned in time to see them grab your dad."

"Did you hear what they said?" Had Dr. Lupine set a trap? *Never trust a Wolf.*

"One guard said they were there to escort your dad into the city and they thanked him for being at the gatehouse so they didn't have to trek all the way to his home. They told him he was wanted for questioning. Then the other guard grabbed his notes, shook them in your dad's face, and said they were arresting him on treason charges."

"My father was supposed to meet with Dr. Lupine to discuss sending medicine to the Wolves. Was he taken too? Do you think he's responsible for my dad's arrest?"

Ethan whistled. "Dr. Lupine wasn't around. Your dad was writing in his notes when I passed him. I don't think Dr. Lupine would set your dad up. He's one of the good guys. But if that's what they were meeting about, then that's a treasonable offense." Ethan rubbed his thumb against the buckle of his courier bag. "What about your friend, the crown prince?"

"No, he wouldn't do that. He promised."

"Wouldn't he? He's a Wolf." His jaw hardened.

"No." She clamped her lips together. He wouldn't. Would he?

"Did the drugs work for the prince? I'm assuming it wasn't *Teo* who was ill." Ethan spat out the name.

"No, the middle one, Bleddyn. ChemTech's drugs aren't working, and he was getting sicker."

"They were the only ones who knew your dad helped him?"

"Yes, but they didn't betray us. Why would they? Dad helped his brother. He was doing better, Teo told me."

"Rumours are swirling in the city. Lots of Wolves are sick, and they're starting to panic. Duko isn't helping himself by not taking it seriously. If ChemTech doesn't come up with an effective drug, the king will have to answer hard questions. The Wolves may rebel against him if they find out your dad has a possible treatment that he is ignoring. Duko will make our lives unbearable. He must have found out about your dad's activities." Ethan took off his glasses and rubbed his eyes. "That or... You're sure the princes wouldn't say anything?"

Rider crossed her arms. "No, they wouldn't endanger their brother. At least not willingly. Something else must have happened."

Had Duko found out that his brother and sons had visited the forest? Perhaps Bleddyn had improved so much after one dose that Duko had suspected their deception. At least that would be a positive in all this, for the prince to have recovered. It would prove that her father's drugs worked. Surely Duko wouldn't reject them. But why would they arrest him?

"I need to go to the city so I can get answers." She put her foot on the pedal.

Ethan grabbed her handle bars. "Wait, shouldn't we stay here in case your dad comes home?"

Rider hesitated; she didn't want to sit around waiting, she wanted to be moving. "They aren't going to let him go." Her heart plummeted at the truth.

"I'm going with you." Ethan released his grip, confirming her gut instinct.

"No. I don't want to involve you."

"I'm coming, so stop arguing. We're wasting time. Is there a way we can avoid the gates? If you're arrested too, you'll be little help to your dad."

"There's a back path in. I've never used it, but my father told me about it once. Follow me."

They rode in silence, swiftly making their way to the city. Skirting the tree line, the city wall to their left, they followed a barely-there path until a clump of shrubs hid the wall. Snapped branches indicated people had recently been through there. They weren't the only ones who knew this path. Was that how they had brought Bleddyn without being seen?

"I don't like this," Ethan whispered nervously.

"It's okay. I think Teo used this entrance when they brought his brother to us. They had to sneak him out."

"Yeah, and now your dad is in jail. They were seen," Ethan hissed.

Rider hopped off her bike and then shoved it under heavy brush. She gathered more branches. Ignoring Ethan's implication, she covered their bikes with foliage until no one walking by would see them.

After slapping the dirt off her hands, Rider squatted before the wall, feeling the mortar around the stones. A small catch snagged her finger. She pulled on a small latch and an opening popped out of the wall. Inching it farther open, they slipped through into an area also covered by shrubs and lots of trees, which had to be one of the only green areas left in the city.

Rider peered around a large tree trunk, studying their surroundings. They was mostly empty and she let out a sigh of relief as she recognized the area and gestured for Ethan to follow. She figured the city gate was as good a place to start. News and gossip flowed freely around there. Maybe Teo would be working.

Her chest cramped. *He's trustworthy, right?*

◆○◆

The silence in the city and at the gates was so loud, Rider wanted to cover her ears. Something was very wrong. Ethan grabbed her hand and squeezed hard. He tilted his head toward the entrance, his eyes wide. The gates were shut tight. In all her seventeen years, she'd never seen them closed. Wolf Pack crawled around like ants, but no one else was in sight. They ducked into a dark alley.

"This isn't good, Rider. I've never seen the gates closed before," he hissed in her ear. "I think we need to leave."

"I've got to find my dad before I leave." *And Teo.*

Ethan opened his mouth, but she covered it with her hand. "I'm not leaving without my dad," she hissed. "If you want to go, then go."

Hurt filled his eyes as he shoved her hand away. "I'm not leaving you."

She wiped a hand across her brow. "I'm sorry. I'm worried." She peered around a filthy dumpster. "We need a plan. Where would they keep my dad?"

"Rider, we're not going to be able to break out your dad on our own."

"I know. We need to find Teo."

Ethan muttered something under his breath and then said aloud, "I don't like this. I don't trust him."

"We have no choice."

"What about Dr. Lupine?"

"He doesn't have the authority to free Dad."

Ethan chewed his lip. "Where do we find the prince?"

Rider scratched her head as she ran through a list of possibilities. Unfortunately, the list was fairly short. "The palace."

Ethan's eyes widened. "No, that's suicide. How are we going to get inside? Are you going to waltz in there and say, 'I'd like to see the crown prince?' Or, better yet, 'I'd like my dad back?'"

"Do you have any better ideas? At least it's a plan. Give me few minutes to figure out the details," Rider growled.

"I can help you with that."

Rider jumped, and Ethan let out a yell.

"By the looks of things, you'll need help with being covert." Teo smirked. "And asking for your dad back isn't going to work." The smirk left his face and was replaced by a grim look.

Rider stared at Teo. Was it possible to feel contradictory emotions at once? Relief washed over her that he was standing there, but at the same time was he responsible for this mess? He didn't look like a scoundrel—worry lined his face and dark smudges coloured his eyes a deep shade of blue. His clothes and hair were dishevelled, but Rider thought he'd never looked better. "What are you doing here?"

"I could ask you the same question. It's too dangerous for you to be in the city." He frowned as he cast a glance around. "How did you even get inside? The gates are locked." He didn't wait for an answer. "We need to get out of here. Now." Teo grabbed Rider's arm, but she shook him off.

"Where's my dad?"

Teo held his finger to his lips. "I need you to follow me."

"How do I know you aren't going to lead us right to the Wolf Pack?" Teo flinched and doubt filled her. Maybe he didn't betray them. She fisted her hands on her hips. "I'm not going anywhere until you tell me what you're doing here."

Teo huffed out a breath and glared at her. "Why would I betray you and your father? I told you I wouldn't, and my word is my bond. Secondly, your father's drugs worked, so again, why would I do that to you?"

Okay, maybe she could accept that. She nodded curtly. "Lead the way. We'll follow you."

Ethan opened his mouth to protest, but she lasered him a look. He muttered to himself again as they made their way out a corridor in the back of the alley. It was a tight fit, but Rider kept her eyes on Teo's back. From there, they hurried to a side street where a small courtyard garden was hidden from the street. Plenty of low-hanging trees to shield them from prying eyes.

"Where's my father?" Rider couldn't bear it any longer.

Teo ran a hand over his tired eyes. "He's with my uncle in the prison located at the wall. My father came back early from a meeting with the county governors and discovered Uncle Alarick about to give Bleddyn the second dose. Father freaked out." He closed his eyes as if trying to block out the memory.

"Did he stop him before he could give Bleddyn the medication?"

Teo's lip trembled slightly before he cleared his throat. "Yes, and now he's getting worse. My father guessed where the treatment came from and he pulled a gun on Uncle Alarick. There was no use denying it because the treatment worked. We hoped Father would see reason. He didn't. We need to get another dose of medicine to Bleddyn or he'll die, which is why I was on my way to your house when I saw a glint in the alley from your friend's glasses. Does your father have any more medicine?"

"I don't know. He was meeting with Dr. Lupine today. The Wolf Pack grabbed him on the way home."

Teo winced. "Dad must have put out the warrant right after he found out about the medicine. At the gates, I heard the Wolf Pack comparing notes about taking Dr. Hood and Uncle Alarick into custody. My commanding officer wouldn't let me work since Uncle Alarick is being held there."

Ethan spoke up. "If we want to go back to the forest, we'll have to return the back way."

Teo slammed his fist into his palm. "They'll be watching your house; I can guarantee it. But we've got to get more medicine."

"*I need* to rescue my father before your father executes him for treason!"

Ethan stepped between them. "Whoa. What I'm hearing is that Dr. Hood has a cure, and if anything happens to him then a whole lot of Wolves die."

"My brother will die if we don't do something *right now*." Teo's jaw tightened.

Did her dad have more medicine at the house? She kicked a rock. "I don't know for sure if there's more medicine. But he would have the recipe written out."

Teo groaned. "That'll take too long to mix up."

"Why not rescue Dr. Hood and take him to the palace?" Ethan scratched his jaw.

Teo shook his head. "It's not that easy. There's no way I can sneak him into the palace. If we get caught, we're all in jail, which helps no one. Bleddyn hasn't much time. The hallucinations are back and he's thrashing around." His voice broke on those words.

"Would your father have kept that second dose he took from your uncle," Ethan asked, "or would he have destroyed it?"

Teo avoided their eyes, confirming what was running through their minds. Duko would not keep the drugs. Silence filled the space between them.

"He'll use Bleddyn's worsening condition as proof that Dr. Hood's drug doesn't work. He's already saying they interfered with ChemTech's, which Bleddyn was administered when he first contracted the illness. But there was no improvement until after he saw your father and took his drugs. My brother needs that second dose."

Rider laid her hand over Teo's forearm. The pain in his eyes was undeniable and her heart ached. "Should we split up? We both have people we need to save."

Teo closed his eyes, his lips a thin line.

There's got to be a way to save both.

He covered her hand with his large one. "You believe me that we didn't betray you?"

She nodded, keeping her hand on his arm. It was warm and she liked the feel of the muscle there; it made her feel safe. *Safe with a Wolf?* Surprisingly—yes. "Your uncle—why is he in jail?"

"My father is using him as a scape goat. He can't arrest his own sons for treason, and he needs someone to blame. He'll deal with us later in his special way."

"That doesn't sound good," Ethan whispered. Rider agreed, but she didn't have time to dwell on that right now.

"What happened to Dr. Lupine?"

"He must have slipped through the cracks because he's not in jail with your dad or my uncle." Teo's eyes lit up. "Would he have any medicine?"

Rider shook her head. "No, Dad didn't take any with him when they met this morning."

"One of us needs to go back to your house and look for more medicine or the formula." Teo faced the street, scanning the area.

"And we need to get Dad out of prison now." The possibility of Duko killing her father loomed, especially if he'd threatened his own brother with a gun. Teo dropped her hand, but Rider didn't back down. If anything happened to her dad, more Wolves would die. She stared at Teo. If he wanted a staring contest, he'd get it.

Ethan flipped his hood up. "I'll go back to your house, Rider, and look for the drugs. That frees you to search for your dad. Teo here can help you."

Rider broke her connection with Teo and grabbed her friend's sleeve. "Are you sure?"

"Positive. I'll go out the way we came. The Wolf Pack isn't interested in me. What am I looking for?"

"When you get to the house, go in through the back. In Dad's office, there's a small fridge with a combination lock. 5555. The drug is in a vial. It may or may not have a label. If it's not in the fridge, then go to his desk and look for a file that says Treatment LF." She handed him her house key.

"Got it. I'll be back before you know it."

Rider hugged him. "Be careful."

"Meet us at the hidden entrance to the city on that back path." Teo tapped a fist against his chest. "Thank you. Please hurry. My brother doesn't have much time."

Rider stared at her friend as he jogged away. Had she sent Ethan into a potential trap?

Chapter Twenty-Nine

Teo

TEO'S EYES TRACED THE outline of Rider's rigid jaw as her friend disappeared into the city. Her pale face was a stark contrast to the hair framing her face. The desire to cup that face almost made him do something stupid—like hold her, tell her it was going to be okay. Instead, he rocked back on his heels, studying the ground as if the answers would magically appear there. Stupidly, all he wanted to do was run to the guard office and demand the release of Alarick and Dr. Hood. He'd end up right beside them on their cell bench if he did that. How were they going to get their loved ones released? Teo drew a blank. His heart raced while panic closed his throat. *Calm down.* He measured his breathing until his body evened itself out.

"How are we going to rescue them?" Her words echoed in the empty courtyard.

"Give me a minute." Once he was able to think clearly, a plan started to form. It wasn't one Teo liked, but it might just work. *It's suicide.* Still, if it meant saving Bleddyn, he'd risk it all. "In high school, I skipped classes now and then. I used to forge my dad's signature, and I became very good at it."

Rider rubbed her forehead. "Why am I not surprised? What does that have to do with getting my dad and your uncle out of prison?"

"Here's the plan. We'll go to the guard house and I'll give them a written release from my dad." *Definitely suicide.*

She scrunched up her nose. "But you don't have a release from your dad. Besides, they aren't going to let you walk out with a prisoner, even if you are the crown prince. That's a crazy idea."

At least they agreed on that. "Trust me. It'll be fine," he lied. "I'm going to the palace where I'll get a release form from Father's office, and then we'll get your dad and Uncle Alarick."

"No." She gripped his wrist and a shock went up his arm. "It's too dangerous."

"Do you want to save your dad or not? This is the only way." He covered her hand with his, gently squeezing it.

"Won't they double check an order like that? What happens if you're caught? What will your father do to you?"

Teo ran his tongue over his bottom lip. "Don't worry, I can handle my father." He forced a smirk, trying to play it cool so she'd buy it. "They won't double check precisely *because* I am the crown prince. It will work." He let go of her hand, afraid she'd notice his sweaty palm.

"Please be careful, Teo."

"I'll be right back. Wait for me here."

"No, I'm coming with you."

Teo stepped so close he could see the freckles dotting her nose. His glance slid down to her full lips, but he quickly shifted his focus away from that particular temptation. What kind of a man was he that he'd be thinking about kissing her when his brother was dying and his uncle was in jail? Selfish. He cleared his throat, pushing away both the desire and the shame. "We can't both get caught. Slipping into the palace unseen is my specialty. I need you to stay safe, here. I won't be long."

Her shoulders drooped but she nodded. Alone, Teo could move faster, and if he got caught, she still might be able to get help. Backing up, he lifted his hand, then ran off. Failure wasn't an option.

⚬

Teo gulped air as he forced his legs to move faster. *Was Bleddyn alive?* He moved to more productive thoughts, rehearsing the steps he needed to take once he was in the palace. The entrance he'd used countless times to sneak out of the palace quickly came into view. After checking that he wasn't being followed, he entered the tunnel that led to the family's living quarters. He sprinted along the dark passageway until he reached the stairwell leading to the entrance. At the top, he tugged it open an inch and peered around it. Silent and empty. He slipped inside, then ran to father's office.

Crossing his fingers with one hand, he knocked softly with the other. No response. He put his ear to the wood but it was silent behind the doors. Panting slightly, Teo jiggled the knob; it didn't budge. Digging around in his pocket, he found his key ring that held a lock pick, something that had come in handy over the years. Inserting the long pick into the lock, Teo wiggled it around. *Click.* He checked behind him and, seeing no one, slipped inside.

The king was a man of habit, and he had always kept paperwork in a filing cabinet along one wall. Teo rapidly flipped through the files until he came to the one he wanted. *Bingo.* He stuffed the pardon paperwork into his jacket pocket, along with a pen from his father's pen holder. Duko didn't count his pens, did he? He froze. *Don't be ridiculous.* After making sure everything was as precise as he'd found it, he stepped into the hallway and locked the door.

Once in his own room, Teo grabbed his military coat and hat. No more than fifteen minutes after entering it, Teo crept out from the hidden passageway. He slipped on his coat, hoping it covered his casual wear enough that no one would become suspicious. He secured his uniform's hat low on his forehead and hurried to the garden.

—◆—

Where is she? Had she gone and done something stupid? Teo groaned as made his way past the entrance to the garden. His heart stuttered. Had the Wolf Pack found her? His eyes scanned the area. Movement by a large tree captured his attention, and relief washed over him like a tidal wave.

Jenna ran to him. "Did you get it? Do we have time to go before we meet Ethan?"

"Yeah. We'll free them, meet Ethan, and get the medicine to Bleddyn. Let's go." There was no time to lose; his brother's life depended on it.

Chapter Thirty

Rider

I MIGHT BE CRAZY. Rider panted as she ran to keep up with Teo's long strides. Was she really trusting an enemy of the forest—the Wolf crown prince, no less—to save her dad? True, Teo hadn't acted much like an adversary. But still... She cast a quick glance at him. His strong jaw was firm, his focus forward. *Handsome.* Yes, he was definitely that. And he was risking everything to save her father.

"We're closing in on the offices, so we need to slow down and catch our breath."

Rider blinked, heat pooling in her cheeks. Had he noticed her staring? Sheesh. "Sorry. I got distracted. What did you say?"

The left corner of his lip curled up. Yes, he'd noticed. His features smoothed out. "I know the scenery is spectacular, but stay focused. We can't make a mistake."

"Don't be so conceited." She concentrated on the road ahead. "My dad's life depends on us. I'm all in." *Are you?*

As if reading her mind, Teo murmured, "I'm not going to let you down. Here's the plan. We'll go to the guard house. Stay with me, because family members occasionally accompany the guards when prisoners are released. We need to look legit."

The determination in his voice soothed her doubt as the office buildings at the gate came into view. Before her eyes, Teo transformed into the persona of a crown prince who was also a member of the Wolf Pack. Shoulders back, chin lifted, Teo straightened his hat and marched up to the offices with a purposeful stride. As though he belonged. *No, like he ruled the place.*

Rider stepped behind him, feeling the need to hide in his tall shadow like a little kid. For a Forester, the offices were intimidating. Guards sat around a fireplace in what looked like a staff room while others hurried to their posts. She and Teo attracted a few glances but most didn't look up from their card games or coffee mugs. They were used to the princes, Rider guessed. And Foresters were still nobodies. Teo ushered her down a side hall.

He rapped sharply on a green door, and a booming voice ordered them inside. An older man sat behind an ancient wooden desk, his large muscular frame stuffed into a small chair. If Rider wasn't so tense, she probably would have found it amusing. Glasses sat on the edge of his nose and his red hair had grey streaks in it. His presence commanded respect. Or fear, if you were a Forester. Rider, barely breathing, stayed firmly behind Teo, who stood confidently in front of the man's desk.

"Sir." Teo saluted.

"At ease."

"Commander Scar, I have papers here requiring the release of Alarick Howell and Dr. Hood." Teo slid the papers across the man's desk with two fingers. The man raised an eyebrow as he drew the papers to himself, never taking his eyes from his officer. Teo didn't blink. Rider's knees weakened as the tense silence screamed.

"This doesn't make sense. The charges against them are serious." The Commander's voice was husky and deep.

"Sir, my brother is very sick. They are asking family to come to the palace."

Commander Scar frowned. "I'm sorry to hear that." He perused the documents, taking his time. Blood pounded through Rider's veins, and the room tilted. *Don't faint.* What if he suspected the papers were forged? What if he refused to let her dad go? *Breathe.*

The commander picked up a pen. "And Dr. Hood?"

"The charges have been dropped because no crime was committed. A mistake in all the chaos of Bleddyn's sickness." Teo voice caught on the last two words. "I mean no disrespect, but there isn't much time. I need to get my uncle back to the palace quickly." He motioned to her. "Jenna Hood is here for her father."

Rider held her breath, hoping the Wolf would buy the pity card and let them go without further questions. News of Bleddyn's sickness was widespread, so there should be enough truth for the lie to be believable. The thud of the stamp hitting the paper signalled that her wish was granted.

He handed the papers back to Teo. "Wait here and I'll send a guard to get them."

The man heaved himself out of his chair and left the room. Rider sagged against a chair, her legs ready to give out, but Teo stood calm as a cucumber. Straightening herself, Rider decided to pretend that she did this every day—forged papers, stood in a Wolf Commander's office. *Fake it 'til you make it.* Teo caught her eye and she saw admiration there. Warmth spread through her chest. She knew she shouldn't put any stock in the approval of a Wolf, but he wasn't any Wolf.

Ten minutes passed—Rider counted every second of them—before multiple footsteps sounded in the hall. She held her breath, only releasing it when Alarick and her father entered the room. Her dad barely got his arms around her before Teo was motioning them out. He was right; they needed to move quickly.

"I'll explain later," Rider whispered to her dad, who kept a firm grip on her hand.

The silent group hurried through the city streets to the secret entrance in the wall, halting, at Teo's signal, a block away from freedom. Here, Wolf Pack patrolled the area in pairs. Teo motioned them behind a couple of huge potted bushes. Rider had always thought what a pity it was that the Wolves planted bushes in pots because they'd paved all the natural dirt away, but, at the moment, she was very grateful for them. The small group silently watched the patrol pass by. Rider huddled against her father, enjoying the warmth and safety of his nearness. The footsteps faded as the Wolf Pack disappeared. Teo stook a step out but quickly jumped back as another pair came into view.

"I think they found out about the secret entrance." Alarick's face was grim.

"I'll take care of it." Teo stepped forward once the guards' backs were to him and strode over to them.

Rider's tight shoulders felt as if they would crack as Teo pointed in the direction of the palace. The two guards nodded, heading back in the direction they'd come. After making sure they were gone, Teo waved the group over, practically shoving them through the hidden opening. A loud sigh escaped his lips as he yanked the door closed.

"What did you do, Teo?" Alarick's frown shadowed his face.

Teo waved his hand. "I told them they were needed back at the palace."

"No. I meant how did you get us out of jail?" A pulse beat in the older man's temple.

"Duko ordered it." Teo scanned the area as though unwilling to meet his uncle's eyes.

"Teo..."

"We don't have time to argue. Bleddyn is going to die if he doesn't get more medicine." He turned to her father. "Sir, I hate to ask..."

"I have more at the house."

Rider peered at the path leading to the forest. "Ethan's gone to the house to look for it. He should be back by now." The sun was on its way to setting. How long had they been at the guard house? At least half an hour, plus Teo's trip to the palace, so plenty of time for Ethan to get to her house and back. She made her way over to the place they had hidden their bikes, moving branches to reveal not only her bike but a bag. She lifted it and peered in. *Medicine—but where's Ethan?*

Rider swung her head around, searching the darkening area for her friend.

Her dad crossed over to her. "What is it?"

"Ethan's been here and left the medicine. But where is he?" Her throat constricted and she rubbed at it.

"It's not that I'm not worried about Ethan, but I've got to get that medicine to my brother." Teo held out his hand for the bag.

Rider passed it to him. "Go, we'll search for Ethan."

Teo hesitated. "You need to get away from here." He motioned between his uncle and her.

"I'm not leaving without Ethan."

"Teo!" Seth broke through the entrance, breathing heavily. "Thank goodness I've found you. I've been looking everywhere. One of the guys at the guard house said you'd been there and left with Uncle Alarick and Dr. Hood, which raised red flags, since Father hasn't ordered their release. I'm just happy I remembered this entrance from our trip to the Hoods." He bent over, gulping air. His shoulders heaved and a choking sound escaped him.

A shudder ran through Rider as she realized Seth was sobbing.

"Teo... Bleddyn's dead," Seth croaked.

Thoughts of Ethan fled her mind as Rider gaped at Teo's little brother in horror. They had done this for nothing. Risked their lives only to have Bleddyn die. She clapped a hand over her mouth.

All colour drained from Teo's face and he stumbled backwards. "*No. Take that back, Seth!*" Alaric stepped over to him, but Teo fended him off. "I said, take it back," Teo growled.

Seth hung his head, his shoulders shaking, his sobs an eerie, high-pitched sound. Alarick moved to his other nephew's side and wrapped him in his arms. Teo stood motionless. A stone statue. Her dad crossed to the crown prince, gently laying his hand on the young man's shoulder. Teo didn't acknowledge the touch, only remained motionless.

A lump the size of a rock blocked Rider's throat. *Too late, too late, too late.* The brothers' grief was palpable. She hadn't really known Bleddyn, but he had seemed nice. What a waste. She reached out a hand, but stilled at Teo's low, gravelly voice.

"I'll kill him. If he'd let us give Bleddyn the second dose, he would be alive." Teo's hands clenched, his knuckles turning white.

Alarick, his arm still around Seth, said calmly, "I know you're devastated and this hurts. We all loved him. But doing something rash isn't going to help. Your father will be upset too. I know you don't believe it, but he will be, and that makes him even more dangerous. Approach a wounded Wolf with extreme caution—especially when that Wolf is Duko."

Tears streaked down Teo's cheeks, and he swiped them away. "His hate and his stubbornness killed Bleddyn. I won't let him get away with it." He spit out the words as though tasting something bitter in his mouth.

Seth wiped his face with his coat sleeve. "We won't, Teo. But right now we have to go to the palace. To Mom. And to keep Father away from the Hoods." He motioned to Rider and her dad. "He's going to come looking for you. You need to get far away. He's on a rampage. How did you get them out of prison, Teo?"

"I forged his signature."

"Teo," Alarick hissed.

"I don't care; I was trying to save Bleddyn. He can kill me too if he wants to."

"He's not going to kill anyone else. We won't let him. But Uncle Alarick, you can't go back to the palace either. It's too dangerous." Seth ducked his head. "I'm sorry."

"I knew the consequences when we sought out Dr. Hood's help. My concern is you two, but especially you, Teo. When Duko finds out you forged his name, there's no telling what he'll do."

Seth pursed his lips. "We've got to come up with a story."

Teo shook his head. "No story; I'm telling Father the truth if it comes out. Commander Scar's loyal to Father and won't go along with any lie I tell. Maybe the commander won't notice for a while..." He didn't look as though he believed his own words.

Alarick scratched his chin. "Teo's right; your father won't listen, and the Wolf Pack is loyal only to him. Lying would probably make it worse."

"I'll take whatever punishment he hands out. I'm not sorry I tried to save my brother." Teo's voice choked on the last word.

Rider rubbed at the pain in her chest. What would happen if Duko discovered Teo's forgery? Execution? Jail? Would the king do that to one of his only two surviving sons? *Duko's a psycho.*

Her dad gazed at the night sky. "What if we turn Duko into the hero?" He held up his hand as Teo and Seth started to protest. "Hear me out. My drugs work with two doses, I'm positive. If we can convince the king of that, he can take my medicine and spin it however he wants. I don't care if ChemTech gets the credit. Or Duko takes all the glory. People aren't going to care where it comes from, as long as it works.

The people of Wolf kingdom are restless and angry about the flu and the climbing death toll. Let the king proclaim he's found a cure, so he can be the savior once again. It may just be enough to mollify his injured ego."

"Even if we can convince him, how do we deal with ChemTech? The trade deal?" Teo swiped at his eyes.

"We'll figure something out." Seth tugged on the bottom of his jacket to straighten it.

Alarick cleared his throat. With her concern for Teo, Rider had forgotten this man had lost a nephew. "Yes, yes, I think Dr. Hood is correct. It's the only way to save your skin, Teo. Let your father take the glory, and hopefully he'll forget about you for a bit. Tell the truth that you were trying to save Bleddyn. The Kingdom will have compassion for you. Duko can't afford to look bad again. Unfortunately, you'll have to bear his pettiness inside the palace, but this might save your life."

"It's too late for Bleddyn," Teo spat out.

Dr. Hood gazed at Teo with a look Rider recognized—compassion, empathy, and the desire to make it all right again. She'd seen it many times growing up. Unfortunately, he couldn't fix this. "I know, son. I'm truly sorry for your loss." He turned to the others. "All of you."

"It's getting late and we're running out of time." Alarick laid his hand on Teo's shoulder. "I'll go with the Hoods and we'll start making more drugs. You two go back and find your mother. She'll be sick with worry."

"You won't be safe at the Hoods'," Teo said.

Those words brought Ethan to the forefront of Jenna's mind. "Wait—we don't know where Ethan is." How could she so easily have forgotten him? She pawed a hand through her wild curls.

"Would he have gone home after dropping off the medicine?"

"I don't know. He might have. I'll check once we're back in the forest."

Seth cleared his throat. "We need to move now."

Rider gripped Teo's forearm. Fear for him coursed through her veins. "Be careful. Thank you for helping get Dad back." He nodded, his lips in a tight line. "I'm so sorry about Bleddyn." *Don't do anything stupid.*

His ice-blue eyes watered, but he surprised her by gently pressing his hand over hers, then quickly let go. He hugged his uncle and shook her dad's hand before the two princes disappeared through the hidden door.

Rider dug her bike out from the twigs and branches, not caring that the twigs scraped her hands. The pain felt good and distracted her momentarily from the whole far-fetched plan. Hopefully Duko would take the olive branch and use her father's drugs to save the lives of the Wolves, all the while soaking in the people's praise and glory. The thought made Rider's blood boil because her dad deserved all the credit, not Duko.

Chapter Thirty-One

Teo

THE PAIN IN TEO's chest threatened to overwhelm him. *Bleddyn, Bleddyn, Bleddyn.* His brother was dead and it was his father's fault. The anger that flickered around the edges of his grief stole any comfort. Teo could deal with mad, but the sad would have to wait. His father needed to pay for his actions—his negligence with Bleddyn, the climbing death toll. *I hate him. He can do whatever he wants to me; I will never forgive him.*

Teo's footsteps marched in rhythm with the anger pulsing through his veins. Seth grabbed his elbow, yanking him to a stop. "I know this is hard, but rein in your anger. If you lose it with Dad, this could all blow up in our faces. We can't let Bleddyn die for nothing. If we're to save our kingdom from this disease, it means playing up to Father's ego. He has to agree to use Hood's treatment. If you blow up he'll shut us out, and you'll be in a small cell so fast you won't have time to protest."

Teo clenched his fists so tightly his short nails pierced his palms. "He let his own son die. I want to wring his neck." Moisture blurred his vision and his throat throbbed.

"It makes me sick too, but saving people's lives is our first priority now. He's going to pay for Bleddyn's death, but right now I need you, the kingdom needs you—so please pull yourself together."

Teo shrugged out of Seth's grasp, but he knew his brother was speaking the truth. Teo needed to start acting like the crown prince and do what needed to be done. He shook himself, then straightened his shoulders. Nodding, he said, "Okay, let's do this." They trudged towards their home, where grief and sorrow awaited them as well as a very angry father.

⸺◆○◆⸺

A chill snaked along Teo's spine in the eerie silence. No maids humming or the sound of furniture being moved while they cleaned. The many footsteps echoing on the stone floors had faded, along with the staff that ran the household.

Tea tree oil and lemon assaulted Teo's nose, along with the underlying scent of bleach. They found their mother alone in her study, staring out the window. Teo had always thought this was one of the loveliest rooms in all the palace. Pale pink covered the walls, the furniture was comfortable and muted, and fresh flowers graced the table and desk, leaving a soft fragrance in the air. Teo had spent many rainy afternoons here as a young boy, holed up in a chair reading while his mother worked. Today, the room seemed colourless. The queen didn't move as her sons entered the room.

"Mom." Teo knelt beside her chair and took her small hand in his large one. A single tear tracked down her cheek, and he swiped it away with his thumb. Small lines etched around her eyes that he hadn't noticed before.

"Your father's on the warpath, Teowulf. Alarick was mysteriously released from prison, along with Dr. Hood." Her eyes slid to meet his. "Commander Scar says you gave him signed release papers." She bit her lip. "What have you done? Am I to lose two boys today?"

Teo squeezed his mother's icy hand. "Listen, Dr. Hood has the drugs that can cure this disease. It would have worked with Bleddyn if father hadn't interfered." He blinked at the truth of his words, his breath stalling as the realization of Bleddyn's needless death stabbed him again. His own eyes watered. "I was trying to save Bleddyn, since Father is a foo—"

"Respect your father, the alpha and king." His mother's words cut him off, her tone sharp. "That's what Wolves do, and you didn't do that." Her eyes flashed. "You can't go around undermining your father."

Teo rolled back on his heels, letting go of his mother's hand. "How can you accuse me when Bleddyn is dead because of father's vendetta against the forest and the Hoods? If he hadn't let hate consume him, we would have been on top of this sickness. Dr. Hood would have come up with a treatment before it got out of control. Instead, we turn to ChemTech, an incompetent, inferior company."

"Did you even consider the consequences?" What looked like fear crossed her lovely features, causing Teo to pause. He couldn't remember seeing his mother afraid. His anger evaporated. She took his warm face in her cold hands and rested her forehead against his. "Listen to me. You need to leave until your father cools off."

"No, I'm not missing Bleddyn's funeral. I'm not running away from doing what is right. Scores of Wolves will die if Father doesn't let Dr. Hood help. ChemTech's drugs are worthless. I told him weeks ago that their pain killers didn't work on my migraine. He ignored me. More people are going to die. Is that what you want for Wolf kingdom?"

Tilting her head back, she said, "I want you to be safe. Both of you. That's my only concern right now."

"We'll be careful. But I'm worried about you. Did Uncle Alarick give you the immunity booster? If not, you need to take it."

"I don't care what happens to me, Teo."

Seth moved to the other side of his mother. "Mom, I know you're grieving as we all are, but we can't lose you too. We need you."

"Alarick secretly gave me some," she whispered. With that admission, Teo realized she'd known all along that Dr. Hood had been helping Bleddyn, and she never said a word. *Why didn't she fight for Bleddyn?*

His mother straightened. "I know you think I didn't, but I fought for Bleddyn."

Teo blinked. How did she always know what he was thinking?

"Duko wouldn't listen. He locked me in my rooms so I couldn't get help."

"What?" Teo's eyes widened. Seth gasped.

"I tried, Teo, but..." She covered her mouth with her hand, sobbing.

Despite the pain that his mother's words wrought, hope surged. If they fought together, perhaps they could reason with his father. Doubt killed the hope. His father had locked his wife away to make sure she didn't interfere. He wasn't going to listen. But what else could they do? They had to try or more Wolves would die.

Seth rubbed her back. After she calmed, he said, "If we can convince Dad that Dr. Hood's drugs will not only save lives but will turn his people's loyalty back to him, do you think he'll listen? He'll be the hero once again. Dr. Hood is making more of the drugs right now."

"I don't know. Your father is unpredictable." Her voice wavered. "I'm not sure I know him anymore. He let his own son die."

Teo wrapped his arms around her and held tight while the storm of emotion washed over them. Eventually, she pushed away and carefully swiped a finger under her eyes.

"I'll talk to Duko. But you need to do what you can to save Wolf kingdom because I'm sure he will listen to me."

Teo knew the king wouldn't listen to her, but he only nodded and stood.

"Don't worry, Mom, we'll figure it out." Teo hugged his mother. Somehow they had to find a way to save Wolf kingdom.

⸺◆⸺

Teo and Seth encountered two guards from the Wolf Pack after they left their mother. The guards were older men, loyal to the king. The princes only knew their names, little else.

"Prince Teowulf, the King has requested your presence. We're to escort you to him. If you'll kindly come with us." The guard wasn't asking as he gestured for Teo to follow.

Seth casually fell in alongside them and the guards didn't object. "Did my father say what he wants?"

"Matters of the state."

That doesn't bode well.

Seth pursed his lips.

The guard ducked his head slightly. "I'm sorry for your loss, Your Royal Highnesses. Prince Bleddyn was a good mate."

Teo swallowed, but couldn't get any words past the lump that had taken residence in his throat. Seth murmured agreement with the officer's sentiments. They followed him to their father's quarters, where the officer rapped on the large mahogany double doors.

His father's butler answered, ushering the group inside. The king stood behind his desk, his posture straight and his appearance flawless, his hands clasped behind his back.

"You may go, Officers. Thank you." The king dismissed them.

Teo shifted his weight. Seth clasped his hands behind his back, mimicking his father.

"If I'd known how talented you were with pen and ink, Teowulf, I would have employed you in a few business matters long ago." Cold amber eyes met his own ice-blue ones. "If your mother wasn't already grieving, you'd be in a dank, cold cell. Unfortunately for you, you wasted your talent and energy—your friends and your uncle won't get very far. Grief has tried my patience. I want Hood's blood for my son's death."

Roaring filled Teo's ears. "His drugs would have saved Bleddyn. His blood is on *your* hands."

Seth nudged him with his boot.

"*His drugs* killed my son. ChemTech's were working, but you had to go and give him that poison. Bleddyn would have recovered if you'd only waited. Instead, you run to Dr. Hood and undermine my authority. I am the king, and I know what's best for Wolf kingdom."

"Without Dr. Hood's drugs, Bleddyn would have died sooner. You signed Bleddyn's and all Wolves' death warrants when you made that trade deal with the Falls District and ChemTech. None of their drugs work. I told you that, but you didn't listen.. Why do you believe their lies over your own son?"

Seth's hand landed on his shoulder. Teo clamped his lips shut at his father's shuttered face. A cold trickle of sweat beaded on his spine.

Seth stepped forward. "Sir, we're asking you to consider our information. We aren't trying to undermine you. Like you, we want to save our peoples' lives."

His father's gaze slid to his youngest son. If anyone could get through to their father, Seth could. Teo had already blown it.

"Dr. Hood's drugs work much earlier than anything else we've tried. Bleddyn started to improve only hours after the dose. It gives us a fighting chance to beat this disease before it's too late. Let ChemTech continue to work on their own treatment to improve it, but, in the meantime, why not use Hood's to give us a fighting chance? The people are afraid. If they find out Hood had drugs that worked all this time and you didn't use it? They'll turn on us. They're already protesting and rioting. If you let Hood help, the people will remain loyal to you. You'll be the hero that saved them from this sickness."

And speeches like that are why you should be king.

His father turned to stare out the window behind his desk. Was he considering his youngest son's words? Teo darted a look at Seth, who appeared to be holding his breath.

"What am I to do about ChemTech?"

"Tell them that Hood has come up with a drug that works right now. Ask them to continue to work on their version, but at the moment your priority is to save lives. They're not going to argue with that."

His father faced his sons but ignored Teo. "How many are sick in the kingdom?"

"Two hundred sick and fifty have died, as of this morning's report."

"Say we roll out Hood's drugs to keep this from spreading any further while ChemTech makes the final adjustments, how will we know that Hood's drugs are the ones that worked?"

"Years of solid care from Dr. Hood. His drugs and treatments have always been effective. Why would it be any different now?" Seth avoided using Bleddyn as proof. Wise. Teo had to admire his brother.

Duko sat and opened a folder. "I want a test subject. Find a sick Wolf and give him Hood's drugs and then report back to me." A dismissal. The princes turned to leave. "Teowulf, don't plan on going anywhere in the near future; I have special plans for you." His cold tone froze Teo. "Alarick is dead to me and no longer welcome in the kingdom. I'm sure you'll convey that to him when you talk to him next. Make sure I don't see his face ever again."

Teo saluted, but his father never looked up from his desk. A loud hammering rang in his ears as he followed Seth out of his father's office.

——◦——

"That went rather well, considering." Seth exhaled audibly as they strode along the corridor.

Teo raised his eyebrows at his brother.

He pointed at Teo. "You're not in jail, Hood and Uncle are alive and free, and Father's considering our plan. I'd say that's a win."

"Thanks to you. A win for the people, but not for us. Alarick can't come back. Bleddyn is dead plus countless other Wolves, all because of our father's pride and hate." Teo shoved his hands into his pockets. "He didn't even show remorse that he might have killed Bleddyn by being so pig-headed."

"I want to know what his *special plans* for you are." Seth furrowed his brow.

Teo's stomach coiled into a tight knot. "I don't."

"Until he enlightens us, we've got to focus on saving lives and changing the future. That's the only way I can deal with our brother's death. We can't change the past." Seth stopped and slapped the wall before resting his forehead against it. Teo stood beside his sobbing brother. Minutes later, Seth wiped his nose and they trudged through the silent halls of the silent palace. Already Teo missed Bleddyn's noisy, exuberant presence.

Chapter Thirty-Two

Rider

S OAP SUDS FLITTED OVER the small glass bottles as Rider scrubbed with a small brush. The rhythmical movement eased the tension in her shoulders. Next to her, her father ground dried herbs into a fine pulp with a pestle and mortar. Usually, Rider peppered her father with questions about the ingredients, but today she was too engrossed in her own thoughts and worries. She'd let her dad handle the meds, and she'd keep her hands busy with the grunt work. His body generated heat and energy, and she moved closer to soak up his presence. *I don't know what I'd do if anything happened to you.*

He touched the side of his head to hers for a moment. "I'm so grateful to you and Teo."

"Me too. He was really brave. I hope he's okay."

Alarick measured out the fine green dust into small canisters at a table in the middle of the room. Rider didn't like his grim expression. He hadn't said much since they'd arrived at this new hiding place.

Her father had led them to an old house deep in the forest that had belonged to his grandmother at one time. Rider hadn't known of its existence, so she was pretty sure the king or Wolf Pack didn't either. They had taken a risk and stopped by their cabin to get the supplies they needed. Alarick kept a lookout while Rider and her dad stuffed a few bags with the dried herbs, bottles, and other things they'd need. No Wolf Pack showed up or followed them. Perhaps Duko was too grief stricken to care. At least that's what Rider hoped. She didn't want to think about the fact that Teo may be suffering the consequences of freeing her father and his uncle.

Ethan was still MIA. They had left a coded note giving instructions on how to find them in the courier box. Hopefully, he remembered the old childhood code they had used to set up secret meetings in locations around the forest when they were young. It had seemed mysterious and fun at the time. *Not so much anymore.*

Rider inhaled deeply, holding her breath before letting it out. After grabbing another handful of bottles, she sank them in the sink, bubbles floating to the surface. *Busy hands are good.* She searched for her friend out the small window. *Where are you, Ethan?*

"I'm sure Ethan can take care of himself." Her dad smiled at her.

"He's fast on his bike. Anyone on foot couldn't catch him." She rinsed a bottle, the suds vanishing down the drain. "I'm also worried about Teo."

"I am too, but he knows his father and what is expected of him as the crown prince. His title is protecting him, I think. He's wise to go back to the palace rather than run. Teo will be okay."

Rider swished her hands around the water. "I hope so. I feel so bad for him. Bleddyn's death was unnecessary, and Teo must feel so betrayed by his dad."

Her dad's eyes studied her. "You like him."

She kept her gaze focused on the soapy water. "I've never known a Wolf outside of the doctors and nurses we deliver to. I can't help but notice our similarities, which also make our uniqueness stand out. It's not a bad thing. I think our differences make us stronger. Teo and I worked together as a team. I couldn't have found you without him. Does that make sense?"

"Yes. It's time to come together."

"Although there is one thing between us that can't be ignored." She smiled. "The royalty thing."

Her dad chuckled softly. "There is that." His face smoothed out. "But you're right, we are greater together. Hate and mistrust taught from one generation to the next is what divides us."

Rider drained the water. "Maybe change can start here. With us."

Her dad wrapped his arm around her shoulders. "I think that's a great idea."

The loud rap on the door jolted Rider. Alarick stood, grabbed a rolling pin, then nodded. Her dad opened the door a crack, peering out. His chuckle filled the room as he threw open the door, dragging in a disheveled and winded Ethan.

Rider ran to her friend, squeezing him tightly. "Where have you been? Are you okay?"

Ethan held on to her, his breathing heavy in her ear. "I'm okay. I found the drugs, no problem, and was out in five minutes, but then I noticed a guy on my tail. I led him on a merry goose chase through the forest. Wow, was he tired." Ethan grinned. "Bet he didn't realize how big the forest was. Once I lost him, I left the package with the bike but didn't stick around, as I didn't want to draw attention to the area. Good thing because as I headed home I noticed another spy, so I toured the forest again and lost him. I rode by your house, but I figured you wouldn't be there. Then I remembered the courier box. I found your note and here I am." He smiled. "The old code? Good thing I remembered how to decipher it."

"I knew you would."

Her dad turned the lock on the door. "You weren't followed?"

"No, but, to be sure, I hid in the forest for the last half hour. No one is around."

"Good man."

Rider hugged him again. "You took a huge risk for us today. Thank you."

"Tell me it paid off?" Ethan's face filled with hope.

Rider exchanged glances with her dad. She shook her head, her voice low. "No, Bleddyn died before we could get the drugs to him."

"What?" Ethan ran his hand over his messy, sweaty hair as he slumped against the counter. "It was all for nothing?"

Alarick set the rolling pin on the table. "No, son. Not for nothing. We're going to save the lives of many people."

"How?" Ethan's words echoed the doubt in the room.

Rider lifted her chin. "Teo is going to convince his father to use Dad's drugs. Turn the king into a hero."

Ethan shut his mouth, then opened it again. "He's going to take the credit for it all." Bitterness coated every word.

Dr. Hood waved his hand. "That's not important. All that matters is we stop this flu and save as many Wolves as we can."

Rider wrapped her arms around her stomach. There was one life in particular she wanted kept safe. *Teo's.*

Chapter Thirty-Three

Teo

⟫ · ⟩ · ◆ · ⟨ · ⟪

D R. HOOD'S DRUGS WORKED. The test Wolf had improved significantly since being administered both doses of the Forester's
drugs. *Bleddyn would be alive if not for my father.* Teo picked at a
hangnail. Forty-eight hours later, and his father hadn't agreed to their
proposal. Teo doubted he would. He had spent the last hour trying to
come up with a plan to get the drugs to the people without his father's
consent. He flexed his fingers, his hands as empty as his mind. *What
am I going to do?*

A knock roused him from his thoughts. "Come in," he murmured.

His father's butler entered the room. "Your Highness, your father
wishes to see you in his office. I'm here to escort you."

This can't be good. Teo followed the portly man through the maze
of halls to his father's offices, hoping the meeting was about Duko
agreeing to their plan.

Seth stood waiting outside the double doors. His hopeful eyes met
Teo's. The butler knocked and then announced their presence. As Teo
crossed the threshold, a chill raised the hairs on the back of his neck.
He swiped a hand over it.

His father, dressed for mourning in a black suit, white shirt, and
black silk tie, sat at his desk.

The king pointed to the chairs on the other side of the desk. Teo
studied his face. Lines ringed his eyes and mouth that hadn't been
there a month ago. His long, dark hair was messily tied back. Teo had

never seen so much as a hair out of place on his father. *Maybe he did love Bleddyn.*

The man, who was now more a stranger than anything, steepled his hands and sank back in his luxurious leather chair. "I've made a decision regarding Hood's drugs. Clinics will be set up around the city for people who are sick to go get it." His golden eyes glowed as they glared at Teo. "As far as anyone outside this office is concerned, this drug was manufactured by ChemTech. Do I make myself clear?"

Teo nodded once to show he understood. He was afraid to say anything in case he provoked his father and the king changed his mind.

"The news will be released today, and it will have the palace's official stamp. I'm assuming Hood is already producing what we'll need?" He waited for confirmation. Teo nodded again.

"It's your job to get the drugs from wherever Hood is hiding, which I'm also assuming you know?"

Teo found his voice. "Yes, sir." He'd received word from his uncle earlier that day, but Duko didn't need to know that.

"Set up a delivery system or go get it yourselves, but Hood is to be invisible. If anything goes wrong or word leaks about Hood, the consequences will be harsh and I can guarantee, Teo, that you, especially, won't like them."

Teo's stomach dropped to his feet, but he kept his features blank. He was not going to give his father the satisfaction of knowing he had shaken his son.

"Get the drugs here by tomorrow at the latest. The clinics open the next day at noon." His father picked up a file and started to read it. Apparently the meeting was over.

After changing into street clothes, the brothers hurried along the back halls and then through the tunnels that led to the secret exit out of the city. Once the gate was behind them, they skirted the tree line of the forest, staying out of sight.

"What do you think he means by harsh consequences?" Seth's alert eyes kept checking for tails.

"I don't want to know. He's always so creative when it comes to punishments. It doesn't matter—I just want to get this done and save those we can."

"Will they have enough drugs ready, do you think?"

Teo nodded. "It's been two days since we split up. Jenna's friend Ethan dropped a note off at Dr. Lupine's office from Dr. Hood yesterday. When the doctor checked in today to make sure we didn't have symptoms, he slipped it to me." Teo extracted the note from his jacket pocket. "Order is filled," he read.

Seth raised an eyebrow. "Succinct."

Teo chuckled. "Pretty sure he didn't want anyone figuring out what he was talking about. Dr. Hood sealed a map to this cottage they're hiding out in to the inside of the envelope." He opened the envelope so Seth could see the map, or, rather, not see it. "I spent ten minutes unsealing the thing."

The map symbolized the seriousness of their situation. Silence wrapped around them as they continued on their way, their noses and ears alert to smells and noises that didn't belong. They stayed in the shadows of the forest, the dense brush and trees keeping them hidden from any prying eyes. Although the Wolf Pack wasn't actively looking for the Hoods, it wasn't a good idea to be seen in the forest, especially if Hood was to remain invisible. They didn't need any unnecessary questions fired their way.

Teo breathed a sigh of relief as he and Seth cut away from the main path and moved deeper into the woods. Evergreens grew prominently here, and decaying leaves and needles deadened their footfalls. Only a little light came through the brush and tall trees. The pungent smell of pine and earth tickled his nostrils. They had to be close, since they hadn't passed a home or cottage in the last ten minutes.

A decrepit looking house, partly hidden by trees, came into view. Teo eyed his brother.

"Doesn't look like anyone has lived here in decades."

"I know, but they're in there." Teo had faith in the Hoods. Both of them.

They hurried to the cabin and Teo rapped three short raps.

The door opened a few inches, revealing Dr. Hood's tight face, but his features relaxed as recognition dawned. He opened the door wide and waved them in to a room that held more people than Teo had expected, strangers he didn't recognize. But his gaze didn't linger long because there was only one person he wanted to lay eyes on. Jenna sealed boxes in a corner. Warmth spread through his chest at the sight of her, which was ridiculous. She smiled and a goofy grin spread across his face. A sharp elbow in the ribs from Seth reminded Teo there were other people in the room.

Before he could say anything, his uncle hugged him.

"It's so good to see you alive and healthy. I wasn't sure how Duko would react, but fortunately he's doing what's best for the kingdom for once."

"We don't have much time. I'm sorry." Teo's eyes locked with Jenna's. *I wish I had time.* Time to get to know her under normal circumstances. But who was he kidding? When it came to Wolves and Foresters, there were no normal circumstances.

Dr. Hood handed Seth several sheets of paper, the rustling grounding Teo in his mission. "Here are the instructions for the dosage and all other pertinent information the clinics and doctors will need. Make sure each doctor gets a copy." Seth folded them and slid them into the chest pocket of his jacket, his eyes darting to the four strangers in the room.

"Recruits who are very trustworthy. They won't speak of any of this, but we needed the manpower to get it made and ready."

Teo cleared his throat. "Right." Guess he needed to start trusting the doctor. "That's good because one of the king's stipulations is that this ..." he waved a hand around the room, "... never happened. ChemTech and my father are going to take all the glory." Shame washed over Teo and his shoulders hunched. "I'm sorry we couldn't do more to let the kingdom know of your role in this. One day I'll rectify it. When I'm king."

Dr. Hood picked up a brown bottle and tightened the cap. "Son, my purpose is to save lives, not gain recognition. We're all in this together. Let's end this plague."

Moisture blurred Teo's eyes. This man was the complete opposite of his father—his humility and genuine care left Teo speechless. He cleared his throat. "Thank you."

Dr. Hood nodded at Jenna, and she pushed a cart full of boxes over to them and held out the handle to Teo. His fingers brushed hers as he took it, a jolt of electricity jangling up his arm. Did he have the same effect on her that she had on him?

Her green eyes were the colour of a meadow, and he could stare into them all day. Her soft smile stirred something in him. He wanted to make her proud. Jenna pointed to the handle. "The cart was the best we could do. It has thick wheels, so it should be okay on the rough areas of the forest floor. The vials are small and packed tightly."

Her nearness—the smell of honeysuckle and something all her—overwhelmed him, causing the room to spin slightly. What was wrong with him? He stared at the boxes, trying to regain his bearings. *Focus on the mission.* "Great. Thank you." Teo's heart raced, and his lips lifted like a lovesick fool's. Thankfully, Dr. Hood intervened, holding out his hand to Teo. Teo shook himself out of the stupor and gripped the pharmacist's hand. "Wolf kingdom owes you more than we can ever repay. More than my father will ever acknowledge."

Dr. Hood nodded. "Godspeed."

Teo tugged the heavy cart toward the door, Jenna following close behind.

"Stay safe," she whispered.

"You too. You need to be careful."

"I will." After opening the door a crack, she peered out. "All clear."

Seth shook Dr. Hood's hand and then hugged his uncle. "Thank you. Those words aren't enough but..."

The doctor nodded and then Teo and Seth hurried out, along the path.

"I can't believe Dr. Hood doesn't care that he's not going to get the credit for helping us. No Wolf I know would agree to that." Seth shoved his hands into his jacket pockets. "How can two fathers be so different?"

Teo didn't have the answer. As the wind blew the tree branches overhead, Teo wrapped himself in the memory of Jenna's touch, of her father's grace, and he vowed to keep them both safe.

⸻◦○◦⸻

Ten trusted guards stood waiting for the brothers at the palace. Although they weren't told where the medicine had come from, it wasn't too hard to guess. They split up the medicine into ten packages, and the guards left to distribute them to the clinics and hospital.

Seth wiped his brow. "I hope this works because I don't want to imagine what will happen if it doesn't."

Teo agreed. After storing the cart in one of the palace sheds, he escaped to his room to prepare for his brother's funeral, which was to be held the next morning. After collapsing on the bed, he pulled the navy duvet over his body, hoping to block out the world. But his mind wouldn't cooperate.

Like Teo's own private slideshow, images of Bleddyn laughing at his own jokes and stunts ran through his memory. Bleddyn reading his favourite books in his rare quiet moments. The three of them playing as kids. Teo's throat closed. Bleddyn always had his brothers' backs. He was a true friend. He and Teo were supposed to be each other's wing man and make inappropriate jokes at royal functions. Bleddyn had promised to be his chief advisor and keep him grounded and sane once Teo took the throne. But those dreams had died when Bleddyn ceased breathing. Teo clutched his blankets closer, the emptiness of the room and his brother's absence washing over him. Sobs wracked his body as the anguish and worry of the last few days released.

His body spent, Teo lay there, his mind finally empty save one face. He didn't fight it. Ebony curls and emerald eyes beckoned. The memory of her scent tickled his nose. He was glad Bleddyn had met her. His eyelids drooped and, finally, Teo slept.

Chapter Thirty-Four

Rider

RIDER SLID INTO A back pew, hoping she blended in with the masses for Prince Bleddyn's funeral. From one side of the church to the other, people were packed in like sardines. Everyone wanted to say goodbye to a favoured son. Her gaze roved over the occupants of the front row. Her breath caught in her throat at the sight of the elder prince, slumped between his mother and his youngest brother. Teo was a far cry from the cocky prince stamping papers at the FBC just a few weeks previous. She blinked to keep her vision as moisture filled her eyes. Gripping the edge of the pew, Rider studied each member of the family. Seth mirrored his brother's sorrow, but the king's back was ramrod straight. *Cold-hearted snake.*

Bright blooms of carnations, roses, and daisies washed the front of the cathedral in the colours of the rainbow. A formal portrait of Bleddyn sat on an artist's easel, painted by a renowned artist. It was a beautiful piece of work, but where was the mischievous glint in Bleddyn's eyes and the ever-present smirk that the prince was famous for? The artist had missed the essence of the man.

Rider didn't know Bleddyn well personally, but everyone knew *of* him. His quick laugh, his outrageous jokes and pranks, were infamous in the kingdom. He'd had an exuberance for life from the time he was a small tyke, and it had shown through on all the media specials about the royals. One particularly famous scene had taken place in the gardens of the palace, where Bleddyn had made a mudball and thrown it at the king, hitting him on the forehead. Bleddyn had stood still as a statue, until his father threw his head back and laughed. Then the young boy doubled over, laughing. The clip had been shown thousands of times over the years, perhaps because it was one of the only times anyone had seen Duko that vulnerable. And Bleddyn had brought it out.

Several people pressed tissues to their eyes. Rider swiped her nose in a very unladylike way. Fumbling in her coat pocket, she found a handkerchief and blew her nose softly. *Don't draw attention to yourself.*

She'd snuck out while her father and Alarick slept. They'd never have let her come if they knew, but she had to be here for Teo.

As the priest came through a side entrance near the front of the cathedral, music filled the sanctuary. Rider stood with the rest of the congregation, but her attention stayed on Teo. *You can get through this.*

After a choral interlude from the choir, the mourners resumed their seats, while the priest took his place at the podium. The man spoke of life and death, but Rider only caught snatches. Teo's head stayed bowed. What was he thinking? She remembered hearing somewhere that the two older brothers were close.

As the final song ended, the royal family walked the centre aisle out to the large foyer. The king led the way, his arm around the queen's waist. Seth and Teo trailed behind. Rider willed Teo to look at her, but he kept disappearing from her line of sight. If only she were taller. As she sagged against the back of the pew in front of her, the crowd parted enough for her to see Teo. His eyes locked onto hers, sending a jolt through her body. Then a large man moved in front of her, blocking her view once again. She tapped her foot against the hard marble floor as she waited to exit her row. The royal family would take a car back to the palace, and Rider wanted to get out of the church in time to see them leave. She wanted to see Teo one last time, but the crowd was large and slow moving. Hundreds of Wolves had risked exposure to the Lupine flu to pay their respects to Bleddyn's family. Rider hadn't expected so many people because the drug her father provided for treatment wasn't available until the next day.

Eventually, a space opened, and she edged out into the aisle. Rider hurried through the church's doors, immune to the sunlight's warmth as she searched for the vehicle that would carry the royals. Tail lights glinted in the sun's rays as the car turned out of the parking lot and drove away, taking Rider's hope of seeing Teo again with it. The red lights blurred, and she blinked several times. He was gone.

She strode to the edge of the city, hoping the somber day would make the Wolf Pack less inclined to give her trouble at the gates, which had opened for the first time since the spread of the sickness. Rider pulled her papers out of her pocket, wishing she could erase her last name from them. She might as well wave a red flag under a bull's nose.

The guard beckoned her forward. "Documents."

Rider handed them over, staring straight ahead while he perused them. Heat rose from her chest all the way to the tips of her ears, making them tingle as his gaze lasered in on her. After a minute that seemed like an eternity, he waved her through. Wrapping her coat around her body to ward off the chill, Rider quickened her pace. As she entered the forest, the hairs on the back of her neck rose and she slowed to glance around. A few squirrels chattering and running along the path were her only company. Laughing at the animals' antics, Rider's shoulders loosened. She'd imagined she was being watched. The Forest was safe—it was home. Her mind wandered to the funeral ceremony and Teo.

A shuffling sound came from behind her, and she whipped her head around, smashing her nose against something hard. Rider reared back and opened her mouth to scream, but a gloved hand pressed hard over her face, smashing her lips against her teeth. The large hand restricted her airflow, and she kicked out, but her attacker grabbed her arm and whirled her around and then circled an arm around her waist like a hand of steel. He lifted her off the ground, drawing her back so close to his chest that she couldn't get any momentum.

"Stop fighting." The snarling voice in her ear chilled Rider's blood, as the man, whoever he was, roughly squeezed her. The edges of her vision darkened as dizziness engulfed her. She felt rather than saw a second person approaching. The prick in her neck stung like a bee, which brought to mind that day in the forest long ago with three boys. Before the memory could fully form, blackness overtook her.

Chapter Thirty-Five

Teo

❧ · ◆ · ☙

Teo's heaping plate of food sat untouched in front of him. He couldn't remember who had given it to him, but did they really think he could eat at his brother's funeral? His sick stomach was ready to revolt, so he shoved it away.

The crowded room was filled with the who's who of Wolf kingdom, all invited to this private wake for Bleddyn by their father. Teo spotted the king, deep in conversation with one of his officials across the room. *Like any other day at the office.* Not even the death of his own son halted politics. Teo swallowed the bile that rose with the thought. Where was his mother? After scanning the crowd and not seeing her, Teo figured she'd left. *Lucky her.* A stab of guilt pricked his conscience because, of all people, didn't she have the right to hide? She'd lost a child.

Seth sat at a nearby table, speaking with one of the neighbouring governors and his pretty wife. *Not as beautiful as Jenna.* Teo's chin dipped as he wiped his forehead. What kind of a guy thought about a girl at his brother's funeral? Despite the rebuke, his mind refused to let her go because she'd provided the one bright spot of the day, risking her safety to be at the church. For him? He couldn't believe a Forester would do that for a Wolf. But the warmth and kindness he'd seen in those emerald eyes filled him with hope. Not only for the future of the kingdom, but for himself. Selfish.

Teo rose and walked away from the table, leaving the people who were laughing and chatting, going on as usual, even though the day was anything but ordinary. Didn't they realize that Bleddyn would never again come plowing through the doors, laughing and joking? He would never marry or have kids of his own. *He would've been a great dad.* Teo sniffed as he trudged along the corridor that led to the courtyard.

"Teowulf."

He closed his eyes, his steps halting. He waited a beat before facing his father, who assessed him with cold eyes. "I need to see you in my suite in an hour."

Before Teo could utter a word, the king was gone, leaving Teo alone in the passage. He licked his dry lips, shaking off his father's words, before heading outside. The warm sunshine washed over him, driving the chill from his body. Was Bleddyn responsible for the sunshine today? He shot a look at the clear blue sky. Maybe so.

⸺◆◇◆⸺

Teo shook his arms out as he stood before his parents' suite. What he'd find on the other side was anyone's guess. *Here goes nothing.* A maid answered his knock and ushered him into the large front room where his parents entertained family friends and guests. The room was spacious and the furniture comfortable. A curtain fluttered in the cool breeze of the open window. His father poured drinks at the side bar. His mother sat on a burgundy velvet couch, across from an older gentleman and young woman.

The smile he'd plastered on his face faltered slightly as Teo recognized the governor of Falls District, Mr. Adams, and his daughter. He'd met them a few weeks before at the dinner where his father announced the trade deal. *What's her name again?*

The king handed the governor a tumbler half filled with an amber liquid. "Teowulf, come in and sit. We have things to discuss." His dad motioned him over to a wingback chair. Teo sat on the chair's edge while discreetly rubbing his sweaty palms on his thighs.

Before taking his own seat, the king passed his wife a glass. No one spoke as they waited for Duko. Just what his father loved—an audience waiting with bated breath.

"Teowulf, you remember Governor Adams of Falls District and his daughter, Tania."

Tania. That was her name. Teo dipped his head.

"We're so sorry for your loss," said the governor, before taking a drink. Not sorry enough to admit his drugs didn't work. Or to put this meeting off to another day. Teo swallowed the acrid taste in his mouth.

His father crossed his legs, balancing his drink on his knee. "It's been very unfortunate that we haven't been able to keep our promise of trade with the Falls District. Being forced into using a drug not made by ChemTech was not part of our deal, and, understandably, Governor Adams is upset, as is his county. Although we are claiming the cure is ChemTech's, their people have lost work because they're not manufacturing the drug. I have assured him we will make it up to the Falls."

He'd told them they were using Hood's drug? Why would he do that? "What—"

"Now, Teo," his father glared at him. Teo clamped his mouth shut. "How do you think we should make things right with the governor and the Falls District?"

Blood rushed into Teo's head, a dull roar taking up residence in his temples. His heart hammered against his rib cage as perspiration broke out across his skin. Was this a test? Teo didn't want to know the answer. It didn't matter what he thought because the king had clearly already decided. And Teo was pretty sure he wasn't going to like it.

His father smirked. "No suggestions, Teowulf? Ah well, good thing it's not up to you. I've come up with a compensation plan, which Governor Adams has kindly agreed to. My plan will make both Wolf City and Falls District stronger, united. Which is what the trade deal was intended to do." He paused dramatically, giving the amber liquid in his glass a swirl as the corners of his mouth rose slightly, as if he had a great secret and couldn't wait to divulge it.

"What's the proposition?" Teo rasped. The roaring became a cacophony.

His father lifted his glass as if proposing a toast. "Marriage, of course!"

Teo blinked. "I don't understand." Except that he did. Perfectly. *Please, no.*

"You and Tania will marry this winter to form an alliance between our two great clans." Not a proposition but a command. "With your union, the Falls District will become Wolf City's premier trade partner and ally. Their status in the kingdom will be next only to Wolf City." His father grinned, showing teeth. He never did that.

The room tilted, causing Teo's stomach to flip flop. His fingertips gripped the armrest of his chair as he forced air into his lungs. He'd never passed out before, but this must be what it felt like.

"We'll announce the engagement before Governor Adams and Tania leave at the end of the week. The women can then begin to plan *the* event of the winter season." His father winked at Tania, and Teo thought he might throw up.

The two men clinked their glasses, obviously pleased with themselves and the arrangement. His mother sat, her hands folded demurely on her lap, avoiding Teo's gaze.

Governor Adams turned to him, his smile fading as he scanned Teo's face. The governor placed his glass on the table. "We're honoured. I know you're surprised, and it may not be the best day to spring this on you," he swallowed, "but my daughter will make you a wonderful wife. And it will be a positive step forward for us all."

Teo wanted to laugh in his face. Not a good day to "spring this on him?" Was the man insane? They'd just come from his brother's funeral, and now his father was marrying Teo off to save face. And to punish Teo for using Hood's medicine.

The governor held out his hand. It shook slightly as Teo stared at it. Then the king cleared his throat, and Teo shook himself, grasped the man's hand, and forced a smile in an attempt to pretend that everything was fine. Tania smiled at Teo and held out her hand as well. He managed to grasp it and bring it to his stiff lips. Pink tinged her cheeks. She was pretty with her white-blonde hair and blue eyes, but she was the wrong girl.

Teo studied her. Did she even want this marriage?

"I'm thrilled at the prospect of becoming your wife," Tania said, a little breathlessly. "I've had a crush on you since I was a girl."

Oh. Teo managed a smile, but words eluded him.

"Obviously, my son is overtaken by your beauty." The king laughed, but there was no mirth in it. Teo heard the warning. He stared into the drink that had been shoved into his hands. He wanted to chug it; instead, he sipped, casting a glance over the rim at his mother, who smiled and laughed with the others. His stomach dropped. There was no getting out of this if his mother was on board.

Thankfully, the governor, his daughter, and the queen soon excused themselves, leaving Teo alone with his dad. Teo held his breath, waiting for the hammer to fall. His father's nose came within an inch of his own. "I told you there would be consequences for undermining my authority. You will marry this girl and make the alliance work, for the sake of the kingdom. Because we backed out of our deal, they're very disgruntled. I don't need a revolt. Marriage was the only way to salvage the relationship. You *will* do this."

His nostrils flaring, Teo glared at his father. "Like you even tried to salvage it. You told them we backed out. You've never had any guilt about lying, but now your conscious speaks up? You betrayed us." Teo shoved past his father. "I would rather go to jail than marry her."

His father grabbed his arm, spinning Teo around to face him. "You know, I guessed that would be your reaction, which is why I've got additional incentive for you."

A cold sweat broke over Teo's body. His father's eyes had gone cold, hard. What did he have planned now?

The king picked his drink up off the table and swallowed the last mouthful. "What about your little red hood? How do you think she would manage jail time?"

Teo stiffened. "What have you done?"

His father tapped his finger on the empty glass. "She will be safe, as long as the marriage happens. It's time you grew up, took some responsibility, and put Wolf kingdom first. I won't touch the girl if you do as I say. You have my word. In the meantime, she's out of sight, out of mind." Duko set the glass down with a clink.

"If you even think about..."

His father grabbed Teo by the throat, forcing him up against the wall. "Don't you dare threaten me, or you will live to regret it. I can't say the same about the girl." Hot breath hit Teo's face as he thumped against the wall.

Gasping for air, he tried to steady himself. "I do what you say and she goes free?"

The king let go of him and smoothed his jacket. "That's the deal." His voice was calm, bored.

"Fine." Teo pushed by him and strode out of the room, clenching his fists.

"I knew you'd see it my way." His father's words followed Teo down the corridor.

I hate him. He stopped by a window in the hall and leaned his forehead against the cool glass, letting his heart rate slow. *Where are you, Jenna?*

Chapter Thirty-Six

Rider

Boom. Boom. Boom. Rider groaned. Where was all the noise coming from? She gingerly felt around her temple. The racket was coming from inside her head. Her eyelids weighed one hundred pounds, preventing her from opening them. She tried moving a finger and failed. Voices murmured, but her scrambled brain couldn't make sense of the sounds.

She tried forcing words out of her dry throat, but they sounded like mumbo jumbo. At least the effort got Rider the desired response, as someone pressed a straw against her lips. After sucking back gulps of the lukewarm liquid, Rider resumed her fetal position on the hard mattress. Shadows flicked behind her eyelids. After considerable effort, she squinted into the dark room. Alone. Had she dreamed the voices and the water? Maybe not, since her thirst wasn't as bad now. She forced her body to a sitting position. Who had given her the water? How long ago was that? Where was she?

The room spun around and around, so Rider lay back, closed her eyes. Unfortunately, her mind had awakened enough that her thoughts began to whirl. Images of a funeral—Bleddyn's—and then the forest. She'd been walking home. A gloved hand over her mouth. Rider lunged for the side of the bed and retched. After wiping her sleeve across her lips, she pressed her forehead to the mattress. She'd have to clean that up later. Her bigger worry was figuring out where she was and who was holding her.

From the little she'd seen, the room was basic, with only a single bed, a side table, and a pine kitchen chair. A crude wooden shutter covered one small window. A lamp sat on the side table, emitting an orange glow. The grey cinder block walls matched the cement floor.

Rider shivered and tugged the coarse blanket up around her. A sharp pain shot through her head, and she closed her eyes. Her father's smiling face filled her thoughts. Was he okay? *Does he know that I've been kidnapped?*

⬥

A scraping sound woke Rider from a fitful sleep. Her head ached, but the nausea was gone. Opening one eye, she followed the noise to a man sitting on the chair by her bed, sharpening a wicked-looking knife. He wore a knit cap that covered the top part of his face to his nose. Pale yellow eyes glowered from two eyeholes cut out of the cloth, and Rider shrank against the wall next to the bed.

"She awakens. Wasn't sure if we had a sleeping beauty on our hands." The voice was deep and gruff.

"Who—" She coughed to clear her throat. "Why am I here?"

The blade stilled, and he set it down and reached for a glass of water from the night table. He held it out, but Rider ignored it, even though her throat ached for the cool liquid.

He shoved it at her again. "Drink. It's not poison."

Rider turned her face to the wall, not about to trust her kidnapper.

"Feisty one, aren't you?" He nudged her in the shoulder. "I don't need you getting dehydrated, so drink up."

The desire for answers as well as a drink outweighed her misgivings, so she rolled over and grasped the glass, taking a sip. Cool relief slid down her parched throat. She took a couple more gulps before the man took the glass away. "Easy. I don't want to clean up more puke."

Oh right. He'd cleaned that up? Heat pooled in her cheeks.

She tugged the blanket to her chest. "Why am I here?"

He picked up the knife, wiping it on his dirty jeans. "Above my pay grade. Until I'm told otherwise, this is home sweet home." He picked his teeth with the tip of the blade. Rider winced.

He stood, his hulking frame towering over her. "We won't hurt you. That's our orders. Unless you act stupid. We're keeping you out of the way... for your own protection." He wiped the blade on the edge of the bed. Rider scooted against the wall.

"Told you, I'm not going to hurt you. I just need a piece of this." Before she could stop him, he reached over and cut a lock of her hair, folding it up in paper. After jamming it in his coat pocket, he slid the knife into his boot. Then he was gone, leaving her with no answers, but many questions.

One thing was clear. King Duko had done this. But why *her*? Revenge? Her stomach twisted at the thought of her dad. Was he okay? *The king needs him to make the drugs.* Still, her father would be so worried. Her lips trembled, but she refused to cry. If it *was* Duko who'd snatched her, she refused to give him the satisfaction of breaking her down. Her first priority was to get out of here.

Slowly, she swung her legs to the side of the bed. The room tilted. *Whoa.* She gripped the thin foam mattress until the room levelled out. Once that happened, she stood, regretting the motion as the floor started to rush toward her. She closed her eyes to keep from going down and inhaled, exhaled. Counted to ten. *Better.* Rider forced her feet to make the twenty steps to the window. After yanking the shutter to the side, she squinted at the light shining through the glass and her heart sank.

Metal bars lined the window. She was a prisoner. Shoving the shutter back to cover the bars, she rested her forehead against the cool cement wall. Was Teo looking for her? Was he nearby? Would he risk standing up to his father to protect her like he'd promised?

Silence was her only answer.

Chapter Thirty-Seven

Teo

TEO'S STOMACH HEAVED, AND he swallowed back the bile as he stared at the lock of hair in the small box. The note, in his father's handwriting, said it all. *In case, you doubted my seriousness in the matter.*

Snapping the lid closed, he crumpled the note with his other hand.

What kind of father did this to his own son? *A monster.* Teo slid the box into a small compartment in his wooden dresser, his reflection catching his attention. Was he a monster too? *No.* Icy fear inched down his spine, vertebra by vertebra. He shoved it aside to assess his appearance. Dark circles ringed his eyes. He hadn't slept much since Bleddyn got sick, instead tossing and turning as his mind worried over first his brother and now Jenna. His shirt was rumpled and dirty from yesterday's wear. He ripped it off, throwing it to the floor. Maybe what's-her-face wouldn't marry him if he was a total slob. As if his father would let him get away with that behaviour. He scrubbed his eyes. Did it matter what Teo did? What was the point? His father didn't care about him. All he cared about was his own agenda, his own power. Teo would never measure up.

He stared longingly at the bed. It, too, was an unrealistic fantasy. What he needed was a shower and food—and to somehow pull himself together. Jenna's life depended on it.

His father didn't make idle threats. Ever. A memory from when he was thirteen surfaced. He'd gone against his father's wishes and left the palace to attend a bike race. Upon his return, he'd been escorted to the holding cell in the Wolf Pack's headquarters—to spend the night reflecting about what disobeying his father meant. Teo had gotten the message loud and clear. *Don't cross Duko.* And he hadn't after that until he turned sixteen and decided he was his own master. He'd paid for it ever since.

But now? Jenna would die if Teo didn't go through with the marriage. There was no doubt about that. He dropped his head. He wasn't his own master at all. He'd believed he could be, but that, too, was a wild pipe dream.

What am I going to do?

<hr>

The aroma of smoked meat met Teo as he entered the family dining room. He sucked in his cheeks to stop himself from gagging.

Seth eyed him over his coffee cup. "You look terrible."

Teo barked out a laugh. "Thanks for the support." Before Teo could grab a seat, Seth stood and handed him a travel mug. Teo sniffed the strong brew before taking a fortifying sip. Seth waved his hand for Teo to follow. Silently, they sipped their coffees as they strolled. Teo side-eyed his brother, but Seth shook his head slightly.

Once outside, they headed away from the palace but stayed on the grounds. Walking the gardens provided privacy that the palace couldn't guarantee. His father really did have spies everywhere.

"Uncle Alarick sent me a message." Seth blew on his hot drink.

Teo kept his gaze straight ahead. "What did he say?"

"Dad's got Dr. Hood's daughter."

"I know."

Seth whipped his head in Teo's direction, almost spilling his drink from the sudden movement. "How do you know? And why take her?" Seth stopped at a stone bench and sat. "Insurance so Dr. Hood will follow orders?"

"No... Although that could be part of it. Kill two birds with one stone." Teo perched on the edge of the bench.

"I know you like her. It's obvious."

It dawned on Teo that Seth didn't know about him and Jenna. Bleddyn clearly hadn't told him. A bird trilled a song in the trees, enhancing the silence between them.

"Tell me the truth, Teo."

"I met Jenna awhile back, and we had a couple of run-ins before the ball." Teo smiled at the memory. "At first I was suspicious, but then I got to know her. She's smart and pretty."

"I saw that at the ball. That was some dress."

The memory of that night warmed his chilled insides. After Teo placed his mug beside him, he rubbed his thighs with his palms. "Father's making me marry Tania Adams, the daughter of the governor of Falls District, as punishment for undermining his authority. He found out about Jenna and me. I don't know how."

"Eyes are always watching, Teo; you know that."

"Yeah." There was nothing else to say. He'd known, but he foolishly thought he'd get away with it.

Seth tapped the space between them. "I'm sorry you're being forced into a marriage you don't want."

"He told me he'd kill her if I didn't do what he said. Today, he sent me proof that he'll follow through on that threat."

"What kind of proof?"

"A lock of her hair." Teo flung the last of his coffee dregs on the ground.

"What?" Seth's eyes widened. "I can't believe he'd do that."

Teo studied his brother. "You can't? After all he's done, you can't fathom that? I know you have a better relationship with him than I do, and he wishes you were the heir."

"No—"

"He does." Teo held up a hand. "And he's right, you would make a great king, Seth. I wish I could trade places with you and make you the heir." Teo sighed. "But that's not going to happen. I'm the crown prince—my role is to do as I'm told. I know I've done the exact opposite the last couple of years, which wasn't smart. Bleddyn warned me, but I didn't listen. I'm all ears now though, and, if it will save Jenna, I'll marry this girl. I will turn cartwheels if the king asks me to if it keeps her alive."

"For what it's worth, you'll be a great king one day." Seth pulled his scarf tighter. "And, for the record, I don't want to be king."

Teo didn't blame him.

"I'm sorry you're getting the brunt of Dad's wrath. I tried to help you, but..." Seth studied his shoes, avoiding Teo's eyes. Teo was being punished but not Seth. Any blame for Seth's involvement would fall entirely on Teo's shoulders.

"Don't worry about it. You should be thankful you've escaped thus far. I am." Teo fiddled with his mug. "I have to come up with a plan to find Jenna. And keep Dr. Hood safe. I'm afraid Father will go after Hood once the drug is distributed."

"But he needs him."

"No, he doesn't. Once he gets a good supply, he can hand over the formula to ChemTech to manufacture the old-fashioned way."

Seth scrubbed his jaw. "What are you going to do? Are you seriously considering marrying Tania?"

"I don't have a choice if I want Jenna to live. But you can't be a part of this anymore. The last thing I want is for you to get in trouble. Uncle Alarick is in hiding and Bleddyn is dead. You're all I've got, and I can't lose you too." Which left Teo with zero allies.

Seth's silence confirmed Teo's opinion that there was nothing more to say. He stood and headed back to the palace, feeling more alone than he ever had before.

⚊⚊⚊⚊◆⚊⚊⚊⚊

Two hours. Teo had spent two hours studying the blueprints of the prisons below the castle, and he was no closer to finding Jenna. She had to be down there, but where? His father would want her close, so he could keep an eye on things.

Teo rubbed his tired eyes as Seth stooped over the papers. He hadn't listened to Teo's warnings to stay away. The noon chimes clanged, signalling the half hour before the shift change of the guards. Enough time to snoop around the prison without bringing attention to himself.

"Seth."

His brother roused himself from his study of the basement.

"I'm going to the prison cells." He tapped one of the blueprints. "Put them away. I've got what I need."

"Are you nuts? You can't go down there." Seth grabbed his arm.

"It's the shift change. It's always a bit chaotic. I'll slip in and check out who's being held there."

Seth pursed his lips but didn't say anything.

Teo nodded to the papers, trying to deflect his brother's attention. "What are you looking at?"

Seth frowned. "Something's off, but I can't put my finger on it. See this wall here? It doesn't fit the measurements."

"There are all kinds of secret passages in this castle." Teo checked the clock. "I need to go if I want to make it in time. Put those back in the library archives when you're done with them, okay? I don't want anyone to know we were snooping around."

Seth was already engrossed in the blueprints again. Teo stared at him a minute before jogging to his rooms and changing into his guard uniform, so he could blend into the chaos of men coming and going. The cells were several floors under the residence, and he descended the stairs quickly until, at sub-level two, he caught an elevator that would take him to the cells.

Most of the prisoners were held only temporarily—until they were transferred to one of the jails in the kingdom or sent to the executioner. King Duko was not in the habit of extending grace, so the job of executioner was a busy one.

After the metal doors slid open, Teo stepped out into the noisy foyer, along with two other men. Thankfully, they had been too engrossed in a conversation to even glance at him. Behind him, the doors whooshed closed, while rank body odor and urine assaulted Teo's nose. He stifled a cough, cursing his weakness in letting a little stink get to him. *Breathe through your mouth.*

The guard desk sat to the right, mobbed with both the incoming and outgoing shifts, as he'd hoped. The men were too busy swapping reports and pouring coffee to pay attention to him. He scooted to the left where the cell block was located. Part of him hoped she wasn't here, because this place was a real-life Hades. The other half hoped she was, because then he had a chance of freeing her from his father's clutches.

A large hulk of a guard lumbered toward him, too wrapped up in some papers to raise his head. Time to get the show on the road before anyone noticed Teo. He strode toward the cells, checking over his shoulder to see if he was being followed. He was alone as he started his search among the cells. Dampness clung to his skin as he peered into each one. Angry eyes or, worse, blank empty stares, met Teo's. Snarled threats were flung out from the dark, dank rooms. Others pleaded their innocence. Teo ignored them all as he walked down that aisle straight from hell. One prisoner rattled the bars so hard the floor shook beneath his feet. How did the guards work here? Never had he been so grateful he hadn't been assigned to prison duty. He'd take all the shifts at the FBC any day.

Teo scanned the last two cells. No Jenna. Disappointment competed with relief. He wouldn't wish this place on his worst enemy. *I'll find you, wherever you are.* He retreated, glancing at his watch as he hit the *Up* button next to the elevator. The five minutes he'd spent here seemed like an hour. The heavy door slid open, and Teo stepped inside, exhaling audibly. He hit the ground floor button and listened to the silence as he rode back up to civilization.

⟨◦⟩

It had been a week since he'd toured the prison, and Teo was no further along in his search for Jenna. She had vanished into thin air. In his spare time, he'd visited every abandoned hut, closet, and storefront in the city. He had risked asking casual questions to his commanding officer. Now, out of options and ideas, Teo was at a standstill. Wherever his father had stashed her, he'd made sure she was out of Teo's reach. If he snooped around anymore, Teo was fearful his father would hear of it and hurt Jenna. If Teo meddled, the king would no doubt keep his word to harm her or worse.

The sky was the colour of charcoal, bringing low his spirits. At least the weather was cooperating with his mood. He patrolled the worn path around his section of the wall, but no one was coming into the city or leaving it. The rain kept people indoors. Although why they needed to keep the Foresters out had begun to needle Teo, like an annoying gnat.

Several of the guards who'd been sick were back at work, Hood's drug helping them overcome the illness. If only Bleddyn... Teo pushed back thoughts of his brother. It wasn't his friends' or coworkers' fault that they'd gotten better and his brother hadn't.

Teo had checked in with Dr. Hood and Uncle Alarick a few days ago. They were hard at work manufacturing enough drugs for all the sick Wolves. Neither looked as though they'd slept in weeks. He knew Dr. Hood was as worried about Jenna as Teo was, but the pharmacist kept busy at his job. He didn't have much choice. Much like Teo.

Father will let her go after I marry Tania. I'll make sure he keeps his part of the deal. It was too late for him, but as long as Jenna was safe and alive, that was the priority now. Teo flexed his fingers as he checked the perimeters of the wall. A few Foresters hurried up the path to the gates. Yellow and red rain ponchos made a spot of brightness in the greyness. As long as everyone stayed calm, no one would die. He hoped.

Movement on the road leading into the city caught Teo's attention. Raising his binoculars, he squinted through the tiny holes. His fingers squeezed tightly, his knuckles whitening. *What are they doing here?*

A luxury sedan, the flags of the Falls District waving from the front of the vehicle, drove slowly towards the dignitaries' entrance to Wolf City. *It's weeks before their next scheduled visit.* The binoculars dropped to his chest after the car sped along the city streets towards the palace and disappeared from view.

"Officer Howell."

Teo saluted his fellow officer.

"The Commander has excused you from duty. The king has requested your presence at the palace immediately. I'm here to relieve you."

Cold perspiration trickled down his back. He hurried down the stairwell, leaving his things in the guard house, and stalked to the gates of the palace. It rose behind the black, wrought iron of the fence like a square, polished stone, shining despite the grey day. Turrets with walkways connecting them rose to meet the sky. It had been a favorite thing for him and his brothers to run those walkways, laughing at the thrill of seeming to be suspended in mid-air. Teo pressed a palm to his chest. The hurt of losing Bleddyn had not dimmed in the week since the funeral.

I don't think I'll be laughing today. He closed his eyes as his fingers gripped the wrought-iron posts. People rushed by, ignoring him, busy with their own plans and lives. If they did recognize him, they didn't say anything, for which he was extremely grateful.

"Prince Teowulf?"

Teo watched as a guard from the grounds approached him.

"Are you okay, your Royal Highness? Do you need help?"

Teo cleared his throat. "No, thank you. I was admiring the palace. Sorry, didn't mean to scare you."

"No problem, sir." The guard backed away.

Teo stood a few minutes more, desiring to delay whatever was coming for as long as he could. When he couldn't postpone it any longer, he trudged up to the family entrance. The heavy door clicked sharply as it shut behind him, reverberating through his body. A cloak of unease settled over him. Was it a sign that the door to his freedom was closing?

His father's butler materialized from nowhere. "Your Highness, if you'll follow me."

"Can I at least change out of my uniform?"

"The king requires your presence immediately." The butler led the way, and Teo practically had to jog to keep up. The air about the place was like a museum. He could smell the disinfectant, and the deathly quiet was enough to drive one to the brink of insanity. No maids cleaning or staff going about their business. *No Bleddyn.*

Teo spotted his father and mother drinking from tall flutes along with Governor Adams, Mrs. Adams, and Tania. The five of them were chatting like old friends. Teo hesitated.

"Teowulf, come in. Come in." The smile that graced his father's lips didn't reach his golden eyes. Instead, the smugness in them set off warning bells in Teo's head. "Good news, son. After a lengthy discussion with the governor and his wife, we have agreed to move the wedding date up. You and Tania will be married in a month's time. They are here to plan, and I expect you to cooperate fully." The innuendo behind his words was not lost on Teo.

He met his father's eyes and didn't blink. After a moment, Teo turned to his mother, who smiled at him. "What..." he forced his stiff lips to move, "... what good news that is indeed."

"We're having an engagement celebration tonight for you and Tania. A small affair, since it's such short notice. A few friends." His mother was a beautiful woman, and tonight her eyes gleamed with excitement. Her rosy cheeks, whether from the champagne or warmth of the room, added to her elegance. "Your suit is in your room, hanging in the closet. I had it pressed. All you have to do is get dressed." She squeezed his shoulder.

"Where's Seth?"

"Your brother is on an errand. He'll be back shortly." His father eyed him over the rim of his glass before taking a drink.

A servant appeared at his shoulder, offering a glass of champagne. Teo grabbed it, glad for something to keep his hands busy.

Governor Adams winked at Teo, which made him shudder. "You'll find, Prince Teowulf, that my daughter is a great helper and simple in her wishes. She doesn't require much attention at all." The governor patted his daughter's arm, and she blushed.

What kind of endorsement is that? Jenna would hate her father saying that about her, talking about her as if she was a pet. "If you don't mind, I'll go get cleaned up before dinner is ready." Teo couldn't make his legs go fast enough. He had to come up with a plan to wake up out of this nightmare.

Chapter Thirty-Eight

Rider

THE THUG, AS RIDER dubbed him, dropped the *Lupine Chronicle* on the bed where Rider sat with her legs crisscrossed, staring into space. If Duko wanted to torture or kill her from boredom, he was a genius because all Rider wanted was to stab herself in the eye. She guessed she'd been here for over a week, although the long hours blurred into one another, making it difficult to discern the passage of time.

The headline captured her attention: *Prince Teowulf and Tania Adams to Wed: True Love or A Political Alliance?*

She snatched up the newspaper. *What?* Rider scanned the article. The wedding was to take place in a month. The bride-to-be was the Falls District's governor's daughter. *There has to be a mistake.* The words, however, didn't miraculously morph into a different story as Rider reread the article. Further proof was a photo of Teo with a blonde girl in his arms, smiles gracing their beautiful faces. An engagement photo suggesting only true love was at the heart of these nuptials.

The thug's eyes bored into her as she smoothed out the paper. At the moment, she couldn't care less what he thought or what he might do. All she wanted was to make sense of the words in front of her. Moisture blurred her vision. She flipped the page, pretending to be engrossed in a different article. Why was he still here? He never stayed longer than a minute when he came to deliver food or water.

Finally, he cleared his throat. Rider turned another page, staring at black letters but not reading a single word. "A month, maybe less, and then you'll be free to go, as long as you stay out of trouble. Consider that a piece of advice and a warning." He turned on his heel and left the room.

That was it? She'd be free in four weeks? She flipped back to the front page of the newspaper. The pieces fell into place, as if solving a puzzle. Teo would be married by the time she got out of here. *The failed trade deal.* She was being kept out of the way so Teo would marry this girl. The king had found out about them. *He has spies everywhere. Stupid.* He'd set his own son up.

Rider bit her lip so hard it drew blood, but it didn't erase the pain in her broken heart. Her vision blurred. She threw the paper across the room. What a fool she'd been, convincing herself that she might have a chance with a prince. Even if Teo had feelings for her, Duko would never allow the two of them to be together. *Foresters don't mix with Wolves.* She slumped across the bed, covering her head with a pillow.

—◆—

Every day leading up to the royal nuptials, the guard "accidently" left a newspaper behind. Like an idiot, Rider lapped them up. Most of the coverage was of the upcoming royal wedding and the happy couple. Articles on Tania's obsession with horses and her desire to start a therapy horse camp filled one entire issue. Another reported on Teo's reformation from bad boy to good husband material. Rider snorted out loud at that one. Still others gave detailed accounts of the wedding cake and who was designing Tania's dress—some designer from Falls District. Most mornings, Rider could barely swallow the thick oatmeal her prison guard left along with the newspaper.

If the king was her kidnapper, he was brilliant because watching Teo's wedding play out to a girl he didn't love while Rider sat helplessly by was cruel and heinous punishment. He didn't love this Tania, right? Because Rider was pretty sure she and Teo had a connection—maybe he didn't love her, but they definitely had chemistry. The zings from his touch proved that. If she was honest, it was a connection she'd wanted to explore. But who was she kidding? He was Wolf royalty. The oatmeal scraped her throat like dry toast. Reaching for her water, Rider shoved away any seed of hope that she and Teo had any kind of future, even as friends.

The weeks leading up to the wedding both crawled and flew by. The time in the cell was long, but the closer the wedding day came, the quicker the hours seemed to fly. In the month Rider had been here, she hadn't been able to figure out where she was being held. Her captor hadn't given away any clues. The only thing she'd learned was that her cell opened into another hallway made of cinder blocks. Outside her window, she could see only sky.

The clicking of a key in the lock brought Rider's pacing to a standstill. The door swung open and she took a step back, stopping when she realized who it was. Seth entered her prison cell. Her eyes widened, and he put his finger to his lips as he crossed the room to her.

When he reached her, Seth grasped her arm, drawing her close. "We've been searching everywhere for you. I was studying the blueprints of the castle with Teo, and I noticed that a few things didn't line up. Like there were more square feet listed than what actually appeared to be there. I've been keeping an eye on the area for weeks but couldn't find any evidence this room existed until yesterday. Your guard uses a hidden entrance to get here. I managed to follow him."

Teo had looked at blueprints. "So Teo knows?"

"He knows you are being held but not where. I didn't say anything because it's safer for both of you if he doesn't know right now. And I wasn't sure my hunch was correct until I saw you."

"He's getting married."

"Father is forcing him. He's threatened your life if Teo doesn't go through with it." Seth's glance flicked between Rider and the door. "We don't have much time, so it's imperative that you listen to me, okay?"

"Okaay."

"Teo understands that Father will keep his word, so he is determined to marry this girl. To keep you safe. We need to stop this wedding. I have a plan, but it's risky."

"What's the plan?"

"The only way the king will let you out of here before the wedding is in a box." He locked eyes with her, but Rider didn't blink.

"So, we put you in a box and have it delivered to your father. Does he have a drug that will knock you out and make it appear as though you're dead?"

Rider's eyebrows hit her hairline. "You're insane. What if I don't wake in time and they bury me alive?" she hissed.

"I said it's a risk. Does your father have any kind of drug with that effect?"

She drew in a calming breath. "Yes, he doesn't keep anything like that on hand, but he could make up a potion. But how can you be sure the king will release my body before the wedding?"

"Believe it or not, my father is very superstitious. He thinks it's bad luck to keep dead bodies in the palace for more than a few hours. Which is why Wolves bury their dead quickly. Since you are Forester, he'll be doubly anxious to get rid of you."

Rider did the math. "I'd need the potion by tomorrow morning at the latest, which doesn't give you much time to get to my father."

"It's enough. Will you trust me?"

Rider studied the youngest Wolf prince. "Why are you doing this?"

"I only have one brother left, and I don't intend to lose him to the Falls District. Not to mention that, if something happened to Teo, I would become the heir, and I don't want to be king. Unfortunately, our father is being unreasonable, as usual. If anything happens to you, Teo will kill him." He studied her. "Besides, I've seen how Teo is around you. How his eyes light up when you're nearby. You bring out the good in him. So maybe we've been wrong about you... about Foresters." He buttoned his jacket. "You're the girl who helped me in the forest all those years ago, aren't you?"

Rider's eyes widened. "How did you remember?"

"I've never forgotten your kindness, although I didn't know it was you until recently. I put it together after the trade deal. That red hood of yours, it's distinctive." Seth moved to the door. "I gotta go. Be prepared to drink the potion when it arrives. It will be in a champagne glass with a note attached, *For the happy couple.* Father wants to rub it in that Teo is marrying another girl. He bragged about it to the guard when I was outside his office, which is how I found you. I followed the guard." He grasped the door handle. "I'll make sure that your body is sent to your father. Wait for instructions there. My time's up. Good luck."

He slipped out of the room, leaving Rider staring, stunned. Two thoughts rolled around in her head. Teo had been looking for her. And Seth was an ally. Inhaling deeply, Rider rolled her shoulders and let her mind drift to Seth's plan. *This will work. What could go wrong, right?* Her stomach clenched at the thought. *Everything.*

⚬

The flute of champagne was innocuous enough. Rider examined it, turning it around in her hand, bubbles floating to the surface. Attached to its delicate stem by a sheer gold ribbon was a thick tag made of elegant card stock. *To the happy couple,* was calligraphed on it in dark, rich, purple ink. She yanked the ribbon and the tag fell away. Clutching it in her fingers, she lifted the flute to her nose with her other hand, the bubbles from the champagne tickling it. Underlying the alcohol, Rider could smell the medicinal scent of the potion her father had made. She swirled the liquid in the glass. She trusted her dad, but she didn't trust the king. Would he bury her or do something other than send her body home to her father? Could Seth be trusted? The thought of being buried alive made her want to throw up.

The key turned in the lock. *It's now or never.* Rider knocked back the glass of champagne and then settled on the edge of her bed, waiting for the drug to work, the tag from the glass still clutched in her hand.

Chapter Thirty-Nine

Rider

CONSCIOUSNESS POKED AT RIDER until she forced her eyes open. Ugh. Her eyelids felt a hundred pounds as they closed again. Fighting the urge to sleep, Rider blinked. Still, blackness enveloped her. She fumbled around with her fingers until something sharp snagged her pinky. *Ouch.* She inhaled only to draw in a lungful of dust and the smell of pine. She coughed, but there was no fresh air. A tremor shook her body as she raised her hand until it hit a board only inches from her face. More slivers pierced her palm and fingers. *No.* They had delivered her body to her father. Where was she?

The blackness closed in and screams ripped from her throat, while her fists pounded the wood around her. When she had no voice left, she stopped, her hands lying at her sides. Her heart slowed as she listened to the silence. Despite all her pounding, the coffin hadn't moved. Had they *buried* her? A sob broke from her throat, but she stuffed her fist in her mouth. *Don't panic.* Where was her father or Seth? And what about Teo? She sucked in air. What day was it? Was Teo married? She had to get out of this box.

Perhaps Rider just needed to alert her father to where she was. Using all her might, she kicked her feet against the end of the coffin until her soles burned. Rider screamed and rammed her fists into the top of her coffin, stopping only when blood covered her knuckles. Surely someone was nearby. They had to hear her. *Unless I'm six feet under.* She couldn't breathe as panic blocked her airway. Tears burned her eyes. She was going to die or she was going to go mad. Did anyone know where she was? Were they coming for her? She kicked feebly at the top of the box. Why had she agreed to this stupid plan?

Chapter Forty

Teo

HIS WEDDING DAY—THE HAPPIEST day of his life. Except that it wasn't. Teo flung his arm over his eyes, tired of staring at the ceiling for the last couple of hours, the sheets tangled around his legs. *Jenna will be safe. Keep her safe.* Only that thought kept Teo moving forward, one foot in front of the other. If he was late to his wedding, she would be harmed. He heaved himself to sitting and studied the clock on his dresser. Five hours of freedom left—if you could call being a prisoner in your own home freedom. He'd acquired a *friend* who had followed him everywhere the last month. A not-too-subtle power play on the part of his father. Teo couldn't escape and neither could Jenna.

Today, she would be free to go home and live her life. Her rubbed his eyes. Would she be angry with him? It didn't matter—she'd be safe and that was what was important. He didn't care if he lived or died, but if she wasn't in the world, he didn't want to be either. Even if he couldn't be with her.

Seth entered his room. "Rise and shine." He slapped the foot of the mattress.

Teo scowled. "If it isn't my brother, the deserter. Where have you been the last couple of days?"

"I know you're upset, but I had a couple of urgent matters that needed attending to. I'm sorry I haven't been around."

"Urgent matters? What could be more pressing than a brother who needs support as he faces marrying a complete stranger?"

"Trust me, okay?" Seth pulled the sleeves of his suit jacket over his wrists.

Teo kicked the covers off and swung his legs over the side of the bed. "What are you up to?" Had Seth found a loophole?

"I can't say at the moment, but be ready to go on my signal."

"What signal?" Teo tugged on a pair of jeans and then grabbed a T-shirt off a chair and tugged it over his head.

"Follow my lead. You'll know it when it comes." Seth picked up a picture of the three brothers, running his fingers over the glass.

Teo took the frame from him. "Don't do anything stupid. I want out of this wedding, but not at the cost of Jenna's or your life, you got me?"

"Yeah, I've got you brother. Trust me."

"You keep saying that." But Seth was already gone. Teo opened the drawer that contained the box with Jenna's lock of hair, fingering the edges. *Stay safe.* A lightness spread through his body. Maybe today wouldn't be the worst day of his life.

— ◦ —

Teo stood in his black dress uniform, while his valet brushed at it with his hands. His shoes shone so brightly, Teo thought he might go blind from the glare. His hat and white gloves lay on the bureau. The clock struck one, causing Teo's heart to stutter. The lightness he'd felt earlier had been replaced by a simmering panic. Where was Seth? *I have one hour until I get married.*

He raised his hand to stop the brushing. "That's fine, Phillipe. I think we're good." When the man had departed, Teo parted the curtains, letting the sunshine into the room. Outside, the streets filled with crowds, hoping to catch a glimpse of the groom. Even as he searched the crowd for a red hood, he knew it was pointless. She wasn't out there. *Are you okay?*

Caterers carried loaded trays of delicacies into the kitchens. Yard workers raked one last time before the guests would arrive later that afternoon. Florists wheeled large, colourful bouquets of roses, lilies, and greens, into the palace—probably to the grand ballroom where the reception would be held later that evening. He turned his back on the scene, his stomach roiling. *I wish Bleddyn was here.* His father hadn't allowed for the family to grieve before announcing the wedding—citing the kingdom's need for an event to celebrate.

Moisture burned in the corner of Teo's eyes, and he swiped at it. Someone cleared her throat behind him. Turning, he gazed at his mother, elegant in her midnight-blue dress with matching coat, her hair swept into an up-do.

"Darling, you're so handsome." She glided into the room and grasped his hands in hers as she studied his face. If she noticed the remnants of tears, she ignored them. "I can't believe you're getting married." She squeezed his fingers before releasing them. "I know this isn't how you pictured this day, but it will all work out. It always does. She's a nice girl, and, in a couple of years, she'll be a great asset to you, Teowulf."

Did he want an asset or someone to love?

"You'll be fine." She locked eyes with him as if challenging him to disagree. Under the circumstances, Teo might have laughed. His mother could easily be a general in the Wolf Pack.

She sat on the edge of the bed. "You know, I had cold feet the day I married your father. We'd only known each other a short time, and I was afraid I wouldn't be enough for him, for Wolf kingdom. Our marriage was arranged by our parents." She smoothed the bedspread, avoiding Teo's gaze. He knew their marriage had been set up, but he'd never given it much thought. The king and queen got along and seemed to be happy. Had his mother had doubts? Had she felt like he did today?

She stared at her wedding ring. It was a simple band, which had always surprised Teo. The other rings she wore were gem-studded and loud. "Duko had been in love with another, before me."

What? This was news to Teo.

"I worried about comparisons to her, but finally I told myself to keep putting one foot in front of the other. I could never be her—I could only be myself. And here we are." She clasped her hands in her lap. "An arranged marriage is not the end of the world. It can work out to be a very satisfying relationship." She nodded as though trying to convince herself. Teo rubbed a medal between his fingers as he considered her words. His father had been interested in someone else? And he was still making Teo marry Tania?

The queen stood. "It's all going to work out."

A lump rose in Teo's throat. His mother always supported the king, but a part of Teo had hoped she'd side with him on this. He kissed her cheek. "Thanks, Mom." He had no idea what else to say.

"The car will be around in fifteen minutes. I'll see you downstairs."

"Do you know where Seth is?"

She checked her reflection in the mirror before striding to the door. "No. I'm surprised he's not here with you. Maybe he's still dressing. Did you check his rooms?"

"I didn't, but I'll try there."

"Don't be late." She disappeared into the hallway, leaving him alone.

Teo's watch chimed an alarm. He had ten minutes until the car came and forty minutes left before his freedom ended. He grabbed his overcoat and went to find his brother.

Chapter Forty-One

Rider

T HUMP. THUMP. THUMP. RIDER struggled to open her eyes, and to breathe. The banging, along with the sound of muffled voices, roused her from the suffocating darkness. Clang. Clang. Clang. Her dad needed to stop banging the pots around. It sounded like he was right over her. Her eyes opened wide as reality flooded her foggy brain. Not her dad banging pots—a fist banging on her new prison. *Someone is out there.* Hope leapt from her stomach to her throat and she jolted up, clunking her head on the roof of her prison. Argh. Rubbing it, she whispered, "Please. Please. Please".

Rider kicked hard against the box, while yelling as loud as her raspy voice would allow. She pounded with her fists, the wounds from her earlier attempts stinging.

"Over here," someone yelled.

Scraping. A shovel? *Please be a shovel.* The coffin jerked, and she braced her hands along the sides of the box. A chill went through her. Who had found her? Had the Wolf Pack returned to finish the job? Her chest constricted. No. *Don't even think that.*

"Rider. Can you hear me?"

"Dad." She wasn't certain he'd heard her, so she banged the board above her again. Her prison bumped against something—the ground, maybe?—making Rider slightly nauseated. Suddenly all was still until a loud screech filled the air and then light flooded her space. Nearly blinded, Rider flung an arm across her eyes. Large hands grasped her, lifting her into the fresh air and freedom. Strong arms enveloped her as she breathed in the scent of her dad.

"You're safe." He squeezed her tighter as the tears flowed from both their eyes.

<hr>

Rider wrapped her hands around the mug, not only for its warmth but to steady her shaking fingers. The soft cushions of the couch cradled her sore body. But nothing could take away the pain in her chest. It was Teo's wedding day. Seth had said he had a plan, but she didn't know what it was. What if Seth was too late to save Teo from this marriage? What if...? She shoved the unwanted thoughts away. There was nothing for her to do. She couldn't very well walk into the church and stop the wedding herself. Could she?

She glanced around her living room, glad to be in a spacious place after a month of confinement in her cell and then the claustrophobia of the coffin. After the rescue, her father had brought her back to their house because he felt she needed the familiar comfort of it. Which she did. She gulped another swig of the robust tea."

"Rest." He sipped from his own mug, appearing to need to take his own advice. He looked older than Rider remembered with dark smudges under his eyes and more lines around his mouth. "The wedding isn't for another hour. There's time for Seth to stop it. We just need to be patient until we hear from Alarick."

After digging Rider out of her grave, Teo's uncle had rushed off to meet with Seth at a pre-arranged spot near the border of the forest to discuss their next moves. Would they be able to prevent the ceremony from happening?

Rider set her cup on the coffee table, drawing her knees to her chest. Things hadn't gone according to Seth's plan. Her father had filled her in once they arrived here.

Once the drugs had taken effect, Seth had originally ordered her body to be released into her father's hands. However, the king vetoed that and said to dump the body in the forest near a ravine, not far from the border. Seth had sent word to Dr. Hood where her body was going to be dumped, except that the king's thugs had decided to bury Rider instead. When her dad and Alarick had arrived at the appointed place and found it empty, her father lost his mind. They searched the area and then, not knowing what else to do, they hid in the shrubs in case the king's men were only late bringing the coffin. Muffled banging and muted screams alerted them to Rider's location, and her father had run back to their house for a shovel. It had taken a bit of time, but they'd found her, alive. A shiver ran over her scalp, and she covered her lap with a soft blanket.

Her dad tucked it in around her. "You okay?" He smoothed her hair with his large hand.

"I'm okay, although I'm not planning to go into a cave or other tight places anytime soon." Her attempt at humor landed flat.

He pulled her close. "We got to you in time. That's what counts."

"Does Teo know anything?"

"I don't think so. We'll find out more when Alarick returns." He nudged Rider's mug in her direction. "Drink. It'll help flush the drug through your system. How do you feel?"

"Not bad." She drank the rest of the liquid. The knot in her stomach pulled tighter as the minutes passed and Alarick didn't return. Images of Teo walking down the aisle with his new bride taunted her.

"I know it's hard, but trust Seth. He'll do everything in his power to help Teo. Everything will work out." He stood. "I'll make you oatmeal. You need to get something into your stomach." He went into the kitchen, and Rider could hear cupboards opening and closing

She breathed deeply, her dad's familiar noises soothing her. She'd never believed Duko would honor his word, so she'd doubted she would ever hear those noises again. She was only hearing them now because, as far as the king knew, she was dead. She shuddered at all the *what ifs*.

Alarick burst into the small house, the door banging against the wall. He was weighted down by several bags. After dropping them at his feet, he smiled at Rider. "It's good to see you have more colour. How are you feeling?"

"Better."

"That's good because it's time to get into position."

"Position for what?" Her father asked as he joined them in the living room.

"To stop a wedding." He thrust the bag at her. "Wedding clothes. First, get dressed and then we'll head out."

Rider's mind jumped to thoughts of rescuing Teo. Blood pounded through her veins. For the first time in over a month, Rider felt the cloud that had been hanging over her head lift. As she reached for the bag, the room swayed. Or maybe it was her. Her father grabbed her arm, leading her back to the couch.

"First you need to get your strength back." He scowled at Alarick. "We've got a bit of time."

He set a bowl of steaming oatmeal in front of her. "Eat.." Her dad grinned. "And then we have a wedding to crash."

⸺◈⸺

The old cathedral was a work of art in both architecture and the craftsmanship of the stained-glass windows. The multi-colored light streaming through them hid the worn wood of the pews, shiny from many hands sliding across them over the years. The room smelled like lemon oil and flowers. The front of the chapel was decorated with large bouquets of pink roses and white carnations, done up in large royal purple ribbons and sitting in silver vases. Thankfully, this was not the same cathedral where Bleddyn's funeral had been held.

As the crowd swelled inside the church, Rider ducked her head, pretending to study the invitation addressed to *Lady Jane Dolphus*, which had been her ticket inside the chapel. She didn't know how Seth had arranged it, but here she sat, an invited guest to Teo's wedding. It was all surreal.

Her dress, pale pink with a matching overcoat and high heels, made her feel grown-up, although she had misgivings about the heels. *I hope I don't need to run.* She ran her hand over the sleek auburn wig that covered her dark curls. The black-rimmed glasses completed the disguise. It had worked for Teo...

Her father sat beside her in a gray suit, sporting a blond wig that flopped over his eyes. Rider bit her lip, but it didn't keep her laughter in. "You look ridiculous."

He waggled his eyebrows, making her snicker again. She grasped his hand and gave it a squeeze. *I'm not sure what I'd do if I had a father like Duko.*

A young man appeared at the end of their pew. "The flowers are ready." Since no one else was sitting with them, that had to be their cue. He disappeared down the aisle.

"Show time," she whispered. Glad they had sat in one of the very back rows, Rider and her father casually stood, strolled to the foyer, and then descended the stairs to the floor below. Seth had been precise with his directions, and a long corridor led them to the door at the end that he had told them about. Rider checked to make sure no members of the family were coming to check on the groom. Seth had said he'd provide a distraction to keep them away, and it looked like he'd kept his word. She clasped her trembling hands. If all went right, Teo was on the other side of the door.

Knock, wait, knock-knock, wait, knock. Her father stepped back from the door.

Seth opened the door slowly, just far enough to shoot out a hand and drag them into the room. Rider stumbled as she spotted Teo standing there in his dress uniform. He appeared tall, handsome, and very princely. Ice-blue eyes locked with hers, widening as Teo appeared to recognize her.

"Jenna?" Obviously the glasses didn't work for her.

Rider couldn't stop her lips from curving up. "How can you tell it's me?" A laugh bubbled up from her chest, feeling like light and warmth.

Teo closed the space between them and engulfed her in his strong arms. "I'd know those green eyes anywhere," he whispered against her ear. Her arms circled his waist as she breathed in the smell of his soap and sandalwood. She didn't ever want to let him go.

Chapter Forty-Two

Teo

THE SOUND OF VOICES outside Teo's dressing room instantly made his stomach clench. He did not want to talk to his father or mother. The smug look that would surely be on his father's face might make him do something he'd regret, and Teo had come this far without upsetting the boat. Instead, Seth dragged two people into his dressing room who were decidedly not his parents. His brows furrowed. What was going on?

A man with a very bad, and very obvious, wig, along with a young, auburn-haired woman, stumbled into the room. Something about them... Emerald eyes met his, and his heart stopped, then revved to life, blood roaring through his veins. "Jenna?"

"How can you tell it's me?" she laughed.

The sound warmed his heart. Ignoring Dr. Hood, he embraced Jenna, whispering against her ear, "I'd know those green eyes anywhere." He kissed the top of her head and ran his hands along her arms, assuring himself that she was indeed real. That she was here. Worry that had dogged him for the last month eased as honeysuckle filled his nostrils, the best scent he'd ever smelled. He tightened his hold, daring her closer, and she leaned back, searching his face. He cupped her chin, doing his own once-over. "Are you okay? They didn't hurt you, did they?" His eyes travelled over her body. "*How* are you here?"

Before Jenna could say a word, Seth, who'd been rooting around under the vanity said, "I hate to rush you, but I'll explain later. You need to put this on and get out of here. Now." He pulled out a bag and unzipped it. After yanking out a pair of coveralls and a wig, he straightened and held them out to Teo.

He reluctantly released Jenna to take the clothing Seth offered. After shaking out the coveralls, Teo pulled them on, buttoning them over his uniform. The wig covered his short hair.

"Follow Dr. Hood and Jenna. You're dressed as one of the workers here today. I'll contact you when I can." Seth grabbed his brother by the shoulders and hugged him. "Be careful."

Teo smacked his brother on the back a couple of times. "Thank you." He stepped back. "Seth, if father finds out you were behind—"

"He won't." Seth shoved him towards the exit. "But if he does, it won't matter. I'm not his lackey. I'm your brother and I've got your back." He grinned. "Consider it a wedding present." He pointed to the hall. "There's a big vase of flowers outside, carry it in front of you until you get to the exit. Good luck." His younger brother hurried out the door.

Dr. Hood cautiously stepped out of the room, drawing Jenna with him. Teo followed. Once in the hallway, he picked up the large monstrosity of a floral arrangement, which hid his face nicely. They hurried to a side hall, where an exit sign pointed the way out. Dr. Hood opened it, the sunshine illuminating them for a moment. Teo set the flowers beside the exit before following them into what looked like a service parking lot to the church.

Jenna nodded to a white van parked a hundred metres away. "That's our ride."

The desire to grab her hand and run to the vehicle overwhelmed Teo, but that would look too suspicious. Instead, he stuck like glue to her side. The hundred metres might as well have been a thousand. As they reached the van, someone flung open the side panel. The three of them flung themselves into the vehicle. Teo did a double-take at the driver as he backed out of the parking spot before Dr. Hood even had the door closed.

"Uncle Alarick," A lump grew in Teo's throat at the sight of him. *I didn't think I'd see you again.*

"Teo." Uncle Alarick's eyes sought him out in the rearview mirror before shifting to Dr. Hood, who'd maneuvered himself into the front passenger seat. "Did everything go according to plan?"

"Yes, a little too smoothly. It makes me uneasy."

Teo surveyed the occupants of the van, chuckling. His shoulders eased as the knot in his stomach unfurled. "You've become bandits, have you? Going against the king?"

"Couldn't have you marrying that girl, Teo. She wasn't right for you." Alarick's gaze flicked between him and Jenna.

"Thank you. I'm confused, though." Teo turned to Jenna, who sat beside him. "How did they find you? I've spent weeks going over this kingdom with a fine-tooth comb."

She wrenched off her wig and ran her hand through her long hair, loosening it from the bun that had tied it back. Her long locks swirled around her like a ribbon, mesmerizing Teo.

"Seth found me a couple of days ago, had an outrageous plan that miraculously worked... with a few hiccups."

They filled him in on the details of the secret holding cell that Seth had discovered from the blueprints. Teo shook his head; his brother hadn't said a word to him about it. The story of the potion that had made Jenna appear dead chilled his blood. Intense looks between the other three in the vehicle didn't go unnoticed by Teo. Obviously they weren't telling him everything, but at the moment he let it go. She was here and alive. And he wasn't walking down the aisle to a stranger he didn't love. That was what mattered right now.

"And my father knows nothing?" Teo could hardly believe it. It seemed too good to be true.

"With Jenna dead"—Dr. Hood finger quoted the word—"he seemed to let down his guard. Although he'll know by now that something is amiss, since you've stood your bride up."

Teo fisted his hands. He didn't want to think about any of that.

Jenna reached over and entwined her fingers with his. He gazed hungrily at every inch of her lovely face. He wanted to kiss her. Instead, he winked. Her neck and cheeks turned a pretty shade of pink. He liked that he could make her react that way.

"So, what's the plan now?" Teo forced himself to turn back to the front of the van, to his uncle and Dr. Hood.

Rider's father shifted a little on the seat to look back at him. "We're driving to the other end of the forest, to an old hideout where Jenna-girl used to play as a kid. It's off the map, so we should be safe there until the uproar dies down."

Is he trying to reassure us or himself?

"And Seth?" Every worst-case scenario flew through Teo's brain.

"Seth has an alibi for whenever he needs one." His uncle steered the van around a corner.

Teo raised an eyebrow. "What does that mean?"

"Remember Lady Gwen, from Greystoke county?"

A slow smile spread over his face. "I do indeed. I also remember she was quite infatuated with him."

"Exactly. She was more than willing to provide Seth an alibi as long as she was recompensed in return. I think a lovely dinner or a night at the club would fit the bill nicely."

Teo snorted before the seriousness of the situation took over. "Will Father buy it?"

"I think so. Your father will be so desperate to make sure Seth is innocent in all this that he'll believe the lie. At least, that's what I'm betting on." Alarick cleared his throat. "I'm hoping Duko will see reason eventually, although there's a chance he won't. You'll be exiled from Wolf kingdom. If you have any doubts about giving up the throne, we can turn around and take you back."

Teo rubbed his hand across his chin. His father would never forgive him for this. A squeeze of his fingers drew him back to the moment. Rider's eyes searched his, and a warmth filled his chest. He rubbed at the spot.

"No, I don't want to go back. I don't want to live under the rule of hate and vengeance any more. Things have to change. And my future is here, in this van." He leaned over and kissed Jenna softly on the cheek.

Chapter Forty-Three

Rider

THE HIDEOUT WAS MORE cave than house, carved into the side of a hill on the far side of the forest near the borders of Falls District. It had belonged to an elderly man, but he had passed away when Rider was a child. Her father had treated the man for a skin infection and had brought Rider along. After the man died in his bed, Rider and Ethan had played here, but never came inside because of rumours of it being haunted. She rubbed away the chill on her arms. Since then, the place had become overgrown, and no one she knew ever visited.

Its entrance was hidden by a mass of overgrown vines and branches. Her father swung a machete he'd fetched from an old shed behind the house, hacking away at branches while Teo and his uncle hauled away the cuttings. The outline of a rectangle materialized in the side of the hill.

Once all the branches had been removed, her dad tried the knob. It opened easily, and they entered a great room with a large fireplace off to the side. Rider supposed there was an opening in the roof for the smoke to go through. Surprisingly, the space was quite cozy—crude homemade furniture was set around the fireplace, and a large oak table filled up the middle of the room. Two doors led to what Rider imagined were bedrooms. There was no bathroom or running water.

"There's an outhouse and a water pump. It's roughing it, but we'll be safe. I'm sorry it's not what you're used to, Prince Teowulf." Her father's complexion turned ruddy.

Teo held up his hand. "No, it's fine. Thank you. Please call me Teo. I'm quite sure I will have been stripped of any other titles by now." Briefly, a pained look crossed his face. "Thank you, all of you, for risking everything for me." He glanced at Jenna.

"We knew what we were getting into." Her dad knelt by the fireplace and rummaged in the kindling box.

Alarick searched in his bag, pulling out paper, books, and socks. "That reminds me, I have a radio in here. I hope we can listen to the news." He extracted a small black box from his sack. Setting it on the table, he fumbled around with the dials and a pair of antenna ears.

The sound of static filled the space as Alarick continued to turn the dials. "...the Crown Prince, Teowulf, failed to show up for his own wedding." The crunching of the airwaves took over until Alarick found the frequency again. "The king will be issuing a statement shortly. Let's go to our reporter covering the wedding, or lack thereof." The newscaster laughed at his own joke. "Sheila Snarl, standing by at the palace. Sheila."

Teo's face paled, and Alarick lowered the volume. Rider went over to him and laid her hand on his forearm. Dirt smudged his face where the branches had brushed against it, and the coveralls he wore pulled against his dress uniform. The last thing he looked like was royalty. She knew enough about Teo by now to know that appearances didn't matter to him like they did the king. "We'll figure it out, all of us together. You're not alone."

"Yeah." Teo undid a couple of buttons on his coveralls. Clearly, he didn't believe her. Did he regret coming here?

"King Duko is now approaching the podium," the news reporter stated.

Alarick shot a look at Teo. When he nodded, Alarick turned up the volume.

"He's going to be making a statement. Stand by." The reporter's voice faded, as the sound of rustling paper filled the airwaves.

"Good evening, my loyal subjects. It is with a heavy heart that I come to you tonight. Prince Teowulf, the crown prince of Wolf kingdom, has abdicated his inheritance of the throne by failing to show up for his own wedding. He has been stripped of his title of Crown Prince as well as HRH. He is a fugitive of Wolf kingdom for acts of treason against the throne. If anyone sees him, or discovers his whereabouts, they will be greatly compensated for his capture."

Rider winced at the king's cold tone.

Alarick came over to Teo's other side, slinging his arm over his shoulder.

"Prince Seth of Wolf kingdom is now the crown prince. Losing two sons over the last month has been challenging, and I am asking for privacy as we grieve these two losses. Thank you."

Her father turned off the radio.

Teo's brow furrowed. "What about Seth? Will he be forced to marry Tania?"

Alarick shook his head. "No. If one thing is true about your father, it's that appearances matter. Interchanging Seth for you sends the wrong message, which Duko can't afford right now. It'll be a while before anything is decided or a wedding takes place. He's not a fool. This buys us time to figure out a plan."

"What about the trade deal? That's why the wedding was happening—to make it up to Falls District and Governor Adams."

Alarick rubbed his newly grown beard. "It's a mess, that's for sure. The king will be licking his wounds, but I'm certain he'll figure out a way to come out smelling like roses. Probably the Falls District will be able to ask for just about anything and they'll get it."

Rider's dad clapped his hands together, as though attempting to pull them all out from under the cloud of melancholy that had descended on the room. "I'm bushed and starving. Let's eat and rest. It's been a long day." He unwrapped a round loaf of bread, a wedge of cheese, and dried meat from a backpack he'd been carrying and set it on the table. The strong aromas made Rider's mouth water. She hadn't eaten since that bowl of oatmeal this morning. They gathered around the makeshift meal, Wolves and Foresters, together. Teo smiled at her across the table, and her heart stuttered. Alarick cut slices of cheese, stopping to glance at his nephew, as if to check Teo was really sitting with them. Her dad passed her a piece of bread and winked. Rider savoured every bite of the simple meal, grateful they were alive, and together.

Stir crazy didn't begin to describe how Rider was feeling as they waited for news in this hole in the side of a hill. They had only been here twenty-four hours, yet it felt like a lifetime. No word had come from Seth.

She grabbed a hoodie and tugged it on. Her father napped on the couch, while Alarick wrote in a notebook at the table. Teo, next to him, was reading through a pile of papers.

"I need air," she said to no one in particular.

Alarick laid his pen down. "Don't go far, Jenna."

"I won't." She slipped out. The setting sun cast pink shadows over the forest, one last show before it went to bed. She threw her head back, breathing in the cool night air. The crescent moon had risen bright in the night sky. A hinge creaked and Teo came alongside her. "I love this time of day. It's so peaceful and beautiful."

"Yeah, it is," he whispered.

"Are you okay?" she asked, not sure what else to say. He had given up not only his family but his future for many reasons, one of them being her.

One shoulder lifted. "Yes and no. I'm relieved I'm not married." He grabbed hold of her hand, twining their fingers together.

Rider stared at their joined hands, enjoying the warmth and tingles running up her arm.

"Is this okay?" He lifted their hands slightly.

She smiled.

"Good." He tilted his head back to see the night sky. "I'm concerned for my mom and Seth. Duko is a ticking time bomb, and, if he goes off, I'm not sure what he's capable of. I mean, look at what he did to Bleddyn." His voice cracked.

She leaned into him, resting her head against his arm. He'd never called the king by his given name before. If her dad behaved like Duko, she was sure she wouldn't want to call him Dad either. And Rider didn't doubt his words about Duko exploding. "I'm so sorry. I feel like it's partly my fault."

Teo dropped her hand before sliding an arm around her shoulders and pulling her close in a side hug. "None of this is your fault. We've all made choices we knew would have consequences. I'm not sorry we did everything we could to try and save Bleddyn. Or rescue your father."

He tugged her to him and wrapped his other arm around her waist, settling his chin on her head. A sense of safety and peace cocooned her. They stayed that way for several minutes. Then his hand slid up her arm and cupped her head, his breath caressing her cheek. Her heartbeat kicked up as his lips softly brushed hers, leaving her wanting more. He ran his thumb over her bottom lip, making Rider's knees weaken. If he wasn't holding her so tightly, she'd probably drop to the ground.

"I have no regrets." His voice was low and husky.

"You're sure?"

A twig snapped in the wooded area nearby, and they both jumped. As they peered into the dark, Teo's arms tightened around her waist. A fox darted out of the woods, and a low chuckle escaped Rider. Teo's hold relaxed, although he didn't let go of her.

"We should go back inside." He nudged her toward the building while continuing to glance behind them. The hairs on her neck rose. Teo was probably a bit paranoid, but the blackness creeped her out now. After she hurried inside, Teo closed the door and locked it, blocking out the dark night.

Rider fidgeted with the strings of her hoodie as she stared at the door. *No one's out there, right?*

Chapter Forty-Four

Teo

I T WAS ONLY A matter of time before his father found them. Last night had reinforced his fears, overshadowing that amazing kiss with Jenna. He wanted to sit and replay it, but images of his father and the Wolf Pack storming into their cave kept his mind otherwise engaged. Maybe the fox had made the noise. This time. Still, his father wouldn't stop searching until he had them in custody. *Where is Seth? Why hasn't he contacted us yet?* The only thing keeping him sane was Jenna. Her bright green eyes and smile reminded him this was worth the fight. He had to keep her safe.

Teo picked up a small rock and threw it into the woods. He stood on the edge of the forested area not far from the cave house. The wind whistled through the bare tree branches. He tugged the zipper of his jacket farther up as he listened. There it was again. His stomach turned over as he backed up to the door, his eyes scanning the area. It was empty, but it wouldn't be for long. Faintly, the sound of marching footsteps echoed in the woods. The forest had amazing acoustics. Wolf Pack. And they were headed straight for them. He'd know that sound anywhere.

Stumbling into the dwelling, Teo shouted, "They've found us. Wolf Pack. Dr. Hood, take Jenna and my uncle and get them out of here. Now." Why was no one moving? Teo grabbed his uncle's arm, dragging him towards the door.

"Hurry before they get a visual. There's only one way out." The roar grew in Teo's ears. His heart rammed against his rib cage. He lunged for

Jenna, grabbing her forearms. "My father will kill you and your father if they find you. They're after me, but if you stay you'll be taken too." He couldn't let that happen.

Jenna's face was pale. "Teo, they'll kill you. Your father said..."

Alarick rapped his knuckles on the doorframe, getting everyone's attention. "Let's calm down, everyone. Did you see them, Teo?"

"I heard them. We've got minutes at best."

Dr. Hood folded the papers he'd been reading and shoved them into his backpack. "How did they find us? The only people who knew about this place were the four of us and Seth. Would your brother betray you?"

Teo vigorously shook his head. "No way. Why would he go to all that trouble to stop the wedding, only to give us up now?" At one time maybe Teo had doubted his brother, but he trusted Seth. He'd proven his loyalty.

Alarick grabbed his coat and shrugged it on.

Teo swallowed the urge to yell. "There's no time to debate. We've got to go."

Dr. Hood shook his head as he peered out the door. "It's too late. They're already here." The sound of marching steps filled the silence.

Teo stepped in front of Jenna, trying to protect her from what was coming. *No. No. No.*

Uncle Alarick stood behind Dr. Hood. "Seth's with them."

Wait. What? Teo shoved himself in front of Dr. Hood so he could see over his uncle's shoulder. "I don't understand."

"He's leading the way," whispered his uncle.

"Uncle Alarick, you stay here with the Hoods. Let me go out." He grabbed his uncle's shoulder from behind, ready to push him out of the way.

Rider, who stood beside her father, said, "No. It might be a trap."

"They can't find any of you."

The sound of marching approached the door. Uncle Alarick turned to him. "I'll go with you. Peacefully. I don't think it's a trap."

"I can't let anything happen to you too." Teo's voice filled with desperation.

"Seth isn't going to let anything happen to either of us. Come." Alarick stepped outside. After a pause, Teo slipped out after him. Seth stood in front of twenty guards. *No weapons raised, that's good.* Teo warily eyed his youngest sibling.

"Teowulf... brother." Seth's voice softened. "Your presence is required at the palace immediately. We're to escort you."

"Why? The king has renounced me as heir and son."

Seth stared at his shiny boots before glancing up at his brother. "The king is sick with the Lupine flu. He's refused medication. His pride won't let him admit he's wrong." His brother's voice broke on the last word. "The queen has granted you a full pardon and has requested that you come."

"What about Uncle?"

Seth's fingers curled around his belt. "The pardon is for you only, although no harm will come to Uncle Alarick or the Hoods, provided they stay out of the city. For now. That may change with a switch in leadership." Seth's stare lasered into him. "Mother has granted a full reinstatement of your titles, Crown Prince."

Teo's stomach dropped. If the king died, Teo would take the throne. *No, no, no.* He wasn't ready to be king and he certainly wasn't about to go to the city without his uncle. Teo opened his mouth to object, but Alarick grasped his wrist and spoke before he could.

"Teo, go to your father. I'll make sure the Hoods are safe. You need to do this, or you'll regret it."

Teo clenched his teeth. "Wolves don't leave Wolves alone. We stick together."

"You aren't leaving me alone. I have a job to do— protecting the Hoods. And you have a job, too. You can do this, Teo. I believe in you. Go. Make peace with your father, and then be who you were created to be." Tears filled Alarick's eyes as he released Teo. "We'll wait to hear from you."

Teo looked over his uncle's shoulder at Jenna, framed in the doorway. She nodded as though she agreed with Alarick's words. Their eyes locked, and in those green eyes he read acceptance, belief, and maybe... more. He hoped it wasn't his imagination.

"I'll go with you, Seth, as long as I have your word they will stay safe."

"You have the queen's word, as well as my own." He motioned for Teo to walk beside him. "Keep quiet and walk."

Teo cast one last glance at his uncle and the cabin before marching beside his brother, the Wolf Pack falling into formation behind them.

<hr>

At the gates, all but four of the Wolf Pack broke away, resuming their duties. The small group followed the back path to the palace to avoid curious eyes, but the city was quiet. *It's a ghost town.*

"Where is everyone?"

"The doctors requested a curfew to keep the sick home. There are a few pockets of outbreaks, and they want them eradicated. Mother agreed."

At the palace, the brothers made their way to the family set of suites. His mother sat slumped against her desk chair, but she straightened as they entered. Teo studied the carpet, afraid to read what was on her face.

"Teo." The long, slender arms that had held him when he scraped his knee or had nightmares as a child wrapped around him now. The heavy weight on his chest lightened. The lump in his throat grew, but Teo forced a shaky breath through. She squeezed him before cupping his cheek in her hand, examining his face.

"You're well?"

He nodded.

She gestured for Seth to come close before reaching for each of their hands and holding them in hers.

"Your father... doesn't have much time. I'll take you to him, but I doubt he'll regain consciousness."

"Did he say anything?" *That he loves me?*

Her smooth fingers rubbed his. "No, I'm sorry, Teo. He a stubborn man, and he's going to his grave because of it. You are not him and you never will be. He's wrong about so many things, one of them being you. You will make a great king. I believe in you, son."

Teo bit the inside of his cheek. While he appreciated his mother's words, a part of him grieved that he would never earn his dad's love. *Why am I surprised? I am dead to him.*

Teo sat on the rock in the courtyard outside the palace. He pressed the heels of his palms into his eyes, trying to erase the image of his sick father. The pale, waxy skin was a death mask. The blood stains around his nose and mouth had turned Teo's stomach sour. No matter how long he lived, Teo would never understand the man. He cradled his head in his hands. He'd made it to the palace in time to see his father, but now the king was dead. His heart pounded against his ribcage and he rubbed his chest.

"Teo."

He sensed Seth's presence behind him, but he didn't turn around. The sinking feeling in the pit of his stomach pooled. "What is it?"

"Mother wants you in her study."

Teo closed his eyes for a minute, his shoulders drooping. He knew what was coming. He'd been prepared for it his entire life. He stood, his shoulders back and his head high. The king was dead. The new ruler had been summoned. Not his mother. Not Seth. But Teowulf, the crown prince of Wolf kingdom, who was about to become king.

Chapter Forty-Five

Teo

ONE MONTH LATER

TEO STOOD ON THE front steps of the palace, his mother on his left and Seth on the right. Dr. Hood stood beside Seth. The mic squawked. Teo cringed but kept his smile in place. *I'm not my father.* The sound guy gave him a thumbs up, and Teo stepped to the mic.

"Good morning, and thank you for coming out for this important announcement. We have endured a crisis, although we wouldn't have a victory today without Hood Medicine. My father put his faith in ChemTech, but I have witnessed Dr. Hood's integrity and his intelligence with plants and their amazing healing abilities. We beat the Lupine flu due to his medicine, not ChemTech's." Teo paused and searched the crowd. There. A blood-red dress coat a few rows in. A sense of déjà vu engulfed him. This time he wouldn't let her get away.

"It is with much gratitude that I hand over the job of Chief Medical Officer to Dr. Hood, as well as the responsibility for all production of medicine for Wolf kingdom. He is a trustworthy ally and friend." He picked up the medal lying on the podium. "Today it is my honour and privilege to award Dr. Hood with the Timber Medal of Honour for his role in saving many lives from the Lupine flu." Teo had a big job in making repairs with Wolf City's relationship with the Falls District, but that was a worry for another day.

Teo left the podium and strode over to Dr. Hood. He shook the doctor's hand before hanging a medal around his neck. Flashes went off around them, and a cheer went up from the crowd. His chest warmed as his people, *his people*, showed their gratitude to Dr. Hood, a Forester. Maybe there was hope for change after all. The podium party posed for another photo, but Teo's eyes were trained on Jenna. Her dark hair was swept up, revealing an elegant neck. Her red dress coat hugged her in all the right places. Their eyes locked and she smiled. Man, he could get used to this. He'd asked her to be on the podium, too, but she'd declined, stating that her father deserved the glory. He'd find another way to show her the honour she deserved. *When I can find free time.* His brow furrowed a little. A king's time was not his own. Every minute was scheduled from the time he awoke until he went to bed. He'd had to squeeze in an early morning meeting with the Hoods to tell them about today. That was all he'd been able to manage, and it wasn't nearly long enough to suit him.

His eyes swept the crowd as flashes went off. Standing in the same row but several paces away were two officials from his father's court. Their frowns and crossed arms told Teo all he needed to know. Not everyone was happy with the few changes he'd made already as king. Dr. Hood's promotion hadn't gone over well at the King's Council meeting. But Seth and Uncle Alarick, as well as Dr. Lupine, had stood by Teo, who had been adamant and pushed it through. It had been a busy month.

His gaze returned to Jenna. He didn't want those officials anywhere near her. A little of the tension eased from his shoulders. Maybe it was a good thing she'd wanted no part of the ceremony today. She was part of the story of the success of the cure, but people had seen them together at the masquerade ball, which might raise questions that Teo didn't want to answer. His desire was for the Wolf clan to respect the Forest clan and, eventually, to see them as equals. That particular journey was going to be long and bumpy. It complicated matters that their king was interested in a Forester because Teo wasn't sure his people would accept that. At least right now. He'd been more than relieved when Jenna didn't want to be seen in the spotlight. What did that say about him? Coward. Maybe he was more like his father than he'd thought.

He straightened. No, he could choose to make different choices too. Wasn't he asking Wolves to do that by accepting Foresters as equals?

As the leader, shouldn't that change start with himself? No, he was not his father, and he was not ashamed of Jenna.

His PR secretary took the podium. "Thank you for coming out today. Any other questions, please direct them to my office." She faced the podium party and motioned for them to follow her.

Teo waved at the crowd one last time before leading the party into the palace. He'd see Jenna at the reception to follow. His heart raced at the thought.

Chapter Forty-Six

Rider

Warmth spread through Rider's chest as her two favourite people stood up front. Her father accepting the highest honour a Wolf could bestow was nothing short of a miracle. Teo had made sure her dad had received the recognition he deserved, and she was proud of them both.

Teo, handsome and distinguished in his suit and tie—different than his military uniform, although she didn't mind—exuded confidence, kindness, and charm. He had taken reign of the kingdom with dignity and made swift changes like the one being played out on the podium. He'd only been able to snag a few minutes early one morning a week ago to let them know about the ceremony. She'd refused to take part in the program because she'd wanted her father to receive the honor due him. If she was honest with herself, she wanted to avoid the limelight at all costs. For now, anyway. City people, other than the doctors she delivered meds to, didn't know Dr. Hood's daughter, and Rider wanted to keep it that way. Criticism for her father's promotion and award had already made its way to the news stations and newspapers from several key officials in the kingdom. Rider didn't want to make more trouble for Teo in these early days.

And if anything did happen between her and Teo? She bit her lip. How did one date a king? She sought him out on the platform once more. Tingles ran over her as he hung the medal around her father's neck. *Don't ruin this moment by worrying about things beyond your control.*

The PR secretary ended the ceremony. One of the Wolf Pack stepped forward and escorted the row of VIP's, including Rider, to the palace. A forest bike courier a VIP? Her head spun. Inside the palace, she found her father standing beside Teo and Seth and speaking to Dr. Lupine and a couple other officials. She stayed back, enjoying observing her father. Teo's blue eyes met hers and he stepped away from the group. He grinned as he grabbed her hands.

"Hi," she whispered.

"Hi. You look amazing."

A wave of heat rose over her. "Thanks. You clean up nice too." *Was that too informal for a king?*

"My mother wants to meet you."

"The Queen Mother?"

He chuckled. "Yes, who else would it be?"

Rider licked dry lips. "Uh, sure."

He tugged her over to where the Queen Mother, her new title, stood surrounded by gorgeous women, the wives of prominent Wolves, no doubt. Sweat trickled down Rider's back and she forced her lips upwards in what she hoped passed as a smile.

The ladies stepped back as Teo approached his mother. "Mom, I'd like for you to meet Jenna Hood. Jenna, this is my mother."

Jenna curtsied the way she'd been instructed.

Teo's mother smiled. "So pleased to meet you. Thank you for all your help with the treatment for the Lupine flu."

"Of course." She blinked. *Say something.* "I mean, we had the medicine. Why wouldn't we help?"

"Not everyone would be so honourable." The queen studied her.

Rider's cheeks flamed. The women standing by the queen stared at her.

Teo bowed slightly. "We'll let you get back to your friends."

"Pleasure to meet you, Jenna."

Rider curtsied once more, her mind blank. Teo tugged on her hand, pulling her away from the group.

"See? She's not so bad. She won't bite."

"Easy for you to say. I feel so stupid. I didn't think about the fact that she was the queen—I mean Queen Mother. That I would be in the presence of royalty."

"What am I, chopped liver?" Teo nudged her.

She elbowed him back. "You know what I mean."

Servants passed by with loaded trays of appetizers, but she wasn't hungry. Teo tilted his head toward an exit. She followed him, no idea where they were headed. They moved quickly, avoiding servants who rushed by them. A girl halted, her eyes wide, before she clumsily curtsied. Rider's eyes widened. They were in the servant's hallway.

Teo put his finger to his lips, and the girl smiled before dropping her gaze to her bread basket. Teo picked up the pace.

"Where are you taking me?"

He ignored her question as he led her into a very small room on the left-hand side of the hall. The large walk-in linen closet, its shelves lined with cloth napkins and lace tablecloths in every colour of the rainbow, had just enough room for two people to squeeze in. Lavender wafted through the space. Teo slid the bolt across, a sly smile on his face.

"Should I be worried?" She crossed her arms.

"Not at all. I only want a few minutes alone with you." His hands slid around her waist. "Do you mind?"

"Not at bit." She wrapped her arms around him, enjoying the sensation of his warmth. He smelled delicious—like sandalwood and citrus. She tried not to sniff too loudly. His arms tightened around her, and she lifted her face to meet his. His warm lips sealed with hers, and tiny sparks lit on her arms and spine. She wound her fingers into his hair, which was longer than she had ever seen it. After minutes or hours, Rider didn't know or care, he broke their hold. "I need to get back before they send out the cavalry because no one knows where I am." He rolled his eyes.

"Tough being a king," she teased, twining her fingers with his.

He brushed his lips over hers one last time before leading her back the way they'd come. As they strolled along the hall, Rider snuck a glance at his strong profile. He wasn't perfect by any means, and they had a long way to go to unify the Wolves and Foresters, but King

Teowulf was a good man, and Rider would follow him anywhere he led.

A Note from the Author

This was not a pandemic book.

It's true. I wrote the first draft of *Into the Forest* for NaNoWriMo 2018—over a year before COVID-19 was even heard of.

I remember brainstorming what bad thing could happen that would bring the Wolf Clan and the Forest Clan together but that would only affect the Wolves. I thought, *An epidemic that is specific to the Wolf Clan. And Dr. Hood could help them because he's a pharmacist.*

My sister, who is a nurse and sat on the Pandemic Committee of her city in the early 2000's, used to talk about what would happen in a pandemic because it wasn't if but when it would happen. Most of the information that I originally wrote came from those conversations. Eerily, the COVID pandemic played out very closely to her predictions in 2020.

I also want to make it clear that Duko is not a certain president. Again, his character was imagined and written before 2020. I did revise through the pandemic so there may be some influence from COVID, but not much.

The more I read, the more I am amazed at how what we think is fiction so often plays out in real life.

Acknowledgments

This is the page I love to read in every book I pick up. It's the hardest to write. So many people influence and inspire me every day.

First of all, a big thanks to you, my readers, for reading my books, talking about them to your friends, writing reviews, and posting on social media. None of this would happen without you.

Thank you to my beta readers, Trina, Andrea, Robin—all of whom have read multiple drafts of this story. I couldn't do this without you. Thank you for making time in your busy lives for my stories.

Thank you to my young beta readers who took on reading a draft with so much enthusiasm, Ashlynn Ward and Grace Baker. Thanks for your suggestions and input! You both helped make this a better story.

Thank you, Sara Davison, for once again working your magic and making me a better writer. I am so blessed to have you as both friend and editor.

Thank you to Robin and Brenda—my writing partners. I thank God that He put Robin at my dinner table at that writer's conference and then she introduced me to Brenda. And Ashley—your joy inspires me to be a better person.

To my Guelph Writer's Group, thank you! You make critiquing a joy, and I value your input because there are nights after our meetings when I pinch myself that I get to talk books with you all.

To my cover designer, Jenneth Dyck! Bravo! I love this cover so much. Thank you!

Thank you to my family and family-in-law, who always support and encourage me. Some days it's hard to sit and write, but knowing people are holding me up and cheering me on is a gift.

Finally, thank you to Ian and Ben. You both inspire me. And to Mark, who is my biggest cheerleader.

Also By Jennifer Willcock

Coco Bradley wants to dance, and she's willing to sacrifice everything, *everyone*, to get it. Coco lives by the creed "Ballet First," but she's about to find out in a painful way that there's more to life than dancing. Opportunities, fame, and love all come calling as Coco chases her dream. But in going after what she wants, will she lose the things that matter most?

Be sure to check out Jennifer's newsletter for exclusive and never-before published content. Sign up at https://www.jenniferwillcock.com

www.ingramcontent.com/pod-product-compliance
Lightning Source LLC
Chambersburg PA
CBHW061145210726
48294CB00006B/1586